Postcards from Sicily

ALSO BY NANCY BARONE

Dreams of a Little Cornish Cottage
My Big Fat Italian Break-up
New Hope for the Little Cornish Farmhouse
No Room at the Little Cornish Inn
One Summer in Sicily
Snow Falls Over Starry Cove
Starting Over at the Little Cornish Beach House
Storm in a D-Cup
The Husband Diet
The Little Cottage by the Cornish Sea

Postcards from Sicily

NANCY BARONE

An Aria Book

First published in the UK in 2026 by Head of Zeus,
part of Bloomsbury Publishing Plc

9 7 5 3 1 2 4 6 8

A catalogue record for this book is available from the British Library.

ISBN (PB): 9781035911530
ISBN (ePub): 9781035911516

Cover design: Gemma Gorton | Head of Zeus

Printed and bound in Great Britain by Clays Ltd, Elcograf S.p.A.

Bloomsbury Publishing Plc
50 Bedford Square, London, WC1B 3DP, UK
Bloomsbury Publishing Ireland Limited,
29 Earlsfort Terrace, Dublin 2, D02 AY28, Ireland

HEAD OF ZEUS LTD
5–8 Hardwick Street
London, EC1R 4RG

To find out more about our authors and books
visit www.headofzeus.com
For product safety related questions contact productsafety@bloomsbury.com

To Auguste, with love from Nonna

1

March

Villa dei Respiri Spa
Contrada Belvedere
Lago Maggiore
23024
Italy

Mrs Olivia Dawson
c/o Timber & Thimble Ltd.,
The Oast House,
Ritherdon Lane,
Canterbury

Dear Mrs Dawson,

It is with great pleasure that we invite you, courtesy of Mrs Susan Amore, to a complimentary eight-week stay at Villa dei Respiri Spa, on Lake Maggiore, from April 13th to June 8th.

For details, rules and dress code, please see included brochure.

I crumple the letter into a ball and throw it into the corner of the room. 'Absolutely not. Never in a million years.'

'Come on, Olivia, it'll be good for you.'

'You knew this was coming, didn't you?'

Dad sighs. 'Yes. And I think it's a brilliant idea.'

'Dad, you know I'd do anything for you, but not this.'

'It's just eight weeks.'

'Yeah, eight weeks of prison.'

'It's not a prison, it's a wellness clinic,' Dad says as he sticks our company label on the last of today's packages. 'You need a break.'

No, I don't. Business is booming right now, so even if I wanted to take two months off, I couldn't leave Markus, my incredible business partner, in the lurch like that. Even though it's only March, Markus is in Copenhagen at a Christmas fair getting ready for our next wave of orders.

'You think I'm actually going to accept charity from the woman who abandoned us and check myself into an expensive spa that she's paying for? I haven't spoken to her in almost twenty-two years. Can't you see how awkward that would be?'

'Livvie, your mother didn't really abandon you. She tried to keep in touch.'

'Dad— She just went away when we needed her most. And she never came back.'

'But she always called. You never wanted to talk to her…'

I love my dad dearly, but I can't help but hate that he stayed in contact with my mother after she left. He's never dated anyone else, never tried to move on, always wanted me to see things from Susan's point of view. We have the same conversations every time the topic of my mother is brought up. Why couldn't he understand how I felt?

'Can you blame me?' I ask. 'She never even came to see Cassie and Joe when they were born. What grandparent does that?'

'You know why, Sunflower. When Cassie was born your mother had just had a terrible skiing accident, and when Joe was born, Aldo had a kidney infection.'

I roll my eyes. Aldo is the Italian whirlwind lover that had whisked her off her feet. Away from us. And they still have the temerity to want to be a part of my life. Well, I've never met him and I don't plan to.

'They could have come afterwards, but they never bothered.'

'But they invite us all to Sicily every summer. You're the only one who never comes along.'

I huff. 'Why are you always so nice to her, Dad? She abandoned you, too. She left you for a Sicilian millionaire to live the life of Riley and you've forgiven her. You must be super-human.'

My father sighs. 'Honey, is there no convincing you that your mother loves you? She had her reasons for leaving, even if you don't want to hear them.'

She *had her reasons*? As far as I'm concerned, there is no good reason to leave your husband and child. Moving to a different country just to get your leg over with someone without even considering the consequences of breaking up your family is certainly not a good reason. It's quite selfish, if you ask me.

I have more sad memories with my mother than happy ones. One of the few, and probably last, good memories was in the sitting room, where her old pub piano had place of pride by the window. It was a cozy living room, full of sunshine streaming through the flowered curtains and a view of Canterbury Cathedral.

We were practising a song for the annual student/parent competition at school. She was going to accompany me on the piano as I sang 'All By Myself'.

'Ready, chickie?' she'd asked me during one of our rehearsals as her hands hovered over the piano keys.

'Ready, Mummy...'

I pushed back my braids, squared my shoulders and nodded for her to start.

'Breathe deeply, stay in control of your voice,' she said softly while beginning to play the opening chords.

I watched her as she played, and as I began to sing, the look of pride on her face made my trepidation dissolve. It had been a rare moment at the time, one of the good ones, which were becoming fewer and farther in between. She was prone to long bouts of sadness during which she became distant, barely leaving her bedroom, and there was no dinner on the table for weeks unless Dad rolled up his sleeves when he returned from work.

This would go on with seemingly no end in sight, until suddenly she would descend the stairs like a smiling diva as if nothing had ever happened. She was like that, my mother. Happy one moment, then miserable the next. So I hung onto the good moments, like this one, and tried hard to forget the not-so-good ones.

Just as I was about to start the second verse, she stopped playing. 'You know what, pet? We should really do justice to your voice. How about starting just with you, a cappella? And then I'll come in with the piano on the second verse, what do you think?'

'Uhm, I don't know, Mum.' I was always shy about singing without any music and automatically stopped whenever the music did.

'I know you're afraid, but you shouldn't be. It would make a great intro, something different, you know?'

She was probably right, but again—

'Let's just try it, chickie,' she coaxed me with her glamorous smile.

I knew I was safe with her. She would never lie to me. She was my mother.

'Okay,' I finally conceded. In the privacy of our own home, no one could hear us. No one would hear the flaws in my voice without an instrument to accompany it.

She sat back and bobbed her head to an inaudible beat, urging me to follow. At her deeper nod, I began to sing the first verse. She was right. I sounded very powerful. Just a girl and her naked voice. But it was scary out there on my own, and I tried to shorten that time as much as I could.

'No, darling,' she said, interrupting me. 'Don't rush through it. *Enjoy* the sound of your voice on its own. Feel what you're singing. Feel the pain.'

Feel the pain. I huffed inwardly to hide my lack of confidence, knowing she was right. I nodded. 'Okay, Mum.'

'Good. Whenever you're ready, then.'

So I tried again, closing my eyes to listen carefully to my voice this time. She was right, of course. It sounded much better.

On the second verse, she joined in with the chords, and I relaxed even more, knowing that she was there to back me up the rest of the way.

But then, she left us. I haven't been able to forgive her since, even if my father has. If what she did is so understandable and justifiable, then why don't *I* just dump my husband, Simon, and my two children for someone else? Not that there is a gorgeous European lover waiting for me in the wings, mind you. But it would be bloody nice to have the option.

The difference between my mother and me is that I would never do that to my kids. I would never break their hearts by destroying their bedrock. How could I be happy knowing that I've caused them such pain? Obviously my mother never worried about that.

'Your mother does love you, sweetheart,' my father repeats, fetching the invitation from the floor and trying to uncrumple it. 'Just forgive her and accept her gift. It would make everyone's life so much easier, yours included. And then next time she invites us all to Sicily, you can come.'

Oh, poor, lovely Dad. Always making excuses for the woman he never stopped loving, under the guise of 'keeping the family together'.

I get up from my seat at the work counter and wrap my arms around him, my head on his shoulder. '*You* love me, Dad. And I love you. You are my rock. I don't know what we'd do without you in our lives. You make everything so much better.'

My father kisses the top of my head. 'Then do me a favour, Livvie. Go to this place in the Alps. You need a break.'

'But I don't, Dad. I have everything I need here. With you and the kids and…' I don't mention Simon, because really, I'm thinking about Markus, but I'm not telling *anyone* that.

Markus is a carpenter and joiner extraordinaire. I'd met him in Copenhagen and immediately agreed to work with him. Today, after all this time, he is not only my business partner but a strong, positive presence in my life. My best friend, after my father. We talk about everything and anything. Like my dying marriage to Simon.

My problems with Simon started before I met Markus. But in the very first weeks of our working together in the oast house at the bottom of our garden, I knew I was in trouble. Well, I knew that from the moment I'd met him. I'd just shrugged it off. Because *I* was not flighty like my own mother. *I* was immune to the charm of other men. *I* was a responsible wife, mother and businesswoman. But I haven't been able to get Markus out of my mind ever since.

Delectable, ineluctable Markus who had a thousand girls a day calling him and texting him. Well, maybe not a thousand, but at one point he did have to mute the calls that were very distracting (to him) and annoying (to me). And that was only the start of it. Sometimes the girlfriend of the week would come to see him at work just to sit there and watch while he built a table or a hutch, while I was stashed away in the loft office printing out invoices for our already flourishing business.

The ladies never flinched at the amount of sawdust in there, just as long as they could get their claws into him. But these ladies never lasted very long, and at the end of the day he'd plonk himself onto the stool opposite mine with two cups of coffee and run me through the entire love story, asking me where he'd gone wrong.

The temptation to say that it was because he wasn't with me was on my lips every day, but I soon learnt to quell it. I had absolutely no right whatsoever to talk to him like that. I was married. And a mother of two. Besides, he'd never shown an iota of interest in me. If anything, he treated me like a sister. If it wasn't for him and my father helping me run the show, I don't know where I'd be; I didn't want to ruin everything we'd built with a spur-of-the-moment confession. And speaking of, my father is still waving that blasted invitation in my face.

'Just promise me you'll give it some thought,' he insists gently. 'Just think: luxury rooms, swimming pools, Jacuzzis, fine cuisine, beautiful gardens, no cooking, no ironing, no school runs…'

'Exactly. Who's going to do the school run if I go? You have enough to do here between the house and the business. You're retired, but you haven't stopped since.'

'I'm retired, sweetheart, not dead.' He chuckles. 'Besides, the last time you did the school run you almost literally *ran* over a father.'

'I didn't run him over. I just… over-zealously honked him out of the way…'

'That, my dear, is called road rage.'

'He was being too slow on purpose…' I argue.

Dad shakes his head. 'You are too highly strung lately, Livvie. You need to decompress. Please, take the offer.'

I don't want to admit that he's right. I *am* at breaking point – with my marriage, with the long hours, with my overwhelming crush on Markus – and I *could* use the rest. To reset. But I can't just *leave*. 'What about the kids?' I reason, looking for any excuse to say no. 'Joe's okay, but Cassie? She already hates me. She'll never forgive me for leaving her for two entire months.'

'Cassie doesn't hate you, Olivia. It's just the teenage phase. She'll get over herself.'

'But what if she doesn't? What if she hates me for ever?'

'Well, then you'll know how your mother feels.'

Ouch. That is not like Dad at all. Yes, he's tried to convince me to give Susan and Aldo a chance, but he's never tried to make me feel *bad* about it. Not that I do. My mother did the unthinkable by abandoning us, and she's had to face the consequences.

Which is what I'm suffering from with my own daughter, Cassie. She really, really worries me. When she was little, she used to love me 'to the moon and back'. She'd always wrap her arms around my neck and give me 'star-kisses', as she used to call them. But now she won't even give me the time of day. Anytime I try to speak to her, her eyes will start rolling and she will groan and leave the room as if I've committed a capital offence against her and humanity. If I'm not careful, she'll become like me.

2

My mother's offer to pay for a stay at an exclusive Italian spa hasn't been mentioned again, thankfully. My dad knows when to give it a rest.

And Simon, as always, is against anything that could possibly put him in a position of responsibility towards the kids. If I leave for eight weeks, who the hell is going to take my place in the kitchen?

To think that when we started dating at uni, my friends had warned me about not jumping headlong into such a serious relationship. I was young and in a great hurry to get my life back on track, so Simon and I had started dating immediately, as if there was no tomorrow. We saw each other every day, and soon it became all day. By the end of the month, he had practically moved in with me, taking the place of my roommate, who left me with a tender warning: 'Don't let him take over your life, Olivia...'

If only I'd listened.

As the months rolled by, he was able to take all his classes and take all of his exams as I, burdened by housework and meal prepping and grocery shopping, had started to lag behind in my studies.

When I'd mentioned it to him, he was very apologetic, telling me that he was sorry he'd taken me for granted, and of course he certainly didn't think that I was there to facilitate his success at the cost of my own. So he started helping out more until we got back on an even keel and I resumed my studies. As behind as I was, I had spoken to the Director of Studies, who assured me that I would be okay if I maintained my new pace.

And then, at twenty years of age, despite being on the pill, I fell pregnant. Again. More on that later.

Despite my trepidation, Simon was absolutely over the moon at the news of my pregnancy. He said he'd always wanted a family, but never thought that he'd be lucky enough to find a girl who would want to start so early. Whichever way he looked at it, it was a win for him.

Not to mention that his parents would be absolutely thrilled and willing to help financially – his father owned a law firm that he could work in while finishing his studies. And when he got his degree, they would immediately fast-track him to junior partner. Which meant that between studying and working like mad, the next two years were pretty much sorted for him. In one lucky stroke, he'd obtained everything he'd always wanted.

But what about me? Whichever way I looked at it, for me it was a losing situation. I certainly wasn't ready for a baby at my age, halfway through an Arts degree! But there was also no way I could do what I'd already done once again. Because ending my pregnancy the first time had nearly killed me emotionally.

There was absolutely nothing I could do. I was trapped.

In a sense, I was reliving my father's life. When my mother left, he'd had no choice but to roll up his sleeves and do his damned best to be there with his quality presence: feeding me, making sure I was clean and tidy, supervising homework, coming up to say good night and listening to my endless complaints about Mum leaving. He had been through so much, if my memories were anything to go by.

All week, Dad made breakfast and took me to school, and prepared tea and helped me with my homework when I got back. All the while Mum stayed in bed, hour after hour. I wondered if she was really sick. She had to be, not to badger me into practising our song. Music was her life. And in turn, it had become mine. Singing was everything to me. It was my biggest joy. It cheered me up when I was down. But we hadn't practised in weeks and I was getting a bit rusty.

One afternoon, I knocked on her door. 'Mum? Are you all right? Can I come in?'

But she didn't answer. She didn't even turn to look at me as I poked my head through the door. The room was dark and smelt musty, as if she hadn't opened the window in days. The sheets were rumpled and there was an untouched bowl of tomato soup next to her on the bedside table.

'Mum?'

Still nothing. Then:

'The phone…' she whispered. 'Who was it?'

'No one, Mum. No one's called. Can I get you anything?'

She didn't answer, only stared out ahead of her. I'd never seen her like this before and it frightened me. What if she was ill? What if she died? Who was going to take care of me? Dad worked all day; he couldn't manage on his own for ever.

Every hour or so I'd go in and check on her, hoping that she'd be better, perhaps even sitting up reading a book. But nothing.

She slept for three more days without another word.

'Is Mum going to get better for the talent show?' I finally asked my father on Sunday morning over my crumpets. 'It's next week…'

I felt guilty for asking something so selfish, but my reputation at school was at stake.

'Of course, pet,' he reassured me, squeezing my hand. 'Mum'll be right as rain soon, you'll see.'

But it wasn't all right after that. I had no way of knowing what she was up to.

Whenever I think back on that time, I can confidently say that there is no way that I am going to pull a *Susan* on my kids. Even if I do feel I am just about ready to snap, always a moment away from bursting into tears for God knows what reason. The kids are healthy and don't want for anything. I know I desperately need some time to myself. And I *will* take some time off as soon as it's feasible. Just not right now. And not on my mother's tab.

And as far as people I can trust with my family, I know that if I asked Markus, he'd step into the breach. He practically *is* family, and probably spends more time here than he does at his own house. He always finds the time to kick a ball around with Joe long after we've finished work and to have a quiet word with Cassie when she goes off on one of her teenage rants against me.

I guess I deserve it. Cassie is simply following in my footsteps as an angry girl, part of a chain reaction passed down from my mother to me, and now me to her. We are all connected inasmuch as we are both impatient towards our mothers, albeit for different reasons. I am nothing like my mother, yet Cassie always finds reasons to despise me. I had always thought it was classic teenage girl behaviour, but now I'm beginning to wonder: is she ever going to have a conversation with me that doesn't include monosyllabic answers punctuated by eyerolls?

It hurts me so much to see my baby, my first-born, reject me. I have lived, breathed and dreamt the idea of Baby Cassie. Toddler Cassie. Child Cassie. Adolescent Cassie. Through every stage of her life, every step of the way, I have been there for her. And yet, there is something in her heart that won't let her love me as much as I'd like.

Am I making this all about me? Am I being petulant, selfish, pouty because she doesn't feel the same way I feel about her? It's a mother's nature to love her kids more than they love her, isn't it? So then why am I feeling hard done by?

Are we ever going to become, I'm not saying friends, of course, because mother and daughter should remain as such, in my opinion, but when, or perhaps it's better to say if, she grows out of this, will she ever be able to love me again? Will I ever know what lies in the deepest, darkest layers of her heart and her soul? Will she be happy one day, will she figure it out, or will she be one of those people who never get over the tough times and stay forever bitter?

I realise I've just described myself. I am the same with my own mother. I can't get over Cassie's lack of love for me because I wanted to have the kind of relationship with her that I never got to have with my own mother. But I suppose you can't force these things.

I had hoped that all the love I *thought* my mother had for me hadn't been lost for ever. I had always hoped to recoup it and relive it, like a precious memory, a special memento like a ballerina in a music box. All I had to do if I was feeling lonely was to open that box and be inundated by the sweetness. But it never happened. My relationship with my mother had deteriorated for ever. Perhaps I was asking too much of my teenager to live that unconditional love through her. What does she know about silent grudges that fester over a lifetime? Of unrequited feelings of a daughter's love? She is well-loved, even if she refuses to act like it.

I never got the choice. And this is what makes me angry: that I am giving Cassie everything I never had. But I'm still not good enough. Just like I wasn't good enough for my mother to choose us over a man.

I know that I've got a lot of baggage to sort out, but Cassie is my daughter and she is my priority. How can I not worry about her? How can I not worry that we're destined to become just like my mother and me? That is my worst nightmare. I worry about this more than anything else. And it's getting so bad that I'm almost afraid to talk to her in case I make things worse. Mothers shouldn't be afraid to talk to their daughters, right?

Besides being my personal music teacher on her good days, my mother never really talked to me if not to tell me to sit up straight or I'd get scoliosis, to not talk with my mouth full and to keep my voice down. I followed this advice steadfastly and have done very well for myself, all things considered.

I could have become so many things in my life, and I blame my mother for my lack of success. Maybe if she'd stayed, I could've honed my talents and become a songwriter or a vocalist. Whether I'm right or wrong is another story. The fact is that I let her suck every ounce of confidence out of me when she left. And she left because she was a bad mother. Not because I was a bad daughter. I know that now.

And my crumbling marriage? I know I'm a good wife, despite the fact that Simon is, let's say, not every woman's dream husband.

You could say I should have thought of that when I married him. But back then, I was pregnant and I didn't think there was anyone better out there. All I wanted was the security of a complete family, something I had lacked growing up. For my children to grow up with both parents.

But for years now, whenever I turned around, it was always Markus who was there for them and not, sadly, their father.

They love Markus. And although I would never say it out loud, so do I. I've been playing the role of his best friend for years, acting my arse off, and quite frankly I should be winning BAFTAs and Tonys and Oscars and Golden Globes left, right and centre, because the man has absolutely no idea.

I still remember the day we met at a craft market in Copenhagen. It was in front of a furniture stall opposite mine. I sewed, knitted and stitched pretty things for around the house: tea cosies, tablecloths, curtains, tea towels. And I'd wanted to branch out. Simon always said that I couldn't compete with international products, whatever that meant. So I'd booked a stall to display my own creations and see what was what.

The furniture for sale in the stall opposite mine was very shoddy: the material used for the upholstery was very low grade, the stitching hurried, the quality of the thread sub-par and altogether the designs were just naff. I'd have been embarrassed to display that kind of quality. That was when I knew I had a real chance at this business after all. I already had a series of loyal customers who regularly put in orders at the beginning of every season. I even had one customer who bought everything I made, which was a bit weird. Every time I came up with a new product, they were always the first to order it. I worried that they were trying to steal my designs, but I hadn't been able to find them online.

'What a load of absolute *skid*. Who tries to sell this kind of crap?' came a deep voice from behind me, making me snort my coffee through my nose.

I turned around and ohmygod, was he not absolutely top-notch gorgeous! Early thirties, tall and broad-shouldered, with dark hair and piercing blue eyes, he was the most beautiful man I had ever seen in my life.

'Hello! Mind if I have a browse? I need to get that pile of rubbish out of my eyes,' he said. By the accent he was definitely Scandinavian, which would justify his Jaime Lannister looks.

'Huh?' I said like an absolute idiot. 'Oh, of course not, browse away!'

'Thank you. I'm Markus Sørensen.'

'Olivia Foster.' I use my maiden name at work.

His face lit up. 'Olivia Foster? It *had* to be you! I recognise the quality of the workmanship.'

'Oh? Are you a customer?' I ventured.

'I'm from Creatie. We finally meet.'

My jaw dropped. He was the mystery company that had bought one of everything I ever made!

'Pleased to meet you in person!' I beamed. 'So, uhm, what do you do with all the stuff you've bought from me, if I may ask?'

He grinned, and blimey, let me tell you, the entire market lit up. 'I've been buying to see what you're capable of. I think that you and I should go into business together.'

'Business?'

'I'm a carpenter by trade. I make furniture. But I think that your love for your craft would make my work even better. How are you at upholstering?'

I remember blinking at him. I couldn't quite believe what I was hearing.

'If you're interested in the idea, perhaps we could discuss it over dinner, once the market is over?'

'Uhm… sure.'

'Great! I'll swing by later, then. I can't wait!'

'Me too…'

And the rest is history. Markus came into my life, blindsiding me while I was stuck in a rut in oh-so many ways. It shaped the person I am today, and Timber & Thimble, the business Markus and I created together with such love.

Luckily our stuff sells all year round, not only Christmas and Halloween or Easter. We started out with furniture pieces like armchairs, which Markus hand made, and I upholstered, and eventually branched out into all sorts of furniture and homeware. We have a 'Spring Beginnings' sale where we offer linens and housewares in new pastel colours. We have new plant pots, outdoor furniture, barbecues and bunting, along with indoor furniture, window furnishings, lamps. Anything you can think of, sourced directly from Scandinavia, thanks to Markus.

Our summer themes are in vibrant colours. In autumn, like the leaves on the trees, out come our wreaths with burnt leaves and gourds and chestnuts scented like cinnamon. In December the gourds go but the cinnamon stays as Christmas decorations fill the oast house. And then we kick off the New Year with discount sales of our Christmas stock and a run-up to Valentine's Day with an explosion of red hearts, ceramic hearts, wooden hearts, golden hearts and all things romantic.

And after ten years, we're still going strong.

Even my father loves Markus, much to Simon's displeasure. My husband already wasn't keen on having Dad live with us, so you can imagine how the presence of a Scandinavian god in our home would wreak absolute havoc.

Markus is my measuring rule against other men. And most of the men I know are absolute knobs. Every time I run into any at Parents' Night or a meeting, one of them will always try it on when their wives aren't listening. Is andropause so bad that they need to prove to themselves that they've still got it? That some random woman who just happens to be in their immediate vicinity will actually find them interesting? I mean, have they seen themselves? It's not so much their looks, which was never a deal-breaker for me, but their behaviour. What happened to carrying yourself with dignity and class?

I've a busy day at the shops, today. After I stock up on food for Cassie's study group back at the house, I make my way to the lingerie area. I'm looking for another pair of blue stockings for her. She's obsessed with blue stockings, but she's always losing them and blaming me. So the next time she misplaces them, I'll be ready with a brand-new pair. Actually, they're on sale so might as well stock up. And while I'm at it, I might as well get her some new knickers.

'Never took you for a chaste, cotton knickers kind of girl,' comes a voice at my side. I jump, only to see Brian Halston, the father of one of Cassie's classmates, Jen. He is slimy, always giving me the eye. It's obvious things at home aren't going too well. They aren't in my household, either, but I don't go around stalking men at Sainsbury's.

And now Brian, who is head of the father–son football team, and thus coach to my little Joe, is leaning against the shelf I'm scanning, his arm blocking my escape. I put on my brightest, You-don't-scare-me smile. 'Oh, hello, Brian. How's Gemma?'

But he ignores my question about his wife. 'I'll bet that beneath that perfect mother disguise, you're actually a *loooot* of fun, aren't you?' the slimy bastard says, one eyebrow shooting practically halfway up his forehead.

What is he *on* about? I spot the blue stockings, size S, and snatch them off the rack.

'Right! Must dash, many things to do! Give my love to Gemma,' I call back, barely concealed disgust on my face.

Wow. What was that? Did I have 'Available and dying for it' written all over my forehead? Doesn't he know I'm a married woman? Albeit struggling, fed-up and out-of-love, I'm still married. I don't do messed-up. That was my teenage life. I'm a grown woman now.

3

On the way home, I am royally pissed off by another *idiot* who cuts me off despite it being very obvious that it's my turn to go at the roundabout. Fine. I fire off a string of curses in my head and then force myself to get over it, rather than leaning on the horn as I normally would have done. Perhaps I do have the *slightest* bit of road rage, but despite what my father and Markus say, I can keep my cool. I don't have any suppressed anger or whatever it is they think I have. I simply have a low tolerance for idiots while I'm trying to run around and get chores done.

Oh, great, just great. Obviously not happy enough with the fact that he's cut me off, he is now *deliberately* slowing down. I'm sure he's doing it just to upset me, forcing me to slow down because if I accidentally hit him, it'll be all my fault. All I want is to get home after a long, hard day running around like a headless chicken. But obviously he doesn't give a rat's arse. What is *wrong* with these people? And where the hell did he learn to *drive*?

'Oi!' I honk at him, yelling out the window like the best of stevedores. 'Get a bloody move-on!'

He slows down, looks at me in his rear-view mirror, just staring at me, coming to a slow stop.

I honk again. 'Get on with it!'

At that point, he stops and gets out of the car. If he thinks he can intimidate me, he's got another thing coming. I am a mother of two, a businesswoman and a daughter of an elderly father. I am from the sandwich generation. I am the sandwich generation all rolled into one woman, and I will not be taking any crap from some bloke who thinks that driving is a right. It is a privilege – one that some people don't deserve.

'What are you honking for?' the man demands, utterly disgusted. He must be in his seventies at least. Jesus, he looks like my dad, who is sixty-nine. He could be my dad's twin, with the same scrawny shoulders and age marks on his temples. I can't very well yell at someone who reminds me of my poor old Dad, can I?

And yet, I want to clock this bloke like never before. What's wrong with me? Have I gone mad? I am this close to passing a limit of decency. This is not me, in the least. I have always tried to be a decent human being, but, as it happens, things get in the way. But not this time. This time I've got it.

'I'm sorry, sir,' I whisper as I change gears and reverse.

His eyes widen. It must look to him that I am moving my car back to try and run him over, and he stumbles out of the way as I drive past him.

'You crazy bitch!' he calls after me.

Well, any man who would call a stranger a bitch deserves a little scare. He shouldn't have cut me off in the first place. I start to giggle to myself at the look on his face, and the more I think about it, the funnier it becomes until I'm laughing hysterically to myself.

Then suddenly, it's not funny anymore. At all. And that's when I'm ambushed by an onslaught of tears. The man was right. I am a crazy bitch. Perhaps I should see someone about this. But it's normal in this day and age to be a bit stressed, right? And it's not like I was actually going to knock him down, was I?

A couple of streets away, I park under a tree to pull myself together.

'You've got this, old stick,' I say to the ragged reflection in the mirror. My green eyes are wild with stress and my light brown hair looks like I've been through the tumble dryer. Sometimes I really don't recognise myself.

I get back home to find Cassie and her friends upstairs in her bedroom, draped around every piece of furniture, listening to my old records from my ancient stereo that she's dragged up from the basement. Now that is a blast from the past.

They're bopping to Duran Duran's 'Planet Earth' in a way we never danced to it. Their movements are jerky, but there is something fun about it. Scattered around them I also see my entire Spandau Ballet collection, along with Wham, Culture Club, David Bowie (which was actually my mother's but I stole it because I'd never heard anything so cool in my life).

These records were already old in *my* time, but something about the carefree, bouncy music made me happy when nothing else had, if only for the length of the record. Eighties music was like a drug to me, and it had kept me going throughout those tough years.

'Hi, Mrs D!' the kids chime in unison as Cassie rolls her eyes.

'Hey, girls,' I chime right back, happy to be among nice people again. 'I got you peeps some nosh,' I say, hoping they'll understand me and that they'll think I'm cool enough to be in their hallowed presence. If they'd only seen me at that roundabout a few minutes ago, they'd be staring at me in terror.

'It better not be those healthy snacks again,' Cassie says, turning her nose up.

'I like those healthy snacks,' Rachel says, sitting up as I distribute cups of fruit salad, yoghurt pots, crackers, assorted nuts (I've already cleared the list with their mothers) and cheese cubes.

'Thank you, Mrs D!' they say obediently, though I dread to think what comes out of their mouths the minute I leave the room.

'You girls have fun, but don't forget to do some studying,' I say as I close the door behind me.

'Oh my God, your Mum is like, super-nice,' I hear Nicole swoon behind the door. 'I wish she was my friend while growing up...'

Oh, Nicole... you poor, innocent little girl. If you only knew...

The week goes by without any particular mishaps until Saturday morning when the kids and I are at the shopping centre to get them some school supplies. We must have bought enough coloured pens and pencils and rulers and glue and binders for the entire school. I used to do that when I was a girl, and I usually did end up giving away at least half of it, whether to break the ice with someone, or to deter a bully from beating the crap out of me. I have never, ever in my life fitted in with the In Crowd. I still don't.

I was always the nerd silently reading my book in the school canteen while the other girls were draped around their boyfriends or snogging in the gym, putting the huge space to what they called *good use*. I couldn't do that. And the result of my never having set foot in a gym showed: I was anything but slender, and it made me an easy target for ridicule. But I learnt to appreciate my body for what it is, even if nowadays I can hardly climb the steps to the bedroom without wheezing, I'm so out of shape and worn down. I *do* need a holiday, I know that. But not now. And certainly not in the Italian Alps, so far away from my kids.

After our shopping spree we go to McDonald's, and everything instantly annoys me; the loud music, the smell of fried food, even the people aimlessly milling around. Why don't they just get out of the way and *sit down*?

Once I've set the Happy Meals on our table, I grab one of the chairs and pull it back, perhaps a little more forcefully than necessary. But when I go to sit down, I completely misjudge it, falling arse over tit and smacking the back of my head against the ceramic floor.

At first I don't understand what's happened. One minute I'm standing and the next I'm on the floor with my burger in my lap, stunned, shocked, and with a splitting headache.

The restaurant falls silent as all eyes swivel to the source of the loud noise. This silence lasts long enough for everyone (me excluded) to get over the shock, and soon a few onlookers are sniggering at me, probably thinking I'm drunk as opposed to dizzy, while others, a tiny percentage, feel sorry for me, judging by the looks on their faces. Screw them. I don't need anyone's pity! All I need is for them to stop looking at me.

I scrabble to my feet as fast as I can, my face and ears burning as the din around me increases to a high pitch, and I'm thirteen again, stumbling to the floor in the wake of Amanda Amherst, the most popular girl in Year 9, taunting me. My throat tightens and my eyes burn as I dust myself off, but there's no way in hell that I'm going to cry like I did back then.

'Oh, my God!' calls a woman from behind me, and I can sense her making her way over to our table. The last thing I need is someone fussing over me, making it look like a huge deal and attracting the attention of anyone who may have missed it. I turn to the sound of her voice, ready to defend myself, but she's part of the staff. 'Are you all right?'

'Quite,' I say. 'It's nothing. Thank you.'

'Are you *sure*, Mum?' Cassie asks with exaggerated kindness, but it is so obvious she is enjoying my embarrassment. She must truly hate me. 'You went down like a ton of bricks!'

'I'm all right, thank you, *sweetheart*.' I say the last word through gritted teeth for the benefit of the kind worker who's come to my rescue.

Anyone else probably would have sat down again to finish their meal, the embarrassment passing quickly. I will never be able to finish my meal now. And it isn't because a few people are still watching me, but because, in the space of a split second, the time it took for my arse to hit the floor, I have lost my dignity, and, as a consequence, my appetite.

'You hit your head,' the woman says. 'Are you sure you're not dizzy? You might even have a concussion…'

'I'm *fine*!' I shout at her, and we both jump. Now the entire place is staring at me, waiting for the punches to fly. I know I look like I'm going to lose it. I *feel* I'm going to lose it very, very soon, and I don't even know why. Is my father right? Should I look up anger management classes? Nonsense. I'm fine. I can handle this.

'I'm so sorry!' I whisper to the kind lady. 'I didn't mean to yell. I don't know what's wrong with me…'

She puts her hand on my arm. I would have moved away from another stranger's touch but for the look in her eyes. I need a friend today.

'I've been there,' she whispers, and I trust that she means it. 'Take some time for yourself, if you can. Trust me…'

I look into her knowing eyes and nod. We have recognised each other. I see the lines of worry that have etched themselves into her face, argument after argument with a loved one, sleepless night after sleepless night over a fractious child. She is fighting the fight just like all of us mothers are. She is a kindred spirit who has been where I fear I'm about to go.

'Be selfish for once,' she says.

Be selfish for once? I would love to. Only… I can't. I can't leave my kids, not to mention my dad, in the incapable hands of my husband. I would find the front door swinging on one hinge (a bit like me) when I returned.

'Thank you,' I murmur to the lady. 'Thank you for your kindness…'

She smiles, squeezes my shoulder and disappears without a word.

'Aren't you going to sit down again and eat?' Cassie asks me as she chomps on her fries.

'No,' I say. 'You two finish up, I'm just going to nip to the loo.'

Which of course is an excuse anyone could see through.

I take my time packing up my meal and taking it to the bin. As I watch, my uneaten fries, still hot and crispy, disappear down the chute along with my burger, coming apart piece by piece. Bun first, then the toppings and finally the patty, it all disappears down a great black hole. Just like my life.

This is what happens when you're pushed to breaking point. You bite someone's head off. Or you don't even see what's right in front of you. It's happening more and more lately. I'll be draining pasta and completely miss the sink, ruining dinner. Or I'll be getting dressed and leave the house with my slippers on. Or I'll be talking to someone and stop mid-sentence, not remembering what I was going to say. I know what this means. If I don't decrease my stress levels, I am eventually going to lose it. I know I am. I actually think I've already started to lose it.

Once I'm certain that there is no one else in the toilets, I break into a silent sob. 'Please,' I whisper to no one in particular. 'Don't make me go mad. The kids need me, even if they don't know it yet.'

I've tried to make my marriage work. Some days were better than others, insomuch as we didn't start arguing as soon as Simon walked through the door. I always made a point to never argue in front of the kids, waiting until we were both locked away in the kitchen or the bedroom. But lately we have even stopped arguing, which in my mind is a sign that there really is nothing left to say, and nothing left to *save*. I've all but given up. Sometimes I have these massive bursts of *Save it while you can, don't let all these years be for nothing*, but all my resolutions die the minute he comes through the door looking like he wishes he could be anywhere else.

I'm certain he hates this situation just as much as I do. Who would want to come home to a life where everything looks comfortably ordinary on the surface, but the underneath is swelling with dark, murky words and resentment over things left unsaid? Each lost argument, broken promise, and disappointed expectation that the other will try harder only builds up flaky sandcastles of hope.

And yet, even if you know they aren't going to last very long, you have no choice but to keep rebuilding after every little earthquake. You hang on for dear life for fear of losing the very little that you do have. The most frightening part of it is that you never know if this tremor will be the one that razes all you'd built to the ground once and for all.

I know we both feel the same way, but every time I try to talk about us, Simon gets all defensive and points out that he's not the one to start the arguments. I don't see them as arguments so much as attempts to communicate and save our crumbling marriage. Because it is truly, inexorably, falling apart, no matter how hard I try to catch the falling pieces. At this point, I wouldn't be surprised if he has someone on the side and is just waiting for the right moment to tell me. Who knows?

In the past, I've tried to appease him, but nothing I do is good enough for him. Not in the kitchen, not in the bedroom – the two places he considers women's primary posts. Now, he's not stupid enough to come out and say it, but the look of utter *disappointment* on his face when I fail to deliver in one or the other domain…!

I've tried to appease Cassie, too. I've tried giving her some space, yet by the same token discreetly being there when I think she needs me.

I'm not allowed to ask her about school, her friends, if there's a boyfriend on the scene, even if she's reading any good books. The ones I suggested to her have been sitting in a pile on her desk for weeks now. I don't know what her opinions are, or if she even has any. I don't know my daughter anymore, period. We have completely lost the mother–daughter bond I worked so hard to nurture as she grew up. If I disappeared into thin air today, neither she nor Simon would notice. I'm just an obstacle to their aspirations to greatness with my everyday, practical mundanity. *Can you please take out the rubbish, Simon? Cassie, can you please fetch the post?*

If I disappeared… they would be happy not to have to deal with the encumbrance of having me around. But I am not going to give up on Cassie. I am her mother and will do everything I can to fix this.

The woman at McDonald's was right. I need time to de-stress before it's too late. Even if it means actually going away for a while. My kids need me to be a better person, a stronger mother. They deserve that much.

After a brief debate of pros and cons with myself, I fish for my mobile and dial my father's number.

'Hi, sweetheart,' he says, cheerful as always.

'Okay, Dad,' I whisper. 'I'll go.'

'Well done, old girl,' he whispers back, and I can tell he's proud of me. Proud of his daughter who's finally seen the light. Maybe, just maybe, some proper R&R can put me back on the straight and narrow.

4

I call Markus in Copenhagen to tell him my decision.

'Good for you,' he says distractedly. The usual enthusiasm in his voice is missing.

'What is it?' I blurt, so used to being vetoed by Simon. 'Do you not want me to go?'

Silence, then: 'You're asking *me* for permission?'

'No, but, I mean, can you manage on your own?'

'Do you mean, do I need you? Yes, always. But I'd rather you were relaxed and happy. Besides, this is a pretty quiet time for the business, so now is the best time for you to go.'

Just like that? No Simon-sized drama? 'Oh. Okay…'

And yet I can feel a hesitance. He's right that things usually quiet down after the Easter rush, so I believe him when he says he can cope without me. So what is it, then? Dare I hope that he's like this because he's going to miss me?

'But I can still call you, right?' he asks.

'Of course. It's not a prison or anything.'

'Cool. Then we'll talk as often as possible. In a way, it'll be like you never left.'

'Sort of defeats the purpose though, doesn't it?'

'Aw, Livvie, you know I'm completely lost without you.'

If only it were true. But it's the opposite. He always does and says the right thing. He encourages me to try out new ideas, and listens to me patiently when I need to rant (which, now that I think about it, is pretty often). He takes out the rubbish bins despite it not being his home, and checks up on my dad during the day, maybe even stopping for a cuppa and a few minutes to help with one of Dad's new puzzles. Markus is always available for anything that we need, like a ride to football or guitar lessons or taking my dad down to the pub for an hour or so in the evening. All this makes me think that, in a parallel universe, we could have been together. Had fate been on my side for at least once in my life, we could have fallen in love.

I would be listening to *his* breathing instead of Simon's loud snoring. He would hold me at night, as opposed to Simon, who sleeps on the edge so there's not even a chance of us touching. My children would look at me with his eyes, and not Simon's. Did you get my double entendre, there? Simon wouldn't have.

Cassie would respect me more. Markus would have made sure of that, instead of sniggering at her shots at me like Simon does. We could have had that life together, but it's all, and always will be, only in my heart.

'You'll come back better than ever,' he says with a chuckle and already I feel better. 'You need a break, especially lately.'

'Yeah,' I agree. Markus almost knows me better than I know myself, so I know that he's right. Markus knows everything about me, except this one secret which I can never tell him lest I ruin the beautiful friendship we have.

I can never tell him that I wish he was my husband, that we had children of our own, that I desire him in every way humanly possible.

Simon and I haven't been intimate for years. I'd had no idea that we had reached that point in our relationship where the complicity had gone alongside everything else; the pleasure of just being in each other's company, talking about everything from a new brand of yoghurt at the supermarket we wanted to try, to the children's education. It was all gone. The pleasure of a shared life, the efforts of being a family.

It had made me feel so small. Unwanted. Kicked to the kerb. Redundant. As if there was no use for me whatsoever. I know there is, technically. My family couldn't run without me. At least not without three major crises a day. Not with Simon at the helm. And yet, he's slowly, slowly discarding the pieces of me, each aspect of our life together, every day. Without looking back, not to mention even giving me an explanation. It had been so slow I hadn't even noticed, leaving me unarmed and vulnerable. I know it would be different with Markus.

'So when are you going?' he asks, jolting me out of my fantasy.

'Uh, the invitation is for April 13th. The same day you get back from bloody Denmark.'

'Rotten Denmark,' he corrects me. 'There is something rotten in the state of Denmark. *Hamlet*. Isn't that what you meant?'

I laugh. 'No, I meant that I hate Denmark when you're there and that I miss you! We won't even see each other before I go. For two entire months.'

'It'll make our reunion afterwards that much nicer. I'll be there for the kids and your Dad, no worries.'

'How can I thank you?' I ask.

'By coming back *relaxed*,' he says. 'I'll miss you, *skat*.'

Not as much as I'll miss you.

'Mum fell on the floor at McDonald's today and then yelled at a lady who tried to help her,' Cassie smugly tells Simon the second he walks through the door that evening.

He stops in his tracks, keys still in hand, as if he's ready to run back to the car, eyeing me as I busy myself with the pasta sauce, careful not to spill it. I believe that only the presence of my dad is stopping him from saying anything unpleasant. Because if he said it was all due to the fact that I was too stressed, he'd have to agree that I should go to the spa. He didn't actually answer with more than a grunt when I told him, actually. Such is his disinterest in my life. But now he makes sure I'm the only one who hears him sighing as he washes his hands at the kitchen sink. He says nothing, as he has done for months. His silence is like a neon sign flashing his mantra: not getting involved.

Oh, how I'd love to get into a conversation, the ones he calls arguments. How I'd love to tell him how I feel, that I am so, so lost, that I can't see the purpose of my own life besides raising the kids and running a business. I assume for some people it would be enough, but for me that is merely survival. Is that all there is? What about emotions, love, laughter? I'm missing out on all the good things. You reach your goals and then sit on your laurels until you die? No happiness, no peaks, just one long, flat line.

What can I do to get out of this rut? Is there some magic word that I haven't said, something I haven't done or thought of that might just clinch the deal? I just don't know what to do anymore.

Later, that night, when Simon *finally* comes to bed, I turn to face him. 'It *is* okay with you if I go, right?'

He stops pulling off his socks, his shoulders visibly stiffening. 'Well, it sounds like I don't have a say, does it?'

I sit up. 'What do you mean?'

'I mean that it sounds like you're dying to go off on your own for a bit. A pity *I* don't get that luxury.'

Well, that's really rich, coming from the ever-absent father who spends more time out of the house than he does in it. But I don't say anything, because the last thing I need is another bedtime 'argument'.

'I just think it would be good for all of us,' I whisper.

'Olivia, you are going to do what you are going to do, and that is that. Good night.'

I bite my lip. It's the best I'm going to get from him, tonight or ever.

After another night of complete silence instead of the deep and lengthy conversations I long for from a partner, I tell the children I'm planning to go away for a bit while they help me pack some items for delivery. Joe likes to do a good job with the labels while Cassie's hasty work has to be checked over and over. She doesn't like helping out and has made that fact abundantly clear.

'Are you sick, Mum?' Joe asks.

'No, sweetie, just tired.' *Fed up, actually.* 'Mummy needs a break.'

'From what?' Cassie interjects.

You. And your father.

'From… work.'

'But you work from home. You don't have to drive to work or wear a suit like Jen's parents.'

Ah, yes, I had forgotten about those two even more miserable fuckers.

What kids, or at least *my* kids, don't understand, is that working for yourself is even harder and more stressful than working under someone else. You have to put in more hours, more energy, more of yourself or it's the end of your business. And even if you're lucky enough to have help from someone like Markus, it's still damn hard, riding the wave and staying relevant and interesting.

Markus and I each have our own specialties (we joke that he's the hard stuff guy and I'm the soft stuff girl) but we often cross over to help the other when needed. Over the years I've learnt to plane a plank of wood and he's learnt to cross-stitch, believe it or not!

Markus and I both agree that it's important to be competent in all aspects and facets of the business so that when one of us gets sick and can only give twenty percent, the other swoops in and supplies the remaining eighty. (Something that I don't get in my marriage with Simon, by the way.) But that's how it works with Markus and me.

'So that's it?' Simon asks as he watches me bring down a suitcase from the attic. 'You've really decided you're going?'

I put the suitcase down on the floor and straighten my jumper. 'Did you think I was joking?'

He snorts. 'Actually, I thought you'd change your mind. You realise you're leaving our kids in the hands of an elderly man.'

'Dad is fine. And just so you know, our children will be *your* responsibility, not his.'

Even if I've caught him out, he doesn't miss a beat, I have to give him that. He comes straight back for the counter-attack.

'And what about the business? You're leaving our second income in the hands of Jaime Lannister.'

Jaime Lannister, for those who don't know, is a character of Game of Thrones, and initially not a very reputable one. That's what he calls Markus behind his back. Need I point out the obvious, major jealousy factor? But he's not jealous of Markus and *me*, he's jealous of Markus period. Because, if we're going to be so vain and start comparing them, Simon wouldn't stand a chance against him, on every level.

For the longest time I was adamant that I wasn't going, but now I am defending my right to a break. Maybe Cassie and Simon will finally understand what it means to not have me around. Let Simon make an effort, while someone else caters to my needs for once.

No laundry, no school runs, no ferrying the kids back and forth to their clubs and practices. No grocery shopping, meal prepping, dusting, hoovering, washing floors, scrubbing toilets. I hadn't actually thought of that. I'll be relieved of all mundane chores and anything related to home-making. I can actually reset my brain, my emotions. Calm down, catch my breath for once.

And it's not like I'm going away forever. I don't even have to stay the two months. It's not a prison. I can stay one month, or three weeks, even. I can come home as soon as I want to. What's going to stop me?

5

So with everyone's (well, almost everyone's) blessing, I start packing for this well-being holiday that, at the end of the day, my mother has generously paid for, I can only assume, as a peace offering. Perhaps it's her way of saying that she does care after all. And after twenty- odd years of radio silence on my behalf, I decide to call my mother to make it official. Well, actually, my father decides it's the right thing to do. I put up a modicum of resistance but in the end capitulate for the sake of peace.

'Hello, Livvie!' comes her sing-song voice that hasn't changed in nearly twenty-two years. 'I've been waiting for your call! So you've decided to go to *Villa dei Respiri* after all!'

She *knows* I'm going. She's known all along. Has Dad already told her, and how smug is she?

'So, uhm, I've had a chat with my family,' I say awkwardly. I know I could have said 'our' family, but she's no longer part of it. 'And we've decided I can be spared for a few weeks.'

'I should bloody well hope so!' she laughs. 'It's time for some *you* time!'

'Yes, well, thank you for your… generosity.'

'It's the least I can do for my baby girl.'

I wish she wouldn't call me that. I was indeed her baby girl once upon a time, but not anymore. But yes, to pay for a wellness clinic for me so I can rest is the least she could do for me.

'I will pay you back, of course.'

'Absolutely not! It's a gift, Livvie.'

But why? I almost say but stop myself. I mean, I am curious, but perhaps it's not such a good thing to keep voicing my past grievances, and especially not over the phone. I am an adult now. Or at least trying to be. And besides, it's easier if we just gloss over that kind of stuff, or actually, never mention it, because if those gates open, I'm afraid I'll never be able to close them again.

Our relationship was like that while I was growing up. She was very temperamental so I always avoided saying anything that would hurt her feelings. Any time I did, she would actually start sobbing like a baby, making me feel like a right monster. But she wasn't always that way, and Dad says she isn't like that anymore.

I know better than to believe him. He always saw the best in her, and I guess he still does. My mother is the kind of woman that you instantly like, but only because you don't know her. On the outside, my mother is welcoming, bubbly, warm and nothing is too much trouble. She's very difficult not to like. The kids adore her. My father adores her, despite the divorce, and she adores him. After all these years they're still the best of friends. It's like they all speak a language that I don't understand. Go figure. I struggle to like my own husband more times than not. But underneath all that, she is naïve, vulnerable and prone to making her problems everyone else's problems, too.

Of course, I wouldn't want anything bad to happen to her, but I can't get over all the pain and hurt she's caused me, all the while breezing through her own life choices as if we were a second thought. She left us when I was just thirteen, and for what? To go off to Italy and marry some rich nobleman. Just like that, out of the blue.

To be fair, Aldo has always been polite and very kind to the kids, inviting them over for the holidays for as long as they want to stay. Of course, out of politeness, the invitation is always extended to Simon and me, but I can't exactly say I'm a fan of his. In truth, Aldo Amore is the root cause of my life going down the toilet. And goodness me, did it, the minute my mum left.

What I never expected as a teenager was for my mother to say that she would be moving to Italy. Italy? Who leaves their child to move abroad with another bloke? I don't care that she called every Sunday, or sent mountains of postcards. You just don't do that. You don't give up your kid to be with someone else.

My dad has never said an ill word about my mother and it pisses me off royally. Because at least then I'd have an idea as to how Aldo came onto the scene. But nothing. *Nada.* Or, in this case, *niente*.

Luckily Susan lives all the way down south in Sicily, while I will be staying all the way up north in the Alps, so there is no chance of me accidentally running into her.

'Now listen, my friends at *Villa dei Respiri* will take good care of you. I'll call ahead and make sure you get everything you need.'

'Thank you, Mother.' All I need is not to have to work, cook and deal with Simon. Cassie's strops, I can normally deal with, but lately even she is grating on my nerves.

'Don't thank me. Just relax and reboot.'

Relax and reboot. Actually, come to think of it, I'm really eager to go now. I'll be all on my own, with no one demanding anything of me, for the first time in God knows how long.

April 10th

During the last weekend before my departure, I am in damage-control mode. Joe, as usual, is a dream, encouraging me to take a break and enjoy myself.

Cassie, on the other hand, is in a strop, almost as if I was pulling a Susan on her. But I know she's just trying to make me feel guilty for the sake of it, and secretly she's glad to be rid of me. Dad promises he is fine and that he doesn't need any help with the kids and that he always has Markus to fall back on, just in case.

And then on Sunday night, the eve of my departure, as I am clearing up after dinner, I get a text from Simon:

I'm upstairs. How about a last one for the road…?

What? Is he effing kidding me? After years and years of absolute indifference to me in that respect, on the very eve of what is supposed to be my eight-week window of freedom, *now* he wants to…? Just like that, as if it was a last-minute forgotten packet of crisps that you snatch up at the till on your way out? I mean, really? He must have hit his head hard when no one was looking.

How do I get out of this? Gosh, I don't think I'd even recognise him, or *it*, anymore, it's been so long!

And even for him, I'm sure it would be like something akin to, 'Er, excuse me, madame, have you seen a young woman somewhere around here?' To which I could only answer: 'That young woman is gone. You missed out on her all these years when she was willing. Now, she hasn't had a visitor in years, so I haven't bothered with the maintenance— Oh, sorry about the cobwebs too, but this place has been shut down for quite a while now.'

No. Absolutely not. I don't want to. End of. And I can't understand how he'd even *think* I would want to.

I don't answer his text, instead taking my time scrubbing the bottoms of all my pots and pans, making sure that I get rid of those blackened oil streaks, the ones that have been there for months, and hoping desperately that he gets the hint. I scrub the hell out of those pans. The last time they were this shiny was when we chose them off the display table in the shop.

Once those are dried and put away, in my desperation to bide my time, I turn to the grouting on the backsplash with an old toothbrush I keep under the sink, and some bleach. Not that it really needs doing. It could have waited a few more weeks. But, I cackle gleefully to myself, so can he.

He's made sure all this time that nothing physical happened between us, meaning that, on an emotional level, *everything* has changed between us. There has been a seismic shift in our relationship over the years while no one was looking. And it has left a huge void where there should have been, oh, I don't know, a proper marriage with emotional intimacy, knowing looks, secret couple codes, laughter in the dark during pillow talk and having each other's back. Basically anything that would cement a couple's relationship.

Our marriage is held together by routine, cowardice (at least on my behalf) and insufficient funds to buy another home for the kids and me. They would have to be shuffled back and forth between two new shitholes as neither of us would be able to afford to give our children any of the things they enjoy now. No more school trips, no ballet or football, even McDonald's would be a stretch at that point.

So a proper separation will have to wait until the kids are older, and can fend for themselves.

The cooker needs a deep clean, I decide, so I pull the burners out and start scrubbing them as well, fully aware that Simon is still waiting upstairs, probably in his boxers. The sole idea makes me giggle louder and louder as I fill a basin with clean water and disinfectant to sanitise the inside of the kitchen cabinets that deserve my attention much more than Simon ever could.

And the sad thing is, I know the perfect man for me exists. With Markus I already have the perfect relationship I should have with Simon, minus, the, well, *you know*. It's not like that between Markus and me. We really are good, trusting friends or we'd never have gone into business together. We have each other's back and wouldn't dream of it being any other way. We've even agreed that our spouses (whenever he decides to get married and break my heart, that is) will have no say in our business decisions.

The next morning, the morning of my departure, Simon, who still has the hump from me not succumbing to his nocturnal wishes, shoves his hands into his pockets and says 'Right, then. Keep in touch.'

'Of course,' I assure him as we both stand awkwardly as if on a first date, unsure of whether to kiss or not. It seems odd. It seems dishonest. But for the kids' sake I lean forward for him to kiss me. Surprised, he gives me an awkward peck and moves away immediately, as if he's afraid he'll get the lurgy. And now it must be blatantly obvious even to the birds in the trees that, after all these years, two kids and a home, we have reached stalemate.

I give my dad the longest hug in history as Simon walks down the front path, gets into his BMW and screeches off like it's a hit and run. Just as Markus's pick-up is pulling up to the kerb.

He gets out, his hand on his heart. 'I saw Simon's car leaving so I thought I'd missed you!' he calls as he jogs up to the front door, wrapping me in his embrace.

'Uncle Markus!' the kids shout in unison, flinging themselves at him.

'Hey, you're back early,' I sigh, pulling out of his embrace and pushing a strand of hair behind my ear. My heart starts to do that familiar *boom-bada-boom* thing.

'I took an earlier flight,' he explains, returning the kids' hugs. 'And I've got loads of pressies for you all. I thought Simon was taking you?'

'Yeah,' Cassie snorts. 'Like that's happening.'

'Cassie, be nice,' my father chides.

'Uh, he has work,' I say lamely. 'So I called a taxi.'

'Nonsense, I'll take you,' he offers.

That's all I need: a romantic (at least on my side) two-hour drive and goodbye at the airport with him.

'Uhm, no, that's okay, Markus. My taxi is due any minute, I'm sure it's too late to cancel.'

'Well, okay, then,' Markus says, wrapping me in a bear hug that I just want to stay in for ever and ever, but I make it quick for everyone else's sake.

'Try to relax and have fun. We've got your back here, haven't we, champs?'

Joe loves being called that, and surprisingly, so does Cassie.

'Of course, Uncle Markus!' Joe chimes. 'We've got it all covered.'

I laugh and ruffle his hair as I eye Cassie, who has made sure she's too far away for me to reach out and hug her goodbye.

6

April 13th

During my flight from Gatwick to Milano Malpensa, I sit back and enjoy my me-time. I'm sitting next to a nice elderly gentleman who shows me pictures of his grandchildren. He has a beautiful wife and family, and I find myself smiling. Normally, I'd have shied away from this kind of personal interaction because I am an introvert at heart. But I am already feeling so liberated. I'm in for Italian food, Italian wine and heavenly landscapes. What's not to love?

But. I also feel a bit of lingering guilt for leaving the kids, even if I tell myself that I am a good mother and that there's nothing wrong with taking a break. I work hard at being a parent and I bring home my fair share of the bacon. I do deserve this break.

Only… it's quite a long break. It's eight bloody *weeks*. In that space of time my daughter might grow a bra size or get her first boyfriend. And Joe? He might master a new level of *Fortnite* without me!

I grip the armrests, suddenly panicking. What am I doing? I'm doing exactly what *she* did all those years ago.

I am abandoning my children and putting myself first by jetting off to Italy. Mothers shouldn't do that. Flashbacks of the day my mother left rush back to me, out of the blue. I remember every single detail.

The school auditorium had filled with the fragrance of popcorn from the stand, and the din spoke of a large audience. After a good speaking to from my dad, my mother finally rallied and managed, with his help, to get out of bed and have a shower and get ready for the talent show.

Behind the curtain, I stood on stage, next in line. I ran through my breathing exercises, rehearsing in my mind the song we'd practised a hundred times.

And then it was our turn. 'Ladies and gentlemen, boys and girls, please welcome the mother–daughter duo, Susan and Olivia Foster, as they sing the world-famous song by Eric Carmen, "All By Myself"!'

As the curtains slowly parted, I felt afraid but blessed at the same time. I was doing what I loved, and I was good at it. My father was proud of me, and my mother would be with me every step of the way. What more could a girl ask for?

The stage lights were so bright I could barely see the end of the stage, let alone distinguish the faces in the crowd or see Mum at the piano below the stage.

I stepped forward, nodded to the crowd with all the grace I could muster, and, as agreed with Mum, I sang the first verse a cappella. I sang it with excellent control, not rushing it at all, as she'd taught me, feeling the songwriter's pain and loneliness while pacing myself until the second verse when Mum would join me on the piano.

I kept the beat by gently tapping my thigh with my fingers, ready for verse two, and dived straight into it with everything I had before my voice merged with Mum's piano.

Only I realised I was still singing by myself, and that, in fact, there was no one accompanying me on the piano. But I couldn't stop in the middle of the song!

I strained my eyes against the lights, trying to see her as my heart began to beat in panic. Had the piano not been connected to the microphone? Had Mum tried to warn me but I hadn't heard? There was nothing I could do but continue to sing as I felt myself sink down a deep, deep hole, alone and afraid. I wanted to stop and ask to start again because obviously something had gone very wrong. They normally allowed us to stop during rehearsals, but I doubted it would be possible during the real performance.

When the chorus came I gave it my all, shifting position so the lights wouldn't blind me as I strained my eyes once again to see where she could have gone. And then I saw it: the empty piano seat and my father's drawn face squinting up at me in a mixture of pride and utter misery. The song seemed to last for ever and every new verse or chorus became harder and harder to perform as I was now almost completely engulfed in panic and confusion.

I don't know how I managed to finish the song, and when it ended, I took a bow amid the uproar. The audience gave me a standing ovation. I'd done a good job. Had the act not been called Olivia and Susan Foster, no one would have known there had been a problem and that I'd had to improvise.

'Where is she?' I sobbed when it was all over, grabbing

my father's hands when he came backstage, getting make-up and tears on both of us. 'Where did she *go*?'

'We'll talk at home, sweetheart,' he said, holding me tight. 'Just enjoy your moment of glory for now. You were *fantastic*. I'm so, so proud of you!'

While balloons and streamers filled the stage, all I could focus on was the empty piano bench. Not even my father's warm embrace could protect me from the pain.

The journey home was a blur.

'Mum? Mum, where are you?' I'd called, bursting through the front door of our home, hoping to find her on the settee watching the telly at least, if not up and about cooking a meal in the kitchen. I knew she'd made an effort to get out of bed, so I didn't understand why she couldn't make the effort to sit at the piano and accompany me through one Goddam song!

'Olivia, sweetheart,' my father said softly, taking my hand and guiding me to the dining room table. 'Calm down, now. I have something to tell you.'

'Is she okay?' I asked. 'I've heard her crying a lot lately.'

His eyebrows shot up in surprise. 'Yes, she has been quite sad lately. I'm sorry you had to hear that. Mummy wasn't well so we decided she should go away for a bit.'

'To a hospital?' I asked, my brows furrowed in thought. That was the only place she could be, surely.

Daddy looked at me, halfway between stern and desperately miserable. 'No, Livvie. She went to Italy for a while.'

'Italy?' I asked. 'What's in Italy?'

'A... a friend.'

'A friend?' I repeated. And then I got it. I wasn't stupid.

She had a *boy*friend. How was I not surprised in the least? She was a right flake, after all. Always had been. We could never count on her to do anything, or be somewhere, even if she'd promised and crossed her heart. She just didn't care enough. Her feelings for us were clear. She had a love, someone far more important than Dad and me. She loved him, and not us.

Fine. I didn't love her anymore either. I decided right then and there that actually, I hated her. She did nothing but disappoint us. How many times had she failed to be there for me? How many times was I going to have to forgive her? Well, not anymore, because she wasn't coming back!

'Olivia, please know that your mother still loves you very much. But sometimes… grownups have to go away for a spell and think about what they want from life. What else, I mean, besides a family. I'm sure you'll understand when you're older.'

'Come on, Dad. She didn't even say goodbye!'

It was all very clear to me. We were the reason she had left. Because we, her family, were too much for her to handle.

'Come here, Olivia,' my father beckoned to me gently. He was so loving and kind. I couldn't be cross with him. It wasn't his fault Mum had left.

I slid off the chair and onto my father's lap as I used to do when I was younger. It had always been my father there to comfort me. Never my mother. My mother was always the demanding one.

Dad kissed the top of my head. 'We are a strong pair,' he said in a clear voice. 'We will stick together and be there for each other no matter what. Okay?'

I huffed. 'Yes, Dad…'

'Good. It's late. We can talk more about this tomorrow, but now it's time for bed.'

'Okay,' I reluctantly agreed as he headed up the stairs. I followed, my legs weak.

But inside I felt a rage I'd never felt before.

'Are you all right, dear? Miss?'

I open my eyes. The voice is coming from the elderly man next to me.

I bite my lip. 'I'm all right, thank you. I'm just… missing my kids.' Well, I miss Joe, but because he's my baby. My kind, sweet baby. I *do* miss Cassie, of course, but more than anything I am worried about her. I swipe at my cheek.

'Oh, that's sweet,' he says. 'But maybe Mum needed a break?' he suggests gently.

'Yuh.' I nod.

The man vaguely reminds me of my own father, who at this very moment is probably preparing snacks for when the kids come home from school. That's it, now I've done it. I've drowned myself in nostalgia and guilt, and it's going to take me the entire length of the flight to get out of it.

So much for getting away and enjoying myself. It's a good thing no one at the spa knows me. I am looking forward to complete and utter relaxation. No school gate mums to force-grin at while they tell me the dreary details of how they got Hugo to *finally* eat his greens or poor, *terribly diligent* Augusta to study for *fewer* hours on her cello. Yes, I do need this break, to be secreted away in the Italian mountains for a while. In truth, I'm more of a beach girl, but upon seeing the beauty of the snow-capped Alps from above, I am utterly conquered.

When I finally touch down at Milano Malpensa airport,

I send our family WhatsApp group a text to tell them I've landed safely. But only Dad and Markus text me back because the kids are at school. I'll send them a message later. Simon must be in one of his dreadfully boring meetings. Or perhaps he's still a little miffed at the fact that I've actually decided to leave him to finally do his fair share of parenting.

As I come out of Arrivals, I start looking for the signs to the train station, but a man with an A3 printed sign catches my eye:

MRS OLIVIA DAWSON
VILLA DEI RESPIRI

They've sent a shuttlebus. Wow. Very classy. I lift my hand and he darts forward. 'Welcome, *Signora* Dawson. Please let me take your luggage.'

'Thank you ever so much,' I say, relieved I don't have to lug all my stuff onto a train by myself. Of course I had everything under control as I am a seasoned traveller, but after flying it's always nice to have someone meet you.

'This way, please,' he says politely. He is very well-dressed and handsome. No wonder people like coming to Italy. It is such a beautiful country, judging by what I've heard and seen online. How had I never visited Italy before? There are so many places to see: Rome, Venice, Florence, Naples, Palermo. I make a mental note to research a few of them and perhaps leave the spa a couple of days earlier so I can fit in some travelling.

The shuttle bus I thought he was driving turns out to be a black Alfa Romeo Quadrifoglio. Not that I have any interest in cars, but Joe is obsessed, so I recognise the Alfa

Romeo logo on the front, and the boot says Quadrifoglio with a four-leafed clover. He would be thrilled to know I travelled in one of these. I'd like to take a picture to send him, but I don't want to look like a tit. Oh, who cares about that! I clear my throat. 'My little boy loves this car,' I tell the driver. 'Would you mind if I took a picture?'

The man smiles. 'Of course. Would you like one behind the wheel?'

Suddenly shy, I shake my head. 'Uhm, thank you, that's okay.'

He nods and lets me take a picture before he loads my luggage into the boot.

'How long is it to *Villa dei Respiri*?' I ask as I buckle myself into the back seat. Black leather, very comfortable.

'About two and a half hours,' he replies. 'There is some reading material for you and a snack if you push the green button.'

'Thank you,' I say, trying not to appear to be too eager. I'm practically salivating at the idea of what could be in there, so I wait until we have cleared the airport and are on the motorway before I dart the driver a look and then push the button.

A hatch opens with a soft *swoosh* and a tray pops out with two separate sections to choose from: *Caldo* and *Freddo*. I know that caldo means hot, so I push that button and a pitcher of coffee pops out like in the Jetsons, complete with porcelain cups and saucers, brown sugar, white sugar and even sweeteners. It smells delicious! Next to it is a plate of croissants and another one loaded with mini savoury muffins. Oh, my word! James Bond and Mary Berry couldn't have done it better!

I take one and bite into it: broccoli, bacon and melted Parmesan cheese, yum!

Curious, I decide to open the cold flap, and am rewarded with another small feast: mini sandwiches containing salmon and ham and a selection of cold cuts, such as salame and Prosciutto di Parma and cubes of assorted cheeses alongside some sun-dried tomatoes, tiny onions, artichokes and olives, all drenched in olive oil. I wash it all down with a glass of white wine. I'm probably eating everything in the wrong order, sooo un-Italian, but I'm sure I'll learn.

I realise that I've never even considered visiting Italy before, simply, and stupidly, I now see, because of its association with my mother. But she's down in Sicily, and with an entire *boot* between us I'll be just fine. Grand, actually.

Sated and satisfied, the gentle lull of the car on the road relaxes me, and I decide that it's okay if I let myself nap for a while. We've a long drive ahead.

'Here we are, *Signora*,' a deep voice wakes me. '*Villa dei Respiri*.'

I sit up and rub my eyes, murmuring a *Thank you*. And then my eyes pop wide open.

Villa dei Respiri Spa is a *dream* resort, nestled on the shores of Lake Maggiore.

It is a nineteenth-century, Art Nouveau villa with a peach-coloured rendering, in some places faded but for this all the more genuine, with vast botanical gardens featuring mostly Mediterranean plants such as azaleas, agapanthus and oleander, but also English roses and conifers. Punctuating the landscape here and there are ancient sculptures alongside both antique and modern water features. I feel like Vesper Lynd in Casino Royale, vacationing in a luxury villa with the love of her life, James Bond. And vacationing, in fact, is exactly what I'm doing. Minus the love of my life, of course, whom I've left at home in the person of the unsuspecting Markus.

A handsome man, around thirty-ish, comes to greet my taxi and shows me into the massive, elegant lobby and I just know that Villa dei Respiri is going to be amazing. Through a wide doorway, I can already see lake views with open terraces and white linen curtains billowing in pine-scented breeze, and fancy drinks and foods, and ladies dripping with jewels and gallant men vying to attend to their every need. More Gatsby, anyone?

I'm given a brochure listing Villa dei Respiri's offerings: skin care sessions, lymphatic-drainage massages, Botox (I can only imagine the cost of *that*), different kinds of yoga classes (good luck with that one), Pilates (and that one), cooking classes to learn how to prepare healthy and fulfilling food, and plenty of other learning opportunities clubs, such as arts and crafts, music lessons, singing lessons (good thing my mother wasn't here or she'd be trying to teach the teachers), swimming lessons in their Olympic-sized pool that, judging from the pictures, looks like it wouldn't be out of place in Hollywood. They even have *bocce*. Not that I'd ever play bocce, but still, it's nice to know.

I'm truly looking forward to this fantastic sojourn, secretly grateful to my estranged mother for trying to buy me back. Not that I can be bought, but it's nice to be spoilt for a bit. And why not? Don't I deserve good things, too?

I will probably never have the money she landed in when she married Whatshisname, and I'll probably never live her lifestyle, but while I'm here I'll be damned if I'm not going to make the best of it.

It's a good thing the brochure mentioned the dress code and that I packed some elegant clothes, I muse as I look around me. These people are so obviously changing at least four times a day. Where the hell do they find the energy? I can barely be bothered to change from my pyjamas into my jeans and a jumper, barely washing my face in the morning as I push my hair into a haphazard ponytail and trudge to the oast house at the bottom of the garden where Markus is waiting for me. He would laugh his head off if he saw where I was now, not to mention take the royal piss out of me.

Judging by the fleeting looks from the sportily-clad guests around me, I'm assuming they've just come out of one of their tennis lessons (white with black piping seem to be the unspoken rule around here) and have stopped for a glass of cucumber water and a chin-wag before showering and changing for lunch, which, as I can tell by the diaphanous linen tablecloths billowing in the breeze and the clatter of shiny silverware being placed on the tables along with white porcelain, will not be long now.

All this elegance, and what a gorgeous backdrop! I never thought I'd ever set foot in Italy, but to be sent to this lovely resort at the foot of the Italian Alps is something that might even move *me*. The mountains are so majestic, reaching infinitely up into the cobalt-blue sky and taking almost all of my field of vision. The purest snow covers the highest peaks but down here I can almost feel the warmth of the summer to come.

And my room? Pure white decadence, with a bed big enough for my entire family. The sheets must be silk, and the towels are so thick and soft I could bounce on them all day.

It sounds silly. Juvenile, even, but when I was a teenager, I always dreamt of having a big, beautiful bed and sharing it with a loving partner. It would be a place to celebrate our relationship, with a thick duvet and fresh linen every week. It would be the most comforting and welcoming part of the house.

Every month I'd redecorate the room, change the colour scheme based on the season and always find some pretty object or other as a source of inspiration. In the spring I'd go floral, in the summer I'd go beach hotel themed, while cinnamon-scented candles would bring in autumn and the festive season. You get the idea.

And, for a time, with Simon, it was like that. I made sure it was. He loved it. But then daily life, routine and drudgery had settled in, taking the place of innovation, attention to detail and care.

But now I can't wait to spend the next two months in my own personal bedroom without Simon. I am free to do as I please and am ridiculously happy, like Kate Winslet in *The Holiday*. I'll wear silk or flannel, whatever I choose, because it only matters to me now. For the next few weeks I can pretend that I'm not married. I can pretend I am on my own, independent, and take care only of myself for a change. Have some 'me' time. I'll make a tiny altar to myself in the name of female freedom.

But first, I decide to check in with Cassie. Her silence always unnerves me, even if I pretend not to be bothered by it. Her mobile rings three times before it goes to voicemail. I'll try again later.

As this is an elegant vacation, I've purchased a few suitable items of clothing, mostly white outfits with blue or black piping or accents (like the people in the brochure), perfect for a day out on the lake or an evening out on the terrace. For this afternoon I've chosen a white dress with a thin black hem and collar and a pair of low black sling-backs. Tonight I will change again for dinner, I think excitedly.

And then I think how silly it is of me to get all excited by a simple change of clothes. But it's only right that I get excited. I can wear white without worrying because I have no cooking to do and no artwork to help the kids with and I'm not in the warehouse packing our products.

I'm here, in the heart of the Italian Alps, and I'm free to do whatever the bloody hell I want for the next eight weeks! And now, before I go and settle in by the pool for the rest of the afternoon, I'm going to accept a glass of white Italian wine from the circulating waiters, if you don't mind!

When I make my way down to the heart of the resort, I see a lounger has been reserved for me. Not only has a fresh white towel been draped over the back, but a plate of hors d'oeuvres is sitting on the little table next to it. Blimey! I lie down, close my eyes and take a sip of my Valpolicella wine (that's what the waiter said it was), letting the aromatic, silky liquid wrap itself around my tongue. I could stay like this forever, letting my mind shut down for once, not worrying about what my kids are up to or if Dad is okay. I'll text them later.

And then, as I stretch out, my first decadent Italian fantasy catches me unaware. How bloody sexy and marvellously impossible would it be if Markus was here with me? If he stole away in all secrecy to join me? Every once in a while I let myself go to these fantastical scenes where everything is possible. He and I, together, in love, while Simon conveniently falls off the face of the earth for good.

I know, these thoughts make me no better than my mum, of course. But it's okay as long as I don't act upon them, right? Certainly, in the intimacy of my own mind, I am allowed to imagine him standing over me? Like someone is right now, blocking my sunlight. Certainly not... *Markus in the flesh?*

Of course not. I know that. It can't be. So I open my eyes to see who is robbing me of my Italian sunlight, only to see him standing over me in all his glory.

'Oh my God,' I gasp. 'What are you doing here?'

To which he leans over me and grins his sexy grin, his face inches from my own.

'I'm here to be with you,' he answers as if it's the most natural thing in the world. And to top it off, he puts his marvellously large hands on the armrests either side of me and comes in for the most delicious, exquisite kiss any girl has ever had in real life, onscreen or in the best of dreams.

I shade my eyes as he isn't quite blocking all the light. 'Okay, Markus, cut the crap, please. Why are you really here? Is it Dad? The kids?'

He shakes his head and grins. 'Nothing like that. Surely you knew I'd come so we could be together, sweetheart?'

'Okay, now you're really freaking me out,' I warn him. But is it really that out of this world that he may have feelings for me? And that at home, he didn't have the freedom to tell me that he fancied me, too, and that he'd acted his arse off to hide it? He'd certainly fooled me!

'I've missed you so, so much, honey,' he says. Only... his voice is not quite right. It's kind of high and breathy, actually, and... vaguely familiar.

That's when I blink against the sun, wake up from whatever lucid dream I am having and jump three feet off my lounger.

'MOTHER!' I screech when her face fills my view, coming in and depositing a huge kiss on my forehead.

'Hello, darling! Surprise!'

7

'*Mother?* What are *you* doing here? Aren't you supposed to be in *Sicily*?' *WTF?!*

She grins her beautiful, impish grin that I loved as a child. She hasn't changed an iota after all these years. 'I've come to spend some quality time with my daughter! We're going to have sooo much fun together, Livvie! And because we're shareholders, we get special treatment!'

All I wanted was to kick my shoes off and let my hair down, on my own – or with my Markus fantasies at the most. But this? My *mother*, here, in the same place with me, is the stuff of my very worst nightmares. A moment ago I was finally feeling so happy and alive! Now I just want to die.

Mother is trying to impress me, not so much to win me back but to show off just how well she's done for herself. Of course her husband is one of the benefactors of this place. She *would* have chosen a wealthy man and a life of ease over my father. And now she's trying, in her own twisted way, to make amends without even doing what is necessary to make amends. She thinks just because she has money that I'm suddenly going to want to be her daughter again.

For years I've fended off her exaggerated, pseudo-compensatory gestures of love, leaving the kids to absorb her too-muchness, while doing all I could to ignore her. But here, in the flesh, without anyone as a buffer between us? This is a total disaster!

I haven't seen her for almost twenty-two years. Now in her mid-sixties, she has long blonde, *healthy* hair, huge turquoise eyes that I didn't inherit, by the way, and a beautiful, firm, if round, face.

Her figure is hidden by a loose-flowing, beautifully embroidered caftan. I know from Dad's pictures that in the summer she wears sundresses with huge jewellery, but does she ever manage to look frumpy? Not one jot. I can't even get away with that kind of garb and I'm thirty years younger.

What annoys me the most is that she is always so relaxed and smiling. To get me to smile you'd have to catch my finger in the car door, she often says to my dad, which is an Italian expression. I suppose Aldo must have taught it to her, precisely referring to me. As if he knew me. Ha.

And what's worse is that Mother has never had a single clue about the effect she *still* has on me after all these years, with her loud clothes and her resonant voice. It's like there's no getting away from her. Already she's attracting the attention of various ladies around her, who get up from their loungers in a hurry to come over and have a look. So much for rest and privacy.

'Lucia, Maria! Meet my daughter Olivia,' she says, beaming, while they stretch out their bejewelled hands to shake mine. '*Piacere*, Olivia! Welcome!'

'Thank you,' I grin back, my teeth clenched so tight I hope I don't crack one.

'Look at you, already in the vibe!' the more tanned one says, noticing my dress.

'Very nice!'

'Th-thank you,' is all I can manage, still reeling from surprise and frustration. Is it too late to make a furtive getaway?

'So,' my mother says, linking her arm through mine so her friends can see how close we are. 'Tell your *mamma* about my gorgeous grandchildren, what have they been up to lately?'

I'm of a mind to tell her that I've never called her *mamma*, that Italian is not her first language and that she already knows how her grandchildren are because she and my father speak every bloody weekend. But I really don't have the energy to go down that road, especially not in front of strangers. I pinch the bridge of my nose. 'Oh, you know, the usual…'

She's giving me her undivided attention, nodding and asking pertinent questions she already knows the answer to since she's so up-to-date with everything, and it pisses me off. Why couldn't she be so interested in her own kid back then? Why all this sudden interest in my family now, and not, say, when *I* needed her?

'I think I need to rest a bit. N-nice meeting you, ladies,' I mumble as I make to turn away, hopefully before my head explodes. 'I'm going back to my room for a nap.'

'A nap? You just got here,' Mother protests. 'Come and have a glass of cucumber water, it's good for you!'

Sighing inwardly, I give up and let her pour me a glass which I down in one go, gagging on it in my haste to go.

'What's wrong, isn't it good?' she says, taking a sip from her own glass and making a face. 'Ugh, that's nasty, isn't it? All right, love, you run along and get settled. We'll have plenty of time together. Eight weeks, just think!'

Exactly. Eight whole bloody weeks.

Back in my room, I lock and bolt the door and do my little thing, i.e., dog-whistle scream at the ceiling. It's been my thing since she left when I didn't want my dad to hear me. It stuck with me over the years and now, when I'm so angry that not even a good shouting session will curb my rage, I whisper-scream. It's the only thing that works for me. I'm good at it, too, not letting my rage be heard by others. I practise this at home after an 'argument' with Simon, or when something royally pisses me off. Usually it's connected to Mother's weekly calls and incessant gifts for us all (I can't deny them for the kids, but I've always given my gifts to the charity shop). I haven't seen her or even spoken to her for over twenty years and she thinks she can just pick things up from where she left me?

But today's dog-whistle screaming is accompanied by what I call my own personal Māori haka, where with every wave of rage, I stomp my feet. First my right one, then my left, and on it goes until I'm all stomped out and breathless. Looking at me from the outside I must seem like a child, but I guarantee you it's the only thing that will get something out of my system. It works wonders.

When my throat is raw and my thigh muscles take over the silent screaming, I throw myself onto the bed. Okay. *Think*. There has to be a way to get out of this without making an arse out of myself. I could cite an emergency at home. But then my dad would assure her that everything's okay. I could cite a work emergency. Get Markus to invent some huge business predicament. No. He's not like that. He doesn't indulge in fake drama. He already plays down my bone-fide dramas as it is.

'Livvie? Open up, the door's locked.'

Her again. Shit. 'Mother, can you come back later, please? I'm trying to sleep.'

'Hurry up, I need the loo.'

The loo? Why doesn't she use the one in her own room? And then I tunnel-vision on a door that leads into another bedroom. I didn't notice it before because it was closed, but now that it's ajar I can see it's already occupied, an open suitcase spilling flowy multi-coloured clothes all over the floor. This can't be! I didn't think I'd have to share with anyone, let alone my mother. And now she's banging on my door with a weak bladder.

Trying to suppress my annoyance, I unlock the door and she dashes past me with a 'Thanks, love!', lifting her skirts like a medieval damsel in distress before she's even got to the bathroom door. Someone please kill me now.

Some mothers sing lullabies to their children when they're little. My mother is singing every Italian song she knows to me, at the ripe age of almost thirty-five, while I'm trying to nap, asking me if I remember them when I've never heard them in my entire life. I live in the UK and have no affiliation with Italy. Why would I be interested in this or that Italian singer's tragic life?

If there is one tragedy, though, it's this bedroom. Because this is not going to end well. But have I got the guts to tell my mother that I don't want to have her in an adjoining room? I have never argued with her. I decided never to tell her how I feel about her abandoning us. How can I start bickering with her when she's forcing me to spend eight weeks in such close quarters, and at her expense? I can't very well say that I can barely stand her presence, can I?

Now the long weeks stretch out ahead of me, like a big, black hole ready to swallow me up. I can't do this. There is no way I can ever do this and not physically clobber myself over the head at least a couple of times. And I'm not one for violence, but if I had a brick wall right in front of me, I'd have put a hole through it by now.

'Sorry, I forgot my key,' she says as I get back into bed and, *through the open bathroom door*, she proceeds to tell me about her husband, Aldo, and her cleaning staff at home. She has *staff*. I can't even get my own husband to take out the rubbish. Life is just not fair.

'And Aldo sends his love, of course.'

Of course. I've never met the bloke in my life, but he *sends his love*. Does he also send an apology for his contribution to ruining my life? I've only seen him in pictures that Mother constantly sends to Dad, showing off her new life and really rubbing it in. I mean, who *does* that to the person they abandoned?

'Livvie?' she calls.

I turn onto my side, fitting my pillow over my head to deaden the noise, but it's not working. 'Yes, Mother?'

'Am I talking too much? I'm so sorry, I'm just excited to see you! I'll let you sleep, love…'

'Thank you,' I say begrudgingly.

'Go to sleep, sweetheart. We'll talk when you wake up. You must be absolutely knackered, you poor thing!'

Then her phone rings. '*Ciao, Sandra, come stai, bella?*' she trills and I know I'm never going to get to sleep.

Somehow, I've slept through dinner and the rest of the night. When I wake up, my first thought is Cassie.

When I try her number again, it goes straight to voicemail. She must have seen my call and rejected it. Not that when I'm home she acts any differently. I'm hoping that it's just a (very long) phase, and that sooner rather than later I'll get my girl back.

Down on the eastern terrace, breakfast is a sumptuous affair, with more expensive linen tablecloths and more of the finest porcelain. Even the fruit juices arrive in crystal decanters.

Whatever your palate, there is more than something for you: fruit salads, yoghurt, muesli, nuts of all kinds, bacon, omelettes, pancakes, croissants, toast… My mouth begins to water and I remind myself to err on the healthy side of luxurious, even though Mother is at my side, encouraging me to eat more.

I feel like I'm on the Titanic, and not just due to the perilousness of my proximity to my mother. Apart from her presence, this could have well and truly been a fantastic holiday.

After breakfast, we are given a pamphlet to book our appointments which are, *yay*, included in the price. So I book a massage, a facial, a pedicure and a manicure. That will take me up to at least dinner time without having to talk to my mother.

Or so I'd hoped.

'Hello again, love! Isn't this fun!'

I look up from my facial bed to see that my mother is being rolled up right next to me in her own massage bed. Where the hell did she pop out from? I thought I'd lost her when I abandoned her to her gaggle of girlfriends gossiping away after breakfast.

'I'm so glad we have all this time together! Luckily the director was able to add me to every appointment that you've made, and for your sake, I've made a few more that you overlooked.'

On and on she goes, extolling the virtues of our masseuses amid comments like, *Oh, and doesn't she put those cheekbones right back up there where they belong?* It lasts forty minutes and by the time I'm done pretending everything is okay for her benefit, I need another facial to sort out the muscles in my own cheeks from all the false grinning. It serves me right. If only I was brave enough to stand up to her.

When we're done I pull out my mobile and message Cassie:

Hello, love. Hope you are well? Miss you already! Text me back when you have a minute.

Love, Mum. xxx

Then I text Joe:

Good morning, my darling. I hope you have a wonderful day at school. Be a good boy, as always. I love and miss you! Mum.

To which he answers immediately.

Hi, Mum, we're in the car. Markus is taking us because Dad had an early morning at work.

It figures. I'm mere hours out of the country and already Simon is delegating his duties to Markus. But I promised myself I wasn't going to worry about things like that while I was here. The kids are in good hands.

Lunch is a quick sandwich and a salad as we are having our manicures, followed by pedicures, still side by side, inseparable like a pair of Siamese twins.

Every cuticle is taken care of, nails filed into an elegant shape, buffed and pre-treated with a primer before the lacquer goes on. There is a small machine that emits blue rays into which we have to stick our hands in for a few seconds at a time before the application of the next coat.

'Now, what colour should we have our nails done, love? Shall we go for a mother–daughter match? I think I'd like the pearly white, Damiano, what do you think?'

'It's very elegant,' the nail technician echoes agreeably.

'Yes, I agree. Livvie, what do you think?'

'Pearly white is fine, Mother,' I say, screaming on the inside. I don't want a matching manicure with my mother – I'm not twelve.

Next follows a full body massage from Gertha, a Swiss masseuse who crosses the border every morning to Italy to come to work. She is tiny but when she gets her poky fingers into my bunched-up muscles I know I'm going to love her. The pain is excruciating at first, but I eventually manage to relax as she urges me to and it's not long before I'm ecstatic with relief. All the tension inside dissipates and I'm feeling like a new woman from head to toe. I'm not even clenching my teeth anymore!

'Ah, that was just lovely, thank you, Filippo, thank you, Gertha!' Mother chimes as she slips them a 100-euro bill each.

'I can pay for my tip, Mother,' I say, reaching into my purse.

'Nonsense, this trip is my treat, lovie! Gertha, Filippo, would you be so kind as to get us some juice before you go?'

The two take their hard-earnt tips and bow out, only to return with a trolley laden with decanters full of kiwi juice, orange juice and berry juice, plus a platter of puff pastry goodies of every shape, size and flavour. The power of money.

8

That evening, I text both the kids as usual, but only Joe texts me back. Sighing, I change into a Little Black Dress as we are all invited to a soirée called *Cock & Mock*. I kid you not. Obviously the staff, who were Italian, had no idea of how awful blending the words cocktail and mocktail sounded. It's so awful, and I can't wait to snigger about it with Markus. Which reminds me. I promised him I'd keep in touch. Funny, though, how neither Simon nor Cassie have even answered my message to let them know that I had arrived safely and not, say, crashed into the Alps. Taking advantage of the fact that my mother always takes ages to get ready, I sneak out to what I've decided is my favourite, secluded spot on the terrace overlooking the lake.

'Hey, you…' comes his Scandinavian drawl through the ether.

'Hi,' I breathe. It's only been a day, but it feels good to hear his voice. 'How are you doing?'

'All good here. I'm just looking over some invoices.'

So far, so normal.

'So,' he says brightly. 'What are you up to this evening?'

'I'm having Cock & Mock!' I say mock-brightly as I survey the other guests chatting away in their black and white, high-society eveningwear. We could easily be on an old Hollywood movie set before the advent of colour TV.

He snorts. 'What?'

'You heard me.'

'You could have mentioned to me that you were on a *wild* holiday, Livvie.'

That's an annoying thing about Markus. He is so *au fait* with our friendship that he actually feels comfortable flirting with me. I flirt back, of course, but we both know it's just for a bit of fun.

'Easy, loverboy. It's not that wild,' I correct him.

'Is it that cheesy?' he asks.

'Actually, it's very posh. Very Italian. It's like being on a cruise ship circa the 1930s, only we aren't actually going anywhere. There are multiple gyms, a beauty salon, lots of restaurants and bars and even an Olympic-sized swimming pool…'

'Don't forget the Cock & Mock.'

'How could I?' I giggle. 'And the views are to die for. I hadn't realised that the Alps were so beautiful.'

'So you've been swept away?'

'That's nothing. Do you want to know the real news?'

'I'm listening.'

'Guess who is here?'

Markus pauses for a moment. 'Uhm… Sting?'

'Guess again.'

'Emma Thompson? Kate Winslet?'

'I wish. At least I'd be having a ball with them. It's my bloody mother.'

'I didn't quite catch that. What did you say, you want a Bloody Mary?' His voice crackles over the line.

'No, I said—'

'Sorry, Livvie, the connection's getting iffy, say that again?' he asks.

'My bloody mother is here,' I repeat, slightly louder than before.

'What…?'

'I SAID, MY BLOODY MOTHER IS HERE!' I scream into my mobile and become instantly aware that I have witnesses. And by the looks on their faces, some of them also speak English. Oh, grand, just grand. The last thing I need is someone to tell her about this – that'll set her off.

'Oh…' comes his reply. 'Ouch.'

'Exactly.'

'Did you flip out?' he asks.

'I haven't stopped flipping out since I got here,' I hiss into my phone. 'Not that she'd know. We always have to keep our emotions in check so as not to upset poor little Mother. I never could stand to see her cry.'

'So you're going to stay?' Without even giving me a chance to answer, he says, 'You should stay. Do the mother–daughter bonding thing and all that.'

'I'll stay, because this place is heaven on earth. But the only bonding thing happening here is me tying myself to a chair. Or maybe I'll go on a hunger strike…'

'Livvie…'

'I'm serious, Markus. I don't want her to talk about the past. Because then I'll really let her have it.'

'Are you going to behave yourself out there?'

'Unless she gets all touchy-feely on me.'

'She won't. So what's on the agenda for tomorrow?'

I sigh, already dreading it. 'Ah. Yoga, pilates and a keto cooking class. But apparently they'll be checking my bloodwork and general health, too.'

'What for?'

'They say there's no point in a wellness clinic that doesn't check your health first and foremost, so they can recommend the best ways to make you feel well again. It's what makes this place so expensive, I'm sure.'

'Don't forget to smile and be nice.'

'Ha. I'm always nice. Aren't I?'

'Yes. Snarky-nice.'

'That's still a form of nice, though, isn't it?'

I can *feel* him grin. 'In a way. The Livvie way.'

'So how're things back at the ranch?' I ask. 'How are Dad and the kids? I miss them!' *I miss you, too, but that's another story.*

'Ah, just fine! Joe played extremely well in his football match yesterday, and Cassie is studying hard.'

'Is she?' I marvel. 'Wow. It must be my absence that has a positive effect on her, then.'

'Don't say that, *skat*...'

'I'm not complaining. I'm just happy she's getting on with it. She's doing much better than I was at her age.'

'Your situation was different,' he reassures me. 'How are you going to handle things with your mother, anyway?'

'I wish I could ignore her completely. She hasn't changed. Still superficial, a real social animal.' I sigh. 'She's just so out of touch with people like us, you know? You can never actually get her to sit down for one straight minute and talk about important things.'

'Last I heard, she and your dad speak at least once a week. It seems to me you are the only one that is resisting her charms.'

'And for a good reason, Markus. You don't know her, luckily. She'd reel you right in. But I know what lies behind the smiles and the hugs. She's manipulative, calculating and selfish. Don't be fooled by all the gifts she sends. Aldo has the money, not her.'

'Do you think that now you're together you might start to forgive her?'

'Ha! That's not happening.'

'But you accepted the invitation. It would hardly be polite to ignore her, wouldn't it? I mean, you're her guest.'

'I didn't know she'd be here, let alone that we'd be in adjoining rooms, by the way.'

He chuckles at my indignation. 'Ooh, the plot thickens.'

'That's what she's like. Luckily, besides the appointments she joint-booked me with, she's got loads of friends here and workshops to keep her busy, so hopefully I'll get a chance to breathe every once in a while. It's at night that I can't get away from her constant gabbing. She won't let me close the door between our rooms because she wants to chat.'

'I see.'

I sigh. 'I wish you could. I'm trying to go to sleep but all she does is yammer on about when I was a little girl, and do I remember this party or that picnic, when all I really want to do is scream at her for leaving us.'

'And you've never done that?'

'I never got the chance!' I say, getting heated. 'It's not like she sat us down and told us she was in love with someone else. She just upped and left, Markus! She left me on that bloody stage singing by myself in front of everyone!'

'I know, sweetie...'

'And the letters that she wrote? I never answered them. I let Dad deal with her. And if the kids wanted to see their grandmother, I couldn't stop them, could I? Especially with Dad advocating for her. It's like he still holds a candle for her. My God, Markus! Do you think he still holds a *candle* for her? After all these years?'

Markus chuckles. 'No, I don't think so. I think he's just a very kind man, and he knew it was no use holding a grudge for too long. And that's what you need to realise, too. But first, you have to talk to her.'

'I can't. There's just too much resentment. If I try and talk to her now, she'll only cry and make me feel guilty about it. That's what she used to do to Dad.'

'So you're just pretending everything is okay?'

'Barely.'

'That's no way to live, Livvie.'

'I know. But she brings out the worst in me. I know I have to sort myself out. I will.'

'Promise?'

'Cross my heart. Speaking of, did you send off my cross-stitched hearts shipment to Japan?'

'Yes. But we're not talking about work, remember? Try to relax as much as possible and have that talk with your mum.'

'That's an oxymoron, like "Dying happily" or "Grounded flying". It just isn't going to happen,' I say.

'Miracles do happen, Livvie. Just keep the faith.'

Keep the faith. Huh. 'Talk soon?'

'You bet,' he says. 'Give me a ring when you're free.'

'Will do,' I promise.

'Love you,' he says.

It tears my heart into a million pieces every time he says that. I just close my eyes and all the fantastical scenarios swirl through my brain. If only Markus loved me the way I wanted him to love me. If only I'd met him instead of Simon, all those years ago. There's an entire parallel universe, a parallel *life* that I could have had from the moment we met. It's crazy, I know, but I feel that I've actually lost out on that life, even if it only exists in my deluded, love-sick mind.

'Love you, too,' I say.

The next day I have a meeting with the in-house, wait for it... *shrink*. Because my *mother* mentioned that it might be a good idea to get a load off my mind. And no, she wasn't trying to be funny. I didn't want to give her the satisfaction of being right, but I thought about my conversation with Markus, and decided that *he* would think it was a good idea. In fact, I told Susan that Markus had suggested it first. I don't think it will actually do me any good though. I mean, I understand and respect that other people do, but I don't do any of that emotional spillage. It's messy, and once the Jack is out of the box there's no putting it back. So I'll go, just this once, to appease everyone.

Plus, *Dottor* Giovanni Severini's office is all the way on the other side of the complex, meaning I'll have a nice quiet stroll on my own.

Only it's not a quiet stroll but a veritable schlep up the hill to where the Mental Health Block is. Huffing and puffing, I slide into the armchair indicated to me by the receptionist. Thirty minutes max. I can do this. Once he sees that I have nothing to discuss with him, he'll chalk it up as an unnecessary use of both our time and let me go on the spot.

Just then, the door opens and in comes a tall man in a white coat. What I hadn't realised is that Dr Severini is about Joe's age. Okay, maybe he's not ten, but he certainly looks very young.

He sits down, sporting a broad smile. 'So, Olivia, what brings you here to Respiri?'

'My mother dragged me here under false pretences.'

'Wow.'

'You can say that again.'

'So what issues can I help you with?' he asks, changing tack slightly. I don't give in.

'Nothing, I'm fine. I'm only here because my family think I need a little rest.'

'Okay. Why don't you tell me a little bit about your family?'

'Er, I've got two children, a ten-year-old son and a fifteen-year-old daughter.' And even as I say that, I still can't help but feel that I should've stayed behind with them.

'Married?'

'Indeed.'

He puts his pen down and looks up at me.

'What?' I say.

'How is your marriage?'

He's cut to the chase, hasn't he? Might as well have a

laugh, then. 'Totally fixable. Have you got a million pounds and a husband-a-tron?' I joke.

'What's a husband-a-tron?'

'Nothing. Just something that needs to be invented.' Uh-oh. Have I already said too much? It was just something flippant to say, but it's backfired on me and now I look like a sad tit.

'So let me understand. You put your husband in there and...?'

I shrug, resigned. 'I dunno. You press a few buttons and he comes out different. Like he was when you got him in the first place.'

'Got it. Interesting. And if there was a wife-tron?' he wants to know. 'Would you put yourself in there, too?'

'Wife-*a*-tron,' I correct him. 'It just sounds better.'

He chuckles. 'Okay. So would you put yourself in there, too?'

'Not at the same time as him,' I giggle. 'You don't want a disaster like in the movie *The Fly*. Imagine coming out with his head on my shoulders instead. That would be a right mess.'

'So you would put yourself in there, then?' he persists.

I shrug again. 'Sure, why not? Just my head, though.'

'And why's that?'

'Because that's still fixable, I'm hoping.'

'And what part of you don't you deem fixable anymore?'

'My heart.' I admit. 'That broke a long time ago.'

'Who broke it?'

I snort. 'Would you like a list?'

He folds his hands together and stares right into my eyes. 'Olivia, you are here to be well and happy again. Once you decide what it will take, a million pounds and the husband-a-tron aside, we will help you achieve your goals.'

'So no changed husband, then, I guess,' I quip.

'Not unless you decide to get a brand-new one. And I'm afraid we can't change the one you've got unless he comes here as well.'

I laugh. 'Who, Simon? I have to badger him to get his hair cut.'

'Well, then all we have is you to work with. Here at Villa dei Respiri we aim to reboot our guests. Give them the start they need.'

'Like in *Fantasy Island*?'

He chuckles. 'Sort of. You can take advantage of the healthy menus and the gyms and walks available. No one is going to go through your luggage to check you don't have a stash of liquor or junk food in there. We want you to enjoy your time here, whatever that may look like.'

'Really?' That's actually great, because I do. Four bottles,' I lie. Just to test him.

He is silent for a moment. I must have destabilised him, like those scripts that telemarketers follow to trap someone into buying something. Usually there's a back-up line to get back on track, but I've completely derailed the poor shrink. *Yes, well, get used to it.*

'Were you ever bullied at school?' he asks casually, completely side-stepping my lie.

How does he know that? After my mother left, I became the talk of the town. Everyone knew what had happened; the town was small, and any news always spread like wildfire.

I took a few days off from school, but the second I came back, the kids were on me like sharks smelling blood from a quarter of a mile away. And goodness, did they have a field day with me. I was an easy target in my vulnerable state.

My first bully started on my very first day back to school. I had not kept up with the homework that my besties Hannah or Emily had brought round. Not because I didn't want to do it, but because I simply couldn't concentrate. The pages would become a blur as my mind lived in a world of *Why did my mother get to be happy while not* one *thing ever went my way?*

Mary, my first tormentor, started off by making out that she wanted to be my friend. After the three months that it took me to finally open up to her about my mother's betrayal, she decided she had enough material to hurt me. And on Monday morning, on our first break in the school grounds, she attacked. I was completely blindsided.

'Ooh, look at little Livvie walking around like a lost puppy, with no mother! Don't you want to just slap that sad look off her face?'

'Yeah,' her friend had enthused, delivering me said slap.

At first, I was shocked. How did they think that was in any way funny? Well, it must have been funny, because soon there was a gaggle of snickering girls circling me, wanting more.

'Give her another one, Mary!' someone had called from the crowd.

And so she did, while I just stared at her again in shock.

'What did you do *that* for?' I demanded, too proud to rub my throbbing cheek.

'Because you think you're hot shit just because you *sing*,' she sneered. 'But you're nothing!'

And she was right. I was just a half-orphaned shell. I had nothing left. Not even my voice to sing anymore. Not even to defend myself.

The painful memories fade into a mist and I find myself looking up at Dr Severini. 'Bullied?' I repeat. 'No, of course not.'

'And what about your relationship with your mother, Susan? What is that like?'

Why is the entire planet interested in my mother?

She never returned. It doesn't matter that she often called or wrote letters. She should have come back. At least to visit, for Christ's sake. She should have made an effort to see me grow, rather than say, 'My, you look so grown in the pictures your father sent!'

I don't care that she and my father kept in contact, or that she wrote me letters and sent postcards, or that Dad begged me to speak to her on the phone on my birthdays. She means nothing to me anymore. And yet, here I am, played once again by her wily ways.

Back in my room, there is a knock on the adjoining door.

'Livvie, can I come in?'

No! 'Yes...'

Susan opens the door and comes to sit on the edge of my bed. 'How did your session go?' she asks.

I shrug. 'Fine.'

She sighs softly. 'Livvie, I think that it's time to stop ignoring the multi-coloured elephant in the room.'

Pointless asking her what she means, of course. We both know it.

After she left, for years I had hoped for the impossible – that my mother would ditch her new Italian lover and return home to us in Canterbury. That she would become a completely different person; a better mother, less miserable. But that never happened and I stopped deluding myself after the second Christmas on our own. Presents had arrived, along with cards and photographs. But I hadn't wanted any part of her memory to invade my new life without her. Dad and I had managed to get on with it.

And coming here has, just as I'd expected, thrown the proverbial spanner in the works. Now what? What do I do? I *knew* how to live that mother-less life. I had built my entire existence around it and I had everything going like clockwork because I had built myself a life without her.

Now that I am here, face to face with her, I've had to not only deal with the fact that she's been gone all these years, but that she's been extremely happy with her new life and never looked back once. And she still wants a relationship with me. To have her cake and eat it, too. She wants, even if she hasn't asked for it, my forgiveness. She wants me to act like nothing had ever happened between us. Like she was not responsible for breaking my heart.

I've tried patience, indifference, resentment. But none of them can fill the void inside me. I need to jump over the chasm in the middle of my life that has stopped me from moving on. I know that. But I also know that I'm afraid to make that leap of faith. I want all of this to be over, once and for all. I truly do. But what if I start trusting her all over again and she pulls another stunt on me? I would not bounce back a second time.

'I'm too tired after my session. I think I need to lie down for a bit.'

I fluff the pillow and lie down, making sure to face away from her. 'Okay, Livvie,' she says, and I hear the quiet click of the door closing behind her.

9

Dinner is another Gatsby affair, with piano music and drinks on the terrace. I stop at the top of the stairs, partly out of surprise and partly because it's time to text the kids again.

Joe has answered my text with a string of hearts, my soppy little boy.

Cassie never answers me, but it's okay. At this age, she needs time to process her emotions. I can understand, in a way. Even if it hurts. So I text Joe again, just to make sure everything's okay with her as well.

How is Cassie?

The usual ray of sunshine, LOL. I'll get her to text you back. Right now she's texting her friends. xxx

Ok, love, thank you. Big kisses from Mum.
Give everyone a hug from me.

I put my phone in my clutch and look around me. There

are beautiful dresses flashing past me, and the clink of champagne glasses makes it all the more posh. I have never done anything posh in my life. The only time I dressed up was at my wedding. I breathe deeply, taking in the din. It's a nice, carefree din that I don't have to do anything about.

The tables are covered in crystalware and there are fairy lights above us in intricate patterns. It all looks so glamorous. Mother must have paid a fortune for me to be here. Who am I kidding? Aldo paid for it. I'm surprised he'd agreed to pay for my spot as well. He must be very generous. Or an absolute pushover, which, knowing my father, is more likely.

The waiters pass me by with trays full of swordfish with aubergines, mint and capers, surrounded by a wide variety of grilled vegetables. If I didn't know better, I'd think that this was some sort of healthy eating retreat. But ah, take a look at the dessert tables and you'll change your mind. It is one long line of tiramisù, cannoli, cream puffs, strawberry mousse, apple pies, apple strudels, chocolate and pear cakes, chocolate mousse and anything your heart may desire.

Mother waves at me from a table with her usual gaggle of girls, comprising her two besties, Maria and Lucia. Tonight they are decked out to the nines and I have to say that they look utterly fantastic. I wish I had the courage to paint my lips that colour!

'Come, come, Olivia!' she calls. 'Come and listen to this trollop boasting about her gardener!'

'Well, he was handsome,' the woman says as I wander over. 'And I hadn't had some good sex in a long time, so…'

'Ooh, you wicked lady!' Mother shrieks in delight, giving her a light push on the shoulder. 'Good for you! And did you see him often, after that, or was it a one-off?'

'Oh, not much. Only every Wednesday afternoon while Eugenio was on the tennis courts, of course!'

At that, my mother and Lucia howl in sheer glee, hugging each other and then Maria. I couldn't help but smile. Trollops or not, they took from life what they lacked. Old Eugenio was probably bonking someone on the tennis courts anyway, no doubt.

'You know, Livvie, Italians are much more liberal with their affairs,' my mother says.

'I guess being Catholic helps with the guilt,' I quip, and the three of them explode in hysterics. I grin back at them, unable to resist.

'Exactly!' Maria says. 'Eugenio's entire family is in the church! It's a good thing he escaped, or I'd have never been able to marry into what is only the richest family in Milan!' More raucous laughter.

So I sit with them and listen to their stories of sexual adventures draped in humour, of housemaids that have become their confidantes in lieu of a proper friend, and luxury, all-expenses paid cruises that are thrown their way by busy husbands. Not that I'm judging them. Heaven knows what's keeping me from falling off the loyalty wagon. But I do understand what may cause them to take on lovers. And then it hits me.

How unhappy must my mother have been with my father? To me, he was the best father in the world, but what about the relationship between them? What kind of a husband was he, in the privacy of their own time together? As far as I could see, he was patient and kind, but what if... what if she suddenly woke up one morning and decided that she didn't love him anymore? That had happened to me. Was I my mother's daughter in that, too?

When I finally go to bed, full and not quite tipsy but almost, I go because I *have to*. Meaning I'm absolutely, completely, one hundred percent knackered, depleted, can't-give-any-more-unless-somebody's-life-is-in-danger exhausted. And even *then* I'd still have to make sure it was someone I really, really like.

I'm looking forward to my pre-sleep ritual, i.e., tying my hair out of my face, using one of the complimentary face masks in the bathroom, perhaps sipping some warm milk and honey while reading a chapter or two of Caroline James' book, *Atticus Arnott's Great Adventure*, to relax before going to bed. Which makes me think that, just like Atticus, I should have gone off on a campervan adventure.

So when I say I'm looking forward to my bedtime ritual, it certainly doesn't mean having to listen to my mother (who decided she was exhausted at the exact same moment as me) humming and gargling (often at the same time) while she is taking off her make-up in the bathroom mirror.

When I was young I failed to cope with her absence, and now that she'll be my roomie for two months I'm flailing. Every single thing that was wrong with me as a kid is coming out with a vengeance now. Everything that she was and I wasn't, like gorgeous, confident and happy with her new love, is still true.

As I watch her cleanse her face, I am transported back to my younger self, studying her as she was getting ready to go out. She still has the most beautiful turquoise eyes I've ever seen, and that cheeky spark in her smile is still there. And I can't help but ask myself, how did she manage to push the guilt aside and be happy all these years without us?

Aldo must have been one hell of a trade-off. Well, good for her. I'm on year fifteen of my own marriage sentence and still going for how much longer, no one knows. Any day now, I assume, judging by Simon's warmth over the phone. Because I haven't got the guts to end it. Because I'm afraid to break Joe and Cassie's hearts.

And meanwhile, here she is, my mother, happily chatting away to herself in the mirror. Or at least I thought she was, but it turns out she's talking to me and is now waiting for an answer.

'Livvie?' she prompts, and I jump. 'Livvie, are you listening to me, darling?'

'Yes,' I lie, hiding my book as she sashays out of the ensuite bathroom.

'Well, what do you think?'

'About Maria?' I ask. At least that's the last thing I remember hearing before she called my name. 'Very nice lady, yes.'

She stops and leans on the dresser to stare at me. Uh-oh, I've done it now.

'Livvie, we were talking about that at least fifteen minutes ago. Have you not heard a word I've said?'

Busted. It's no use denying it. 'Sorry, Mother...'

She comes to sit next to me on the bed. 'Are you all right, love? Are you sleeping? Eating properly? How's your sex life?'

'Mother!' I wail.

She *pfffts* me. 'Don't be so uptight all the time, Livvie. We're women. You've heard Maria and Lucia. My girlfriends talk about sex all the time. Even the ones who aren't getting any anymore, poor lasses!'

Ugh, the thought of my mother having sex is something I just know is going to give me nightmares.

'I mean, Aldo and I have always been verrrry compatible in bed if you know what I mean, but my friend Carla, the one with all the make-up and the dark curls? Oh my days, she and Fabrizio are practically swinging from the chandeliers, *despite* the menopause!'

Simon's face flashes past me, and I stiffen. Compatible in bed? Swinging from the chandeliers? Is she effing *kidding* me? I hadn't enjoyed sex since I was with Mitchell, my high school dropout boyfriend. Mitchell, the bad boy whom no one really saw through except for me.

I can still see him, coming to my rescue in the schoolyard...

'Hey, Foster!' someone had shouted. One of the knobs in Year 12. 'You going to be in the talent show this year "All By Yourself"? Why don't you sing a little for us now? What's the matter, cat got your tongue?'

'Stop it, Travis,' Mitchell had said. He was all the rage among the most popular girls for his Bad Boy looks. He had just moved from the United States and was already an icon, despite not being on any of the sports teams and the fact that he spent most of his time smoking round the back of the maths block when he should have been in class.

He took me by my elbow. 'Come on,' he said, leaving my bully flummoxed. 'Don't mix with that scum.'

'Th-thank you,' I managed when we were out of earshot.

'Don't mention it.'

We walked a bit in silence as I tried to think of something to say that would make me look interesting in his eyes, but couldn't think of anything.

'So I heard your mom left your dad,' he said matter-of-factly.

'Yeah…'

'Bummer. How're you coping?'

'Not so well, to be honest,' I admitted. He was the first person, besides the teachers, who'd actually asked me that.

'Yeah, I know it's tough. My dad left my mom for an English chick and now we're living here in a tiny shithole with her and her two sons while searching for a bigger home. Not exactly a picnic.'

'I imagine not…'

'You have any brothers or sisters?'

I shook my head.

'Well, at least you're not living with The Three Stooges. Consider yourself lucky.'

'I guess…'

'This place really sucks,' he said, pulling out a pack of cigarettes and offering me one, which I declined. 'You wanna go for a ride on my motorbike?'

'And skip *school*?' I whispered.

'Yeah, no biggie,' he said, pulling out a lighter next.

'It is for me. I've never skipped school.'

He stopped to look up from lighting his cigarette, a smile tugging at the corner of his mouth. 'Tell me you're joking.'

I shook my head. 'You look like you're used to it.'

'Oh, yeah. Big time. So you wanna come or not?'

'W-where?'

He shrugs. 'Anywhere we wanna go.'

'Anywhere our fancy takes us?' I liked the idea.

'Well, I don't know about your fancy, but I could really use a Mickey D's. That stuff you call school dinners? Barf time.'

I laughed. 'I like them. Well, used to. Not so much anymore.'

'My guess is it's the company that's got you down more than the shitty food. Come on, Foster. Let's go.'

'It's Olivia, actually…'

'Olivia. What a typical English name. But then again, you are a sweet, typical English girl, aren't you?'

'I dunno…' I could feel myself blushing.

He studied me for a moment and grinned, caressing my cheek. I can't explain the sensation. It was as if my entire life I'd only been noticed for the wrong reasons and suddenly this older, bigger-than-life guy, noticed me for the right ones. *Me.*

'Yeah, you are sweet. Come on then, Livvie. Let's go.'

'Easy there, *pardner*,' I said in a very bad American accent. 'I barely know you.'

'But I'm offering you the opportunity to *get* to know me,' he reasoned.

I pictured my next few years in school, toeing the line and killing myself studying. And I groaned. Why did I have to always be a good girl and do all my chores and my homework and be thoughtful and considerate when the one person who was supposed to be teaching me all that had gone rogue and thrown the rulebook away? If she could go off the rails, so could I. Besides, it would be fun to walk on the wild side for once.

'Okay,' I said, feeling a sense of foreboding, yet freedom at the same time. 'I'm in.'

So go we did. We went everywhere that afternoon, all afternoon. And that was the beginning of my downfall, I knew it. Let this be on her conscience, if she even had one.

Because I knew that I probably wouldn't have even given Bad Boy Mitchell the time of day if my mother hadn't left us.

The same mother who was still waffling on about her rich friends as I'd zoned out. But I gather I hadn't missed much because she was still boasting about their sex lives.

'And Margherita, the lady with the big hair? She's got a toyboy half her age, Marco, who is an absolute god, and *she* told me that he likes to—'

'*Mother!*' I beg, covering my ears and face with the coverlet.

At that, she stops. From under the covers, I can only assume she's studying me.

'Darling?' she says. 'Are you and Simon not having sex? What's happening in your marriage?'

'Nothing,' I snap, throwing the coverlet to the floor and running for cover to the bathroom where I lock myself in, fuming at my reflection. How dare she stick her nose into my private business as if we were the best of friends? How very *dare* she?

'Darling? Darling, are you all right? The door's locked. Are you ill? Have you got an upset stomach? You did look a little pale at dinner. Have you been? Come out and I'll give you a laxative. They're herbal and very effective. Take one now and tomorrow morning—'

Arrrrgh! I silent scream into my hands. I've tried everything. To be honest, I was up all last night thinking of various ways to get out of this. But even my demonic mind couldn't come up with anything that wouldn't make it too obvious. Because, despite my resentment for my mother, the last thing I want is to see her cry. I really don't want to deal with that right now.

She cried when she was sad, when she was happy, and even when she was proud (that was actually quite nice, though). So the less she engages in emotional overspill, the better. But I can't avoid feeling like a heel. She really is trying. I have to give her that. 'I just need a few minutes, Mother…'

Seven weeks to go. I might as well make the best of it by filling my schedule with spa appointments, massages and manicures. At least when I go home I'll *look* refreshed, even if I feel like I've been through an emotional mangle.

10

A few days later, it's time for another fun-filled afternoon, i.e., another session with Dr Severini. He's already in place, knives out and smiling. I don't know why I have elected to take advantage of this service. Probably because a stranger may have the best perspective on things. Dad and Markus are always telling me to get on with my life rather than harbour anger towards my mother. Simon, on the other hand, says nothing at all because I stopped confiding my deepest feelings to him years ago.

'I'm ready, Hannibal, bring it on,' I say before I can stop myself. I realise it's rude, but I can't bring myself to apologise. He should be apologising to me after all that prying around the last time I was here.

Instead, he looks up with an amused smile. 'I enjoyed our last session,' he says, catching me off guard.

'Well, no offence, but someone has to.' Is it me, or are we both enjoying the antagonism?

'Even if you've been holding back,' he says amiably, ignoring my quip.

I don't know why I resent him so much. Probably for

the same reason I resented my very first shrink. I had been acting up at school and at home under Mitchell's influence, becoming a proper nightmare, and I resented anyone who tried to help me at that time.

'You are a lot of work, did you know that?' he says.

'Sure, I'm a regular Lorelai Gilmore.'

'A what?'

'Lorelai Gilmore. From *Gilmore Girls*. Don't tell me you've never seen the series?'

'Can't say that I have.'

I gasp in exaggerated surprise. 'So you know about *Fantasy Island* but not *Gilmore Girls*? Are you in for a treat!'

'Do all of your cultural references come from the entertainment industry?' he asks.

'Where else? I grew up glued to that thing.'

'And why is that? Didn't you have any friends?'

Straight in again.

'My daughter watches it,' I lie. She watched it once but as soon as the mother–daughter theme emerged she dropped it like a hot potato. 'And if you want to see a dysfunctional family par excellence, let me introduce you.'

'They're fictional.'

'Yes. But they are real types.'

'So you identify with this Laura—?'

'Lorelai. A lot of women do. Her mother is a real—'

'What have the two of you got in common?' he asks.

'Her mother and me?'

'No, you and Lorelai.'

'Huh.' I pause, thinking. 'Well, we both have impossible mothers. But at least hers never left her.'

'Your mother left you?'

'When I was a kid; didn't you know?'

He shrugs. 'How am I supposed to know?'

'Not that she would ever tell you any of her sins, but isn't she your patient?'

'She's one of the shareholders. And by the way, we don't refer to our guests as patients. This is a wellness centre, after all.'

'You could have fooled me,' I say. 'I've seen more doctors than I have beauticians. What does a girl have to do around here to get a hair appointment?'

He sits back and looks at me coolly. It's obvious I'm here because I have to do the talking.

'So let me get this straight,' I say. 'You know absolutely nothing about me?'

'Absolutely nothing.'

'Oh my days,' I say almost gaily. This is going to be fun!

'I know Susan is your mother, but that's about it,' he clarifies. 'So, tell me more about your children. What are they like?'

'Joe is a dream. Top of his class, very sporty, very affectionate towards everyone.'

He nods. 'So then it's Cassie who worries you.'

'I never said that…'

'You didn't have to. I can see it in your face. Besides, teenagers are always problematic.'

'Even yours?' I ask.

He takes off his glasses. 'How did you know?'

'I can see it in your face. You're happy to see that yet another parent is struggling. I'm not offended. It's the way the world turns. It makes us all feel less lonely, less of a failure.'

'Amen,' he says.

'How old is she?' I ask.

'My teenager? How did you know it's a she? Never mind. You're good at reading people, you know?'

'Maybe I'll have a change in careers,' I joke.

'Maybe you should,' he agrees, smiling. 'So tell me about Cassie. What's her problem?'

'Me, if you ask her.'

Dr Severini chuckles. 'Are you an overbearing mother?'

'Doctor, I come from an overbearing mother who abandoned me. You do the maths. Of course I'm not overbearing.'

'But you're always there for her?'

'Clearly!'

'Then maybe that's the problem. Maybe she needs to figure some things out for herself.'

I shrug. 'You're probably right. But, you know, I want to make sure I'm always there for her, even when… she screws up royally.'

'Like you did?' he asks.

'How did you— Never mind.'

'What was his name?'

I sigh. 'Mitchell. His name was Mitchell. He was… everything I thought a boy should be. He was strong, he was kind. He didn't talk too much, but I liked it that way.' *Especially because it allowed me to fill his silences with my teenage girl fantasies, turning him into an absolutely perfect mix of things a boyfriend should and shouldn't be.*

'So in other words, he was there for you,' Doc says.

I nod. 'Yes, he was. One call and he'd run to me.' I look up, expecting to see a negative reaction on his face, but he's as cool as a cucumber.

And as if pushed by some invisible force squeezing all the feelings out of my mouth, I begin to open up despite my fears. 'We fit perfectly for two main reasons, neither of which were that romantic, but who cared? I had him and he had me. I needed someone to always put me first.' Apparently my dad wasn't enough for my bruised ego. 'And Mitchell always ran to me because he *needed* to be needed. It truly was a win–win situation for both of us.'

'That's very profound,' he says. 'Most people don't realise what their other half needs.'

'Oh, I realised and more, even at that age. I had to grow up quickly after everything. When I vented to him, he knew he was no longer the only one suffering, or the weaker one. With me, he had someone else who was worse off, in his opinion. Between the two of us, I actually don't know who was worse off, but we were starting to become more and more similar each day, as if our troubles had rubbed off on one another.'

In truth, we would often cut school to go and smoke somewhere, discussing our own version of history and politics and world events. For someone who was hardly ever at his desk, Mitchell was quite versed in these subjects and I soon fell under his spell. His ideas became mine, albeit in a more watered-down version because I really had no idea about much of any of it, too immersed in my own little world of self-commiseration.

'I had lost all interest in everything else. After numerous desperate attempts to reel me back, my two best friends –

my two only friends – Hannah and Emily, had stopped trying to fix me. Because I couldn't be fixed. The sadness inside me was constant, and no pyjama party could erase it.'

And for some reason, I continue to talk about my childhood.

'I used to get invited to parties all the time, but then everyone must have got sick of asking. I couldn't blame them. Actually, I didn't care anymore. I could barely get up to go to school on some days. It was just too much of an ask.'

Dr Severini leans forward sympathetically, and I can feel the embarrassment at spilling all my secrets threatening to rise to the surface, but I'm on a roll. I don't want to stop now, so I ignore him, and just keep talking as if he isn't even in the room.

'Sometimes even... *washing* was too much for me, but Mitchell didn't mind. He wasn't all that squeaky clean himself, sometimes sleeping in his clothes and then rolling out of bed and straight to school – on the rare occasions that he did go.'

'And your father? How did he take it?'

I groan inwardly. Poor Dad. 'I put him through hell. I had changed so much, become a real rebel, he hardly recognised me, asking me where...' I swallow. 'His... good little girl had gone...'

'Do you still carry the guilt?' Dr Severini asks softly.

I look up. 'Guilt? Have we met? I am made of guilt.'

'I know. It's the ones who bear the weight of guilt who try to shake it off by being angry at the world.'

'You know, Doc? I think you're starting to understand me.'

'So I'll see you next week?' he asks, leaning back in his chair.

'After my facial, maybe,' I say, getting up.

He beams up at me, happy that I seem to have melted like the proverbial butter in his hands. 'Good. Looking forward to it, Olivia.'

I sigh mischievously. 'Ah, Doc, I wish I could say the same.'

Truth be told, Mitchell and I hadn't spent *all* our time evaluating philosophical theories and political views, and after a few months I missed my period. When I rushed over to his house in a panic to tell him, he'd grinned. Grinned! 'Wow, that's so cool, Liv!' he'd said. 'We'll make great kids, you and me.'

Which was nice to hear on one hand, but where was his practicality in all this? What were we going to do with a child, and not one GCSE between us?

'But *we're* still kids, Mitchell. I'm only fifteen.'

'Nah. It'll be all right. If you're pregnant, you're pregnant. Besides, my dad's loaded. He'll put us up, we'll have a great life.'

'But what will we do, besides raise a kid? What jobs will we have?'

'Jobs?' he'd said, surprised. 'Honey, this baby will be our meal ticket. We don't have to do anything as long as we live, now.'

'That's not exactly how I see my life unravelling, Mitchell,' I said. 'I want to do stuff. Become someone I can be proud of.'

He shrugged. 'No one's stopping you. Once the baby is born and settled, you can do whatever you want.'

All words some people may dream of hearing, but not me. I wanted to start my own company, run operations, make things and sell them. Be my own boss. I was too young to resign myself to motherhood, just like that. I had had a shit life until then. When would I actually start living if I had a baby?

And Mitchell? His plans were to sit on his arse all day and drink beer while minding the baby as I tried to put a business together? Not my idea of a dream life. Which was why I, the bullied underdog, left the cutest bloke ever to grace the hallowed halls of the school.

'I can't keep going on like this, Mitchell,' I'd whispered after a couple of weeks of debating how to tell him.

'What's that, hon?' he said distractedly, one hand on my hip as he turned the page in his *Classic Bike Guide* magazine. We were in his bedroom, lying around like dead dogs on a hot afternoon. But my mind was running a hundred miles an hour, and in a completely opposite direction to his.

I sat up. 'It's been great, Mitchell, acting out, being free to do whatever I wanted. But I got it out of my system and it's not who I want to be anymore. I owe it to myself to do more in my life.'

Mitchell put his magazine down. 'What are you saying?'

'I'm saying that I am not keeping it. And I think it's time we said goodbye, once and for all.'

He stared at me, his eyes wide. 'But... but... if you're pregnant, you'll need me to come with you and...'

There it was again. *You'll need me.* What he didn't understand was that I didn't need him, especially if he was going to continue to be happy dragging me down like this. I hardly recognised myself. I was supposed to go to music college, perhaps become a songwriter. But where was I going like this, a school dropout on a fast track to absolute nothingness?

Enough. Enough of the laziness, enough of this self-doubt. Mitchell had seen me when no one else had, but it was fair to say that he hadn't had a healthy effect on me. On one hand he had given me what I'd needed at the time: he'd made me feel carefree for a while, and he'd made me feel beautiful and special. No one had made me feel like that. But I needed more. I wasn't the me I *wanted* to be.

'I'll be fine, Mitchell. Honestly. I'll just go and see a doctor and sort it out. I hope you understand, but I'm too young.'

'Olivia, come on! I thought we really worked together! You're really, really sure you wanna do this?'

I nodded, resolute 'Yes. I'm sure.'

'Damn. I really like you. I like you better than anyone I've ever liked. In fact, I think I might even love you, Liv.'

It was all I could do not to cry. But I was determined this time. 'I'm sorry…'

He dragged out a long, pained sigh. 'Well, if you ever change your mind…'

I threw myself into his arms in a grateful hug. The last thing I wanted was to hurt him when he'd been there for me as best he could, but it simply wasn't what I needed anymore. So I got to my feet and straightened myself up. The shorts I was wearing were wrinkly and somewhat overused. Time to go home, have a shower and do some laundry. Time to do a lot of things.

'Thanks, Mitchell, for understanding. You're the best first boyfriend a girl could ever want.'

He rubbed his face and ran a hand through his spiky hair and smiled a sad smile. 'I guess I just gotta let you go, then. Bummer. Big bummer, but hey, easy come, easy go…'

I took his stubbly face in my hand and kissed him one last time. 'I will never, ever forget you, Mitchell. Thank you. See you around?'

He snorted. 'Yeah. Maybe if you go back to school, I might be persuaded. I'll miss you, Liv.'

'No, you won't,' I said with a grin but inside I was crying. I truly loved Mitchell, even with all his weaknesses and shortcomings. But even at my age I knew he was not for me and that he would only tether me down to a non-life. A mere existence, and I wanted more. 'Take care of yourself, Mitchell. I will always love you...'

Oh, sweet, sweet Mitchell! I hadn't dredged up the memory of him for quite a while and now that I have, the pain of it all comes crashing back. My first boy-induced heartbreak.

I pause at the suite I'm sharing with my mother and wipe my eyes. I can't let anyone see, let anyone know that I'm still hurting over what happened after that. No one knows. Not my father, not Simon, not even Markus.

I open the door, relieved to see that I am alone, and that I can actually lie in my bed and cry for a bit, thinking about what happened after I left Mitchell.

The 'procedure' had been quick. I went on my own. No witnesses to the saddest moment of my life yet. But the doctor was very kind and considerate, explaining to me what I needed to do afterwards.

I went home on my own and lay in bed all weekend, absolutely gutted and empty. But I did my best not to mope around listlessly. And on Sunday evening, I was caught by a cleaning/cleansing/rebooting raptus. I can still remember it clearly.

The first thing I did was throw the dirty laundry into the machine, then I wiped down all the countertops in the kitchen, putting odds and ends away and binning the useless stuff that had been lying around despite Dad's best efforts to keep the place clean.

Then I vacuumed the entire house, from top to bottom and proceeded to do all the dusting, and not just feather-dusting around objects but actually doing it properly. From now on I was only going to do things this way. No more half-arsed jobs.

Next I moved into the sitting room and threw open the windows, which I washed, deciding to do all the others while I was at it. By the time I'd finished changing the sheets on both beds and tidied some more, the house hardly looked like ours anymore. It was unbelievable what a bit of TLC could do to a home. Because this was still my home. Dad was still my dad and I would do my best to make this entire shitty year up to him.

By the time he got home, he didn't know what had hit him. I met him at the door with a kiss, wearing a clean, proper dress and my hair in a neat ponytail.

'Hullo...?' he said, looking around him and breathing deeply while still hanging onto his toolbox. 'What's all this? I smell furniture polish, disinfectant, you've tidied up and... look at you, Livvie, you look amazing! What's happened?'

'I've left Mitchell, Dad. I'm going back to school to get my GCSEs. From now on I'm going to be the daughter that you've always wanted.'

At that, he dropped his toolbox at his feet. 'Oh, Livvie…! You are the *only* daughter I've ever wanted. You are my little baby girl, no matter what! I'm always proud of you!'

'Thank you, Dad. But I'm serious. I want to study design, continue with my sewing and study business to start my own company,' I blurted out before I could think.

'Oh, sweetheart, that's fantastic!' And then he started to cry.

'Dad…?'

'Tell you what, love – I'm going to clean out the oast house at the bottom of the garden and make a little workshop for you, how's that?'

I gasped, my hands over my mouth. 'We can do that?'

'Of course! I'll help you in any way I can!'

'Will you promise me something, then, Dad? If it goes well and I manage to bring some money in, will you retire from your job?'

'Oh, sweetheart…'

'I don't want to see you killing yourself on construction sites anymore, Dad. You're as thin as a rake. But I'm going to take care of you, now, just like you've taken care of me!'

He laughed and played with my ponytail. 'Let's see how things go, first, yes? It's a bit too soon for me to retire. But when I do, I'll be able to help you even more in your business, okay?'

'Deal!' I agreed, and we shook hands like real business partners. I knew I could always count on my dad to be there for me.

I even patched things up with Hannah and Emily whom I'd abandoned during my Mitchell phase. But, being the good friends that they were, they were happy to have me back.

I'd vowed that from that day my life was going to change for the better, with no bad men, no need for shrinks, and that my mother would be a distant memory. So much for all that.

11

Relieved I've made it through another day, after I've called home (Cassie is still refusing to talk to me) we all convene for drinks on the western terrace to enjoy the sunset before dinner, and the funny stories of my mother's friends: Carla, the seventy-year-old woman with dark curls and lots of make-up; Maria, the one who had an affair with her gardener while her husband named, er, let's see... *Eugenio* played tennis; and finally Lucia, who... wait, what did she do? Or rather, *who* did she do? I can't remember for the life of me, but I remember it was hilarious.

'The important thing is that you don't do it *here*,' Carla is saying, clad in a gorgeous caftan ruined by what must be her entire collection of necklaces spilling into her tanned cleavage. 'That's a big no-no now, after someone was caught in the sauna a few years ago. And they were both married, and both spouses were actual guests at the time. Imagine if *they* had been the ones to walk in on them!'

'That must have been embarrassing,' I muse, suddenly interested. Not that there was anyone here I could see myself having sex with – but fancy the idea of getting your leg over with someone of your choice in this beautiful setting?

'Well, now there are cameras everywhere, so unless you're into that sort of thing, it would be quite difficult to get it on.'

'If I could, I'd do it in the pool late at night,' sighs Elsa, a new entry for me but an old friend of my mother's. She's in her late sixties but looks like she could be my mother's mother. All the years of sunning herself haven't been kind to her skin. For a wellness clinic, it doesn't seem to me like anyone is trying to age gracefully. If anything, they're trying to cheat a natural process.

'What about you, Susan? Where would you do it?' Carla asks.

At that, she smiles.

'What?' we all say in unison.

Elsa sniggers. 'Susan's been here quite a while. She and Aldo have baptised every single corner of this place, haven't you, you naughty harlot?'

My mother, who isn't denying it, looks very smug.

'They're not one of the main benefactors for nothing,' Carla says. 'Which was the best place, Susan? Tell!'

But she just continues to smile and it is obvious that some raunchy, sordid memory has just crossed her mind. I am stupefied to say the least. I knew she didn't have any morals, but that is more than Mitchell and I ever did. And even *I* eventually grew out of my wild child phase. Is my mother planning to stay young and sexy forever? And what about the rest of these ladies here, battling the inexorable advancement of time, some more or less desperately?

But I have to hand it to them for their youthful spirit. And, to be honest, their depth. At first glance they had seemed rather frivolous, but now that I'm getting to know them, I'm beginning to change my mind. They are turning out to be quite entertaining, but in an insightful manner. Miriana, another new entry for me but the oldest of the lot, tells us about her boob job gone wrong and how it ruined her back, causing all sorts of balance issues.

At first, I think it's funny, but then she tells us about all the mind-blowing pain she had to endure that her meds never fully dulled, and the ensuing infections and the scars that never healed properly, and I find myself actually flinching in sympathy with her. It must have been absolute torture.

The next hour is spent listening to everyone's botched work: the nose jobs that had left them unable to breathe properly, the face-lifts that had left them with expressions that didn't belong to them and the boobs that had exploded during a flight to the Caribbean. The sores that never healed and all the money spent on suing these so-called doctors.

And all those parts of me that I'd wanted to fix one day? Forget it. Going under the knife is not for me. Unless I'm at risk of dying. That's a different story. But to rashly give myself up into the hands of someone with a scalpel, no matter how skilled they are, is not happening.

These women have shared their stories about their most vulnerable moments with me, simply because I'm Susan's daughter. But to me it's more than that. I am truly touched by each of their stories. Marriage, unhappiness, dreams that never came true, loneliness, fighting against depression, over and over again. We are all fighting the same battles, the same fears.

But as it all becomes more morose, my mother jumps up from the table. 'Enough of these long faces! Time to sing and dance. Follow me!' she beckons and catapults herself onto the piano bench in the corner, then starts pounding out and singing the first bars of 'Gold' by Spandau Ballet. Immediately everyone follows suit, waving their hands in the air, mimicking the drums and the sax.

'Come on, Livvie!' she calls out to me as I'm the only one not singing or flapping my arms around like a drunken bat. 'You love singing! My daughter has an amazing voice!' she calls out to everyone, who all 'Ah!' and turn to me expectantly.

The truth is that I can't remember the last time I sang, even in the shower. It brings back too many hurtful memories.

'Come on, Olivia, join in!' everyone is saying, looking at me expectantly.

And suddenly, the smell of popcorn fills the room, and in my mind a spotlight finds me, just like that night many years ago in the school auditorium when I was left to sing alone. So I turn around and run.

'So, how did it go this week?' Dr Severini asks with a grin as I collapse, resigned, into his armchair. He's moved me to his last slot on Friday and it's like I can unload the entire week on his shoulders. 'Any family dramas unfold?'

'No more than usual,' I say. There is no point in telling him that I still haven't spoken to Cassie and that she's not answering my messages because he'd only point out to me the similarity to my relationship with my mother, which I'm already well aware of.

'I'd like to talk more about Mitchell. What happened between you two after you split up?' he asks, knowing that there has to be more. Clever man doesn't have all those framed certificates hanging behind him for nothing. I'm beginning to think that he can actually help me. Or maybe he can't, but I still need to talk to someone who will not judge me (or at least not that much).

I stare at him, swiping at a tear. Slightly surprised, he holds my gaze for a minute, but then drops it to his hands, something I've never seen him do before. I'm probably scaring the crap out of him.

'I… we split up…' I begin. 'And then I had an abortion.'

If I'm expecting an *I'm sorry* or even an *Oh* of sorts, it's not happening. It's an extremely sensitive topic and he knows better.

'And how did you feel about that?'

I groan. 'Like crap, as you can imagine.'

'Yes.'

I'm trying not to break down, taking deep breaths and swiping repeatedly at my eyes, but I'm not doing a very good job of it. It's a struggle to get the next bit out, a memory that I've always tried to supress. 'We didn't keep in touch, as I thought it would be easier for both of us to move on that way. A few months later, he died in a motorcycle crash. A freak accident.' And then I collapse into a heap in my chair, crying silently while taking huge gulps of air. I am definitely one hot mess.

'I'm sorry, Olivia,' comes his soft voice as he hands me a tissue.

I shrug, wiping my nose, trying to catch my breath, but it's useless. The dam has come apart under all the pressure of such a long-kept secret and it's all I can do to stop myself completely falling apart.

'It was unbearable,' I sob. 'Losing him… twice… and a baby that we could have raised together.' And then I laugh. An unsteady, unhinged laugh. Even though I knew I had made the right decision, I couldn't help doubting myself after that. 'Just think, Doc, I had lost another potentially dysfunctional family right there. A second one, gone down the drain… and now my present family is falling apart… I can't… I don't know how to keep it together…! I'm losing, losing on every level! I've abandoned my kids for two entire months! Who does that? I am a terrible mother, just like mine was!' The tears are falling thick and fast now, and I'm struggling to take a proper breath.

'You don't mean that,' Doc says soothingly.

Of course I do, but what does he know? To study guilt and grief and loss was one thing, but to actually live with it, every single day? It's not a life.

'Perhaps your relationship with your mother isn't just about the two of you,' Doc suggests. 'Perhaps it's also due to your own burdens.'

Who knows? Is it? All I know is that I don't want to be like my mother, never have been, and yet here I am, putting myself first, and still full of all sorts of problems.

And Cassie will never forgive me for this, just like I never forgave my own mother.

We sit in silence for a moment as I calm myself down. Doc hands me another tissue. 'Better?' he asks as I straighten up in my chair and blow my nose.

I nod. 'Better, thank you. Same time next week?'

He nods as I get to my feet. 'Same time next week. I'll get some more tissues.'

'Get the expensive ones, though. These ones can't withstand a good cry.'

And I'm out of there.

I check my watch and decide that I'm going to skip the group walk up and down the mountain paths nearby and get a facial instead. Try and put my blotchy, cry-baby face back together again, as if nothing had ever happened. I'm good at that.

The next night is 1980s Foreign Music Night, my mother's absolute favourite music period, as she's been telling me all day.

When I was a child, I dreaded birthday parties. My friends would immediately forget it was my birthday and they would all gather around the piano to sing along with her rather than play games.

When I was thirteen, Danny, the boy I liked, brought his guitar to my party. At first I'd been touched by this gesture, but all too soon I'd realised it was so he could perform a duet with my mother. My *mother*. On my *birthday*. I practically grew up in her shadow. And even now, it seems, I can't come out from under her huge presence. I'm like a tiny egg that's trying to get out from under its huge, meddling, dominating mother hen that stifles her baby chicks before they can take their first breath.

'Come on, Olivia, join in! Have some fun with us!' she insists as she plays the intro to 'Against All Odds'. Apparently my escape from the music room the other night meant nothing to her. Why does she keep doing this to me? Doesn't she understand?

Have fun. After twenty odd years, she still doesn't get how much it hurts to be in her shadow. To not sing as well as she does, to not play the piano as well either because she left and there was no money to pay for a piano teacher, to not be as beautiful or sociable or happy. After all this time, she still doesn't understand that it viscerally hurts to be her daughter.

'No, thank you,' I repeat through a clenched smile. It is becoming more and more difficult to maintain a semblance of civility, but she is truly getting on my nerves with all these efforts to make me be like her. Why is she doing this to me? Doesn't she remember that the last time I sang with her was before she abandoned me on a stage? And why won't she accept that I'm not like her? We see life in a different way; I can't be happy or have fun if someone I love is having a hard time. Take Cassie, for example.

We are going through a rough patch. Only she chooses not to talk about it. The irony is certainly not lost on me here, but with all due respect, I've always been there for my family.

'Oh come on, Livvie!' my mother calls. 'Live a little!'

Live a little? My whole life has been ruined because of her and she has no idea. Her lover came before her own child. If there's someone who's lived more than just a little, it's definitely her.

'I'm okay,' I repeat, firmer this time, my nerves ready to snap, but I hang in there. After all, we're not alone.

'Come on, chickieeeeee!' she shouts again, only this time into the microphone so everyone can hear. 'Why won't you join in?'

'Because not everyone is a party animal like you!' I snap, slightly too loud.

Her eyes widen and I expect her to stop playing and the room to fall to a hush at the audacity of my reaction.

But no. As if she hasn't even heard me (or perhaps she hasn't, so wrapped up in her own talent that our pseudo-dramatic exchange was only an aside to her), she continues to sing and is soon lost in a new verse, bringing everyone else in with her. It is indeed like standing alone in this great hall, and I am suddenly transported back to my childhood birthday parties, where it didn't matter whether I was there or not, because this was the fun part of the evening for everyone.

It would be easier just to leave the hall, but I stick it out and simply wander away from the piano so at least she's not in my line of vision.

I never pretended to be more important than anyone else, of course. My father had taught me better. But growing up in a family where we had to walk on eggshells so as not to hurt my mother's feelings was a bit much. I had never been allowed to have teenage outbursts that my parents would softly coax me out of. Oh, no. The only one who could lose their rag was our mother. Which she often did.

But then she swung straight to extreme gaiety, leaving us flummoxed, to say the least. We never knew quite where we stood with her from one moment to another. And I still don't know. When you expect her to have one of her tantrums she instantly brushes it aside, and when she should be happy she's absolutely miserable.

When she finally comes to bed later that night I pretend to be asleep. An argument with her is the last thing I need right now.

I listen to the soft sounds of her getting ready for bed: the way she lifts the chair at her make-up table to not wake me, how she softly opens and closes her cream jars and how she shuts the bathroom door before turning the lights on in there so as not to blind me. These are all things I have taught my own kids. I thought I'd picked them up from my dad, who was the mildest man you'll ever meet, but obviously these were traits that they both had. Funny, because my mother is a steamroller during the day. It is only at night, when all is quiet, that she seems to tune in to her surroundings.

Breakfast is the usual luxury experience. Everyone else at our table is as vibrant as ever. It's only my mother who keeps her eyes glued to her plate, as if she's never going to speak to me again. How do I feel about it? Like when she was living with us: regretful that I've rocked the boat, yet at the same time seething about the fact that only she was allowed to express disappointment.

Not one reference to the night before, but trust me, it's all there, in the awkward space between us.

'Would you like to go for a walk?' Mother asks finally as they clear our plates, literally shocking me out of my rumination.

'A walk?' Of course, this is her olive branch and I have to take it for both our sakes. 'Sure, some fresh air will do me good.'

'Okay, then. Meet me at the gates after your spa appointment.'

This could be a good time to have a private chat with her. I don't expect an apology for leaving almost twenty-two years ago, but perhaps she wants to apologise for being so pushy last night. I would graciously accept, of course, because I don't want to provoke an argument. If I know myself, I'll probably end up apologising for ruining her fun last night. It's so much easier this way.

Someone once said, 'You can be right, or you can be happy.' I'm never either of the two, but it's okay. I'm a big girl. I can take it. It's what I learnt to do a lifetime ago.

She's right on time, waiting for me at the gates, just like she said. I confess I'm actually surprised she's remembered to show up, what with all her friends vying for her time. Pleasantly surprised, indeed.

'Hello!' she chimes, waving to attract my attention. As if I could miss her, in that turquoise gym suit and sparkly turquoise sneakers. She's wearing a silver glitter baseball cap and her face is, of course, done up completely. Who does she think we're going to meet on our walk, George Clooney? Nevertheless, she still looks great, and not just for her age. She's curvy and luscious and I stop to wonder why I don't look like her in the least.

'I'm ready to go,' I say, pushing down a sense of jealousy and forcing a smile. I can't be jealous of my mother. How loser-y would *that* be?

'You look nice, Livvie,' she says. Well, at least she's making an effort.

'Thanks, Mother. So do you. Shall we hit the road?'

'We need to wait for the gang,' she tells me.

'The gang?'

'There they are!' she sing-songs, pointing to her friends ambling slowly towards us. 'Come on, you lazy bones!' she calls out to them, waving her bangled arms. 'Let's get *going!*'

Oh. I should have figured. Why would she want to spend one-on-one time with me? Especially now that I've made it more or less clear that I'm not an emotional spiller? What would we talk about, the two of us on our own, anyway? We would probably end up quarrelling about which bend to take. Perhaps it's for the best.

But as we set out on this glorious late spring day, surrounded by towering pine trees on one side and the dizzying escarpment above Lake Maggiore on the other, I can't help but resent how many friends she has, and how at ease she is with the world and herself.

I should be happy, too! I deserve to be happy. And yet, here I am, in my mid-thirties, lagging behind a bunch of over-sixties who are all used to these fitness walks, while I am wondering if my next step is going to be my last before I collapse to the ground.

But it's not just about me and my well-being. It's about my family as well. Not only should I be happy, my daughter should be happy too, but she's angry at me for coming here. I would never have left if I'd had the slightest inkling that she didn't want me to. I'm used to her treating me like a burden, so I'd figured she'd be relieved if I went for a while.

We're walking downhill now, which isn't so bad. We are surrounded by Mother's squawking friends and I've pretty much disappeared into the background, so I take the back foot and concentrate on calming my breathing. Up this high, the air is different. Almost… rarified. And… the path down is so steep I feel like any minute I'm going to blow a hip joint or a knee-cap. And my lungs? They're on fire. The breath is soughing in and out of me like a loud wind howling through a narrow cave, and I'm wondering how long I'm expected to last.

Yes, Cassie is most definitely cross with me. We haven't spoken since I got here. Not that it's any different at home, but I was hoping that a little distance would have made me more precious in her eyes. Well, the joke's on me. Precious my arse. She reminds me so much of myself.

12

April 26th

After two weeks of putting up with my mother and her chaotic friends, I get a chance to be alone on the second Sunday there. Everyone is going to Madesimo for the day except for me. I've complained about an upset stomach so I spend most of the day in my room reading and watching my favourite Netflix shows that I never get to binge-watch at home because I simply don't have the time.

At lunchtime, someone knocks on my door with a tray. Delightful! It's an asparagus soup with lemon chicken, string beans and tiny, perfectly rounded potatoes drizzled with olive oil and oregano. Healthy but tasty. I gobble that up in six minutes flat and, then, smacking my lips, look around the room. I am now officially bored.

I go over to my mother's room to look at the pictures on her dresser. There is one of my kids, one of me as a kid, one of my father, believe it or not, and one of her and Aldo looking incredibly well. Younger. As a matter of fact, they look much, much younger! I take a closer look. In fact, it's during their honeymoon. I remember that photo. She'd dared to send it to us as a final slap in the face. I swear,

I don't know how my father even speaks to her. I don't know how any of us speak to her.

By the afternoon, I've worked myself up into such a frenzy that I need to go for a brisk walk. I'm not feeling adventurous enough to leave the compound so I just explore the halls and evening areas. They look different in the light of day without the fairy lights. I go down the stairs and start exploring the bowels of the building, stumbling upon a room with another piano in it.

I haven't played the piano in years. I doubt I still can. I sit down on the bench, staring at the keys, like the first time my mother had tried to teach me.

I can almost hear her younger voice: *You see, Livvie, this central key here? It's called the middle C. The scales are made of octaves…*

I was keen to learn, back then. I hung on her every word. When she played and sang at the same time I thought she was a goddess of some sort, with her long, blonde hair and shapely but slender figure. She sang a lot of ballads, and when she closed her eyes, I always marvelled at how she never needed to look at the keys. 'It's something that becomes second nature,' she'd explained to me once.

Before I realise it, my hands are caressing the keys in a regular rhythm. *Those* chords again. They have obsessed me for years after I refused to ever play or sing this song, or any other one, again. I remember learning it in five minutes flat. Of course I never knew that it would become the leitmotif of my life, haunting me despite the fact that I'd tried to push it back down into the shadows of my mind.

I'm playing the chords in a loop, endlessly, as if trying to psyche myself to get into the song. But I can't. The humiliation of that night is holding me back. I cannot get over the loss, the fear, the sadness of my own mother abandoning me in the moment I needed her most, the very night of our mother-daughter act.

Without realising, I come back to the here and now, practically halfway through the song. My fingers are stroking all the right keys at the right time, but somehow it just doesn't sound like my mother used to play it. Nor can I bring myself to sing it as I had that infamous night, between the sniggering of the students and the pitying eyes of my teachers. It is precisely that memory, rather than other happier ones, that has stayed with me all these years. It's that moment of panic that had gripped me, when I realised I was on my own, just like the song said, that accompanies me even today. Whenever I get upset, it's the smell of popcorn, and not the taste of my tears, that fills my senses.

But tonight, sitting on this piano bench on my own, go figure, I'm knocking it out of the park. And this voice that I'm not familiar with, a grown woman's voice singing my childhood song, belongs to *me*. I didn't even know I could still sing. I hit the high notes like the song had been written for me, holding it even longer than necessary, just to prove to myself that I can. I have lung capacity that translates to the stage and not onto the mountain paths, go figure!

I'm soon lost in the song, loving every single note, avoiding every single bad memory, because just this once, I want to jettison the weight of that night, the pain and sorrow.

When I'm done, I'm sweating like a dog, but I'm happy. I look around me, half-expecting someone to come out of the shadows and clap, telling me how surprised they are at discovering I have my mother's talent. But no one claps. I am completely alone.

That night, I wake up drowning. Whatever I do, there is no air coming into my lungs. I open my mouth wide but nothing is happening. It's as if the four walls have closed in on me, and my mother's voice sounds like it's coming through layers upon layers of mattresses, muffled by my own hoarse, desperate gasps. And like in the movies, I see my entire life flash by me in those few seconds.

I see Cassie, just born, in my arms, and then Joe, and his very first smile. I see my father giving me piggy-back rides and Markus unloading items from a delivery truck into our oast house out back with his usual grin.

And then there are doctors in my room and my mother is sobbing and the next thing I know, an oxygen mask is slapped onto my face and they won't let me speak.

Soon it is dark but there is a feeble light above my head and my mother's face hovering over me.

'It's all right, love,' she says. 'You're okay.'

'Mmiodhsdnc,' I say.

She frowns. 'What's that, love?'

'Mudnfuoefu,' I try again.

'Yes, Mummy's here, Livvie. Just try to get some sleep and tomorrow you'll be right as rain. Don't speak.'

Mmmm... motherfff.

I mean, what the actual F...? I had agreed to come to this place to get away from myself and my life and instead I'm having to confront every single one of my problems all in one go? At home, I can make them go away. Just like not facing my deteriorating relationship with Simon is feasible, or downplaying my daughter's resentment towards me, or my thousands of other issues.

As Markus always says, I am software on the inside. Definitely hardware on the outside, no bones about it. But inside? I'm pure mush. I am capable of solving only one issue at a time. Which is funny because I am an amazing multi-tasker if we're talking about practicalities. Like most women, (on a good day) I can synchronise my laundry-hanging with my cooking and baking and homeworking the kids like a well-oiled machine. I know what I'm doing. But throw in a personal emotional crisis and I'm lost. I can talk anyone down from a ledge but when I'm up there, that's it. I just don't do interior crises.

The next day when I'm wheeled back into my room, Mother is there waiting for me as expected. Her face is drenched in tears.

'Oh, sweetie, I thought I was going to lose you…!'

'I'm all right, Mother,' I dismiss her, leaning away from her embrace. The last thing I need is her pity after all these years!

If she's realised I'm avoiding her, she does a great job masking it by smiling brightly. I can't stand it when she over-reacts, which is pretty much all the time.

'The doctor says it was only a panic attack,' I explain.

'Yes, I spoke to him. He also said that if you wear a CPAP mask for the next few nights, you should be okay.'

'Uh-uh. No CPAP.'

'But, darling—'

'I said no CPAP!'

Still fuelled by the adrenaline of thinking I was dying, I call home. I don't plan on telling any of them what I just experienced, but right now I need a dose of home. Only Simon's the one to answer the phone.

'Have the kids eaten?'

'Yep.'

'Done their homework?'

'Yep.'

'Had their showers?'

'Yep.'

So he's actually doing his duty. Dad must have had a word with him. Perhaps he can *learn* empathy. Maybe there is hope for him after all. I should make a point of calling him regularly. If he doesn't understand that it's the decent thing to do, then I should set the example. And hopefully, in time—

'Olivia, did you want anything? I'm sort of busy here.'

It's useless. He lives in his own world. He is completely oblivious to anything outside his personal sphere. Not even the kids worry him, because he knows that my father, Markus and I have got their backs. He doesn't need to do anything, in his mind.

I had sleep apnoea due to anxiety, I want to tell him. *I thought I was dying. I'm still shaking a little. But I'll be okay.*

But instead I say: 'No, just checking in.'

'Right. Talk if and when something happens, yes?' he says distractedly.

'If and when something happens,' I echo him and we ring off simultaneously. If anything, I feel worse.

The GP assigned to me, *Dottoressa* Micheli, sits me down to explain our next steps.

'Now, you have high blood pressure which could be due to the altitude, so we'll monitor that all week. In the meantime I suggest you wear a CPAP mask. It's a—'

'I know exactly what it is. No, thank you.'

'But, Olivia—'

'I said no. I'm not going to look and sound like Darth Vader.'

'But your life depends upon it...'

'Hardly,' I snort. 'I've lived this long, haven't I?'

'Pure luck,' she says.

Eh? Okay. She's a tough-love kind of girl. I can do tough love.

'Thanks, but I'll take my chances.'

'You'd have to sign some papers relieving us of any responsibility ...'

'Then let's. Thank you.'

She studies me. I know what she's thinking. I know she's right, but I didn't come here to relax only to be told that I had life-threatening issues. What a load of bollocks.

'If you change your mind...'

'I won't. Thank you, Dottoressa Micheli.'

From the rooftops of Villa dei Respiri, the views are even more gorgeous, taking me aback for a moment. To the east is the lake, only about five kilometres wide, and over sixty in length. (I only know that because I've just googled it.) But what is absolutely stunning is the shade of blue of the water, a deep cobalt, much more brilliant than the sky, and framed by forests of luscious pine trees of a fragrance so intense you want to inhale forever, capture in a bottle and take home with you.

From this altitude, the little towns hugging the coast are but a series of pink and salmon dots all connected by a coastal road, and I can even make out a Ferris wheel at the end of a pier. This place is lovely.

The next morning one of the staff, Amalia, marches into our room with a box.

'Good morning, lovelies!' she coos. 'I have something for Olivia.'

I baulk at the sight of it. Because I know exactly what it is. Dr Micheli, the harpy. I'd *told* her that I wasn't wearing that dreaded thing. That it was just a nightmare I'd had. I wasn't really dying, let alone drowning, for Christ's sake. I'm not ninety and I don't need a bloody CPAP machine strapped to my face all night, thank you very much. Can you imagine me actually having to wear this thing at home, with the kids around? I'd scare the living crap out of them, poor little things.

Simon, on the other hand, wouldn't be affected in the least. His mother has one and he's used to it.

'That's very kind of you, Amalia,' I tell her. 'I was just sitting here thinking how I just couldn't wait to try one of these on.'

She laughs and turns to my mother. 'This daughter of yours has your same sense of humour, she does! Come on, Olivia, let me show you how to use it.'

Panic rises inside me. This is it. If I have to wear this thing and talk like Darth Vader, I'm officially no longer young and healthy. I don't want to be old and sick! I'm too young to be old and sick!

She plugs in a few cables and switches it on. Immediately an asthmatic breathing sound ensues. Amalia finally pulls out the mask and places it over my face. My first instinct is to back away, and she senses it, because she says, '*Calma, calma,* Olivia.'

Calma? How am I supposed to keep calm? Even listening to it makes me anxious, let alone wearing it. It feels like an octopus has invaded my face, squeezing my cheeks. And it's immediately in charge of my lungs, practically breathing for me. I'm waiting for the exhale to happen and I find myself on the edge of my seat. This thing is supposed to make me feel *better*? I'm already a nervous wreck, imagine sleeping with this thing on my face all night!

'You'll get used to it in no time,' she soothes. 'Just lie here for a half-hour to start getting used to it and soon you won't be able to sleep well without it.'

And how is that supposed to comfort me, knowing I can't breathe on my own? I mean, of course I can breathe on my own, but if I miss a beat or two, apparently this thing will shake me back into place.

'I'll sit with you, love,' my mother says, adjusting the straps around my ears as Amalia grins at us on her way out. Somebody please wipe me out now…

'So how are things at home?' she asks.

I stare at her. 'Why are you asking?' is what I wanted to say but it comes out muffled. Still, she seems to understand.

She shrugs. 'Just trying to understand where all your anxiety is coming from, Livvie. But have I hit a nerve?'

I flinch. She's definitely lost all traces of Britishness. Back home, we of the stiff upper lip don't ask personal questions, especially to semi-estranged family. But Mother has always been different. Excessively outgoing. Free of any stigma. She used to embarrass me sometimes with her gung-ho attitude, especially in front of others. *Come on, chickie, don't be shy! Sing!* Or *Dance!* Or *Tell the truth!* Always pushing me to stand out and be different when all I wanted to do was just fit in. She never cared if people were watching and judging her. In a way, sometimes I wish I'd inherited that gene. But I haven't.

'No nerve hit, Mother. Everything is fine.'

'You know, chickie, I was thinking about Cassie. She reminds me very much of you when you were young. And you remind me of me.'

'How? I never hated you while you were with us. I mean—'

'I know what you meant, love. But Cassie doesn't hate you.'

I snort. 'Oh, she most certainly does. But the difference is that I never did anything to cause this hatred. I've only left for two months.' I stop short, shocked at my own bluntness. This extra oxygen must be going to my head. 'I'm sorry, I didn't mean it to sound that way.'

She sighs. 'It's all right, Livvie. I know how much I've hurt you. I was selfish.'

So we're doing this now? Okay. I take a deep breath before answering. 'Yes, you were. It was terrible growing up without you. But Dad was absolutely fantastic.'

'As I knew he would be.'

So I might as well ask her what I'd always asked myself while crying myself to sleep after she left. 'How… could you just… leave?'

She looks into my eyes and takes my hands with her own soft ones. 'It killed me to leave you, truly it did. But Aldo and I… we had been in love since we met in Rome one summer when we were teenagers. Life separated us. Then I met your father and got pregnant with you. And then, through some mutual friends, Aldo found me and we realised that our feelings hadn't changed. It was a young love, just like for you and your Mitchell.'

'How did you know about Mitchell? Did Dad tell you?'

'Of course, love. I never missed a single event of your life. I watched you from a very big distance, but I was there with my heart.'

'And yet you never came back. You loved Aldo more than your own family…'

'Not more than you, chickie. Certainly not more than you. But Aldo needed me.'

'More than I needed you?' I plead, sounding like my thirteen-year-old self.

At that, she sighs softly. 'Aldo was very ill. He needed a kidney and I was the only one who could give it to him. He had siblings, but they were not interested in donating, so as soon as I found out, I got tested. We were a perfect match. I knew that my life would be over if I lost him…'

I did not know about the kidney. She'd actually saved his life, then?

'And the only reason I'm asking is because I hear you talking to Joe and your business partner and your father, but hardly ever to Simon and even less to Cassie. So what's going on?'

'Oh, nothing out of the ordinary. She's not my biggest fan at the moment.'

'Daughters never are. Until they are.'

Now how would she know?

'They go through years of resenting you, feeling misunderstood and unappreciated.'

'That sounds about right,' I comment. 'I guess I deserve it, after all those years of ignoring you. What comes around goes around.'

'Oh, no, sweetheart! Parenting is not a punishment. It's a privilege, and I… made a dog's dinner of it. If you want to be closer to Cassie, your parenting has to change from teaching to influencing. That's the way you create a connection. The moment you try to tell her something, position yourself as an authority, you lose her. And teaching by influencing is the biggest privilege you'll ever have. God only knows I let that pass me by, but I don't want you to suffer the same.'

She rolls her eyes at herself. 'I'm not trying to contradict myself by teaching you something, Olivia. I suppose I'm simply trying to apolo— No, not just that, I'm trying to tell you how truly sorry I am for leaving you when I did. It seemed like the right thing at the time. I underestimated you. I thought you wouldn't care enough to suffer so much. You always were Daddy's girl. But I realise now that I was just making excuses for myself.'

She takes my hand and it's all I can do not to flinch. I don't want her to know just how much she broke me by leaving. I've locked it away deep inside my heart and I cannot cope with it at the moment. Not when everything else is absolute shite. I have to have at least *one* good thing going in my life for me to hang onto as a safe place from which I can deal with my two major problems right now, i.e., Cassie and Simon. I really don't have the strength to take on any other issues right now, not in this moment in time.

'It's okay, Mother.' I brush the issue away as kindly as I can.

'No, it's not, Livvie. I know the damage I've done to you. I've followed your life thanks to your father. Good old George never knew how to keep a grudge. Life has been too good to me, Olivia. And it's time I start passing it on. So let me help you. Not only to make amends, but to be of some use to you now with Cassie, if you'll accept it.'

'It's not that I don't accept it, Mother,' I try to explain. 'I'm not all that good at… talking about… feelings.'

'I know, love. And it's my fault.'

'Is it? I don't know, Mother. Cassie is her own person and I just don't know how to deal with her anymore,' I confess despite myself. 'I'm only trying to help her but everything I say is stupid or crass or too forward or—' I bite my lip. It's as if I'm describing my own mother now.

She smiles and nods. 'It's not only you, Livvie. You both need to find the right groove. You need to be empathetic and let her grow up on her own if that's what she wants. Don't give her any advice. Let her make her own mistakes. Just wait in the background until she realises that she still needs you'

'How do you know all this?' It's not as if she's had a lot of experience.

She smiles at me wistfully. 'Years and years of therapy.'

'Therapy? What for?'

'Oh, just my sense of guilt for leaving you…'

I can't believe it. 'But you never looked back. I never thought you felt guilty?'

'Ah, my pet, if you only knew. A mother's love doesn't disappear because she's far away.'

'So, wait, just to be clear,' I say. 'You were unhappy because you did what was supposed to make you happy? And for this you went to therapy?'

'I am still going,' she says with that smile.

'Wow. So after you left England, you and Aldo didn't just ride off into the Sicilian sunset?'

She laughs, a throaty, genuine sound. 'If you only knew. We, too, have had difficult times. Love itself, despite what many poets and musicians say, is not enough. And what I mean by that is that even if you and Cassie love each other deeply—' She coughs. 'Sorry. What I meant to say was—' And again she coughs for a spell. 'Oh, dearie me, sorry about that.'

'Are you okay?' I can't help but ask at her reddened face.

She waves me away. 'Yes, yes, I'm fine! What I meant to say was that with Cassie, you just have to try these little tricks. Try to reduce the drama in her tantrums – not the importance of her pain, just the level of how she manifests her distress – and she'll respect you all the more for it, you know.'

'I don't know about that, Mother. Cassie is particularly resistant to opening up to my love,' I say, feeling my own cheeks reddening.

'Give it time. You'll see.'

13

The next morning, my eyes are barely open and Mother is hovering over me again, making me jump in fright. 'Yea-ahhhh…!'

'Good morning, love! Did you sleep well? You sounded like you did. Come, come, wash your face with cold water to get rid of those wrinkles.'

I sit up, groaning inwardly. Wrinkles, too, now? I'm not even thirty-five yet.

'Oh, and speaking of plastic surgery,' she said (which we weren't), 'did you know that Lucy Jones had a facelift? She looks at least ten years younger.'

Facelift? Here we go, always searching for ways to be even more beautiful than she already is. Some people are just greedy, greedy, *greedy*. Unless she's suggesting that I have it? With her you never know.

'Of course, it's expensive, but worth the pain, I suppose. No pain, no gain and all that.'

I sigh. 'Mother, you heard your friends the other night. Why would you even consider something so dangerous? Aren't you happy enough? You live in a beautiful villa by the sea with the love of your life, why do you need to be the most beautiful person in every room you walk into?'

'Who said I'm considering it? Why would I want to look any different to what God gave me?'

'Oh, I get it. So you want *me* to get a facelift or something? Is that what they do here? I've seen the pulled faces at the dinner table, but I hadn't put two and two together. Is that why you dragged me all the way here? Is that what this place is?'

She blinks. 'I didn't drag you. I only wanted you to feel better.'

'Not to look better?'

'You are already beautiful, Olivia,' she says. 'But I sensed that you needed to change the way you feel.'

There she goes again, with her superior state of knowledge in every single field. 'Did you really?'

'Of course.'

'No other reason?'

'What reason could I possibly have, besides spending some quality time with you?'

Please. Don't go there. Please don't start with the quality time spiel. We had spent quality time together as a family, but then you broke that family up when you chose to leave us.

I bite my lips to keep from saying any of this. Last night was emotionally exhausting enough as it was, without getting into it all over again this morning.

So I take a deep, deep breath. Those always keep me from doing or saying anything too drastic. Markus always says I'm too dramatic and maybe he's right. I should tone it down and avoid any confrontations. And that's precisely why I haven't kept in contact with her all these years, precisely why I let her and Dad organise the kids' trips to Italy. And even *that* is only because he insists it isn't fair that my children and my mother grow up without even knowing each other.

That alone for me is a loaded gun, because I could come up with at least twenty years' worth of *why* it is extremely fair, and actually more than that. It's *generous*, because my instinct would be to let them be strangers. I groan to myself. 'Moving on…'

'What?' she says innocently. 'What have I done to upset you now?'

I look at her, with her fine features, rounded chin and shoulders. But it's her bright turquoise eyes that steal the show. They attract you immediately, and you would have considered her beautiful even if her other features had been less than perfect. She looks like Grace Kelly at an ashram, with all her charm.

And she's driving me nuts. To think we had an almost pleasant conversation about Cassie last night. We'd almost connected, yet here we are back to square one. But I'm okay. I won't tell her how I feel about her. I've done well for all these years, why break the tradition of submission now? Believe me, it's so much easier to nod and grit my teeth rather than escalate to something I just can't handle.

Her mobile rings and she jumps up. 'It's Aldo,' she informs me, her face lighting up as if it was George Clooney. '*Ciao, amoooooreee*,' she breathes, reverting from her act of concerned mother to her usual, frivolous self.

I don't know what annoys me more, her girly voice while on the phone with him, or the fact that she is *always* on the phone with him. I mean, what's the point of coming all the way up to the Alps if you're going to be talking to him all day, every bloody day? If you need a break, then for God's sake, just take a bloody break.

I get that Simon and I are on the complete opposite end of the spectrum, barely managing one call a week despite the fact that we have kids and a household in common, but this is ridiculous. Their love is so... in your face. There. I've said it. It's like only their love matters in this world. It's the kind of love... that I wish I had.

I keep my mother's wedding invitation in my wallet. It had arrived the day of Mitchell's funeral. I kept it. Not as a lovely keepsake, but as a constant reminder of what she did to me. I know it off by heart. It says:

My Dears,

Aldo and I are getting married! Would love it if you could make the trip. I have so much to show you and to tell you as I embark on the second half of my life!

Mum/Susan xxx

My mother got married in the spring. The ceremony was performed in the private chapel of the groom's villa in Sicily. There were three hundred guests. The menu included all the local dishes but with a modern twist. The bride wore a cream-coloured dress of organza and was radiant.

I know all this not because my family attended (we didn't) but because of the letter containing photos of the ceremony and reception. And yes, my mother did describe herself to my father as 'radiant'.

I still don't understand why she felt comfortable inviting us or sending us information even after we (my father) politely declined because he didn't want to leave me on my own. Nor do I understand how my father could have forgiven her for walking out on their family, the one they'd built together.

All I know was that my father seemed genuinely happy for her. I didn't understand him.

Wasn't it ironic? My very first boyfriend had died at the age of seventeen just when my mother was getting married again. Even now, just as my marriage hits a low point, she is running off with her phone to speak to her perfect husband. The more deeply I fall, the more my mother flourishes. As Mitchell used to say in that American drawl of his, *Life sucks*.

As I'm pondering this, my mobile rings too. It's Simon. I'm praying it's nothing serious as he never calls me unless he needs something. I hope the kids are okay. They should be, because only half an hour ago Joe responded with three hearts to my hug emojis. In any case, it's only early afternoon and Simon's always at work at this hour.

'Hello?' I say, bracing myself.

'Hi,' he says brightly.

'Hi!' I chirp, surprised. 'How's it going?'

'Not too bad,' he says, but he already sounds distracted, as if he was only calling to make sure I was still alive, and seeing that I am, he's lost all interest again. Why is he calling me at this hour? He never does. He only remembers I exist when he needs something.

'So what's up?' I say encouragingly, hoping that my mother has witnessed his effort to call me. And I certainly don't want to scare him off if he's planning on making these calls regularly. It must never be for *my* lack of trying.

'Not much,' he says and I can hear tapping. 'Just finishing a report.'

'Right.'

'I need to run something by you.'

I glance at my mother, who is smiling into her mobile like the Cheshire cat and playing with one of her curls, completely oblivious to the fact that I'm on the phone with my husband as well. 'Tell me,' I say.

'Well, there's this conference in Manchester my boss wants me to go to.'

'Right…?'

'It would be for a week.'

'When?'

'In three days' time.'

Now, normally, I never had a problem with Simon going away for work, but what with my being gone and my father being frail lately… 'Can't he send someone else?' I ask. 'Or at least wait until I get back?'

I know the minute I say that he's not going to take it well. He already thinks I'm being selfish by accepting my mother's invitation to Italy for the best part of two months.

Simon sighs. 'It's not up to me to decide when or where, Olivia. Unlike you, I'm not my own boss. I can't just leave everything at the drop of a hat whenever I feel like it. I have *responsibilities*.'

'And I don't?' I counter. 'It's because of all my responsibilities that I'm here in the first place. I need a break.'

'And you're having one.'

'Fine. But how can you be comfortable leaving the kids with my father? He isn't as strong as he used to be, you know?'

'This is rich,' he says. 'It didn't stop *you* from leaving, did it?'

'That's because the kids had *both* of you looking after them, but if you go to Manchester, it all falls on him. That's not fair.'

'Then why don't you come back?' he suggests.

'What?'

'For the week. As soon as I return you can go back if you so desperately want to.'

'I can't just leave now,' I say. 'I made a commitment. And it would be rude to my mother. It's not that I was dying to come here in the first place.'

'Well, I suppose I should be impressed that you managed to tear yourself away from Markus in the first place.'

'Okay, Simon,' I snap, getting hot under the collar now as Mother laughs at something Aldo's said. 'First of all, I have told you time and again that Markus is practically family. Dad and the kids love him.'

'And you?' His question hangs in the air.

'Of course not. I mean, I love him, of course, but not the way you seem to think.' What else can I say? That he's spot on, that I miss Markus like crazy? I haven't got the heart or the courage to tell Simon that. Because that would really be the end of our… thing that's been dragging on, like roadkill on the tarmac. Dead. Finished. I can't bring myself to do it. Not while the kids are still young.

He sighs. 'It doesn't matter. So I'm going, okay?'

'Fine, go, do whatever you want,' I answer. 'I have to go now.' And I hang up before I give him a piece of my mind.

So much for atonement. I tried. I really did. I've been trying for years now and all I'm doing is failing, time after time. He might be a piece of work, but I'm not that much better. What kind of a mother leaves her kids for two entire months? What the hell was I thinking? I want to call him back to tell him I'll go back while he's away. But then he'll think I've capitulated. I don't want that. For years I've been trying to earn my stance. I'm not letting him walk all over me again and again.

Mother starts blowing kissie-kissie bye-bye noises and for a good two solid minutes they negotiate on who will have the heart to hang up first. She sighs, content, but then she remembers I'm still there.

'What's wrong?' she asks. 'That was Simon, wasn't it? Did you have a fight? You fight often, don't you? It's easy to tell when people are used to having fights. They are less articulate than younger couples who still make an effort to communicate despite their differences. You and Simon don't do that, obviously. You use the word "fine" a lot. "I'm fine, it's fine. Fine. Everything's juuuuust fine." But is it?'

Well, not only have I got Shrink Severini on my case, now I'm being psycho-analysed by my mother as well? But she is right about the fighting thing. Simon and I stopped trying to make the other see our way a long time ago and we have been at the Fine-do-whatever-you-want stage for some time now. For once my mother is right.

Maybe she would understand me if I told her? She seems to know about arguments, even with her own happy marriage. But of course, she knows from her previous marriage to my father, no doubt.

It would be so good to be able to talk to my mother and explain to her how I'm feeling, and how I've been feeling for the past one hundred years. Confessions from woman to woman regarding matters of the heart, motherhood, financial struggles, self-esteem and body issues. You name them, most women have them. Yes, it would be nice. Only she can't relate because she really doesn't have any of these problems.

Because after all these years, not only are my mother and I still strangers, we also have absolutely nothing in common. There is no way on earth that she could ever understand my real-life problems while she's living in a mansion by the sea, with the love of her life.

They have everything for a good life: cleaning, cooking and gardening staff and picnics on the beach and formal parties and fêtes where the entire village is invited. She is practically a queen in someone else's country.

In comparison, my life is an absolute failure. I'm married to a man I don't love anymore and who obviously couldn't care less about me. My daughter isn't speaking to me for the sole reason that I exist, and I have a mother I'm not speaking to for the sole reason *she* exists. My father is aging faster than lightning and I worry about him all the time.

I would love to tell my mother all these things, everything I've been through and all, but once I unleash the truth about my own personal hell, then what? You can't put Pandora back in the box once it's out, can you?

'It's *fine*, Mother.'

'There you go,' she sighs. 'The F-word again.'

14

That night, I have a dream. I am in the woods. It's after sunset, in autumn. The leaves are gently riding the breeze, softly falling down on me. I watch them as they descend towards me, suddenly realising that they are not leaves after all, but musical notes jumping off an invisible staff as if they had a life of their own, like little birds flocking around me.

Semibreves, minims, crotchets, quavers, semiquavers, all swirling around my head. I am aware that I have lost track of my mother, who had been walking by my side until only a moment before. I whirl around, frantically, in sheer panic, but she is nowhere to be found.

'Mum?' I call out. 'Where are you? Stop playing games, Mum. It's not funny, you know!'

But she doesn't answer. If anything, the forest has become unnaturally quiet. Sounds that were present only a while ago, like the fall of our footsteps under the crunchy autumnal leaves, or the bird calls, have all been hushed, suffocated, like under a heavy, soundproof duvet.

'Mum? Where have you gone, Mum? Come back! Everything is sooo hard! Why can't you just come back?'

And I'm suddenly lying on the ground, unable to move my limbs and get up. Leaves, no longer notes, are collecting around my face and any minute now I will be covered by their endless fall. I am going to be buried and no one will ever be able to find me, assuming anyone realised or cared.

'Mum!' I call in one final, desperate attempt as the last of the leaves cover my nose and mouth. 'I forgive you, but come back! Mum? Mum! *Mummyyyy...*!'

'I'm here, sweetheart, it's only a dream, you're okay...'

A dream? I'm okay? I open my eyes, afraid. But if I'm opening my eyes, I'm alive, right?

'I think you might have had another bad dream. You really should use that machine they gave you, but we can talk to the doctors again tomorrow if you'd like. Try to sleep now, love.'

There is no way I'm going to get back to sleep after that whammy of a nightmare.

'Shall I sing to you?' she asks.

'You want to sing to me?' I echo stupidly.

'Yes, like I used to sing to you when you were a little girl.' And before I can say *No, thank you*, she is sitting on my bed, singing me a lullaby that I barely remember. It was one that she had written for me a long time ago.

Her voice hasn't changed in the least, nor the position she's sitting in, hovering over me, her cool and soothing hands on my forehead. And that's when, out of the blue, I burst into tears and cover my face with the blanket so she can't touch me anymore.

That evening the din of the diners is really getting on my nerves, so I sneak out as Mother is holding court with our table as usual. I'm not in the mood to gossip about everyone's salacious sex lives right now.

I pull out my mobile and see I have a missed call from Simon, so I dial his number. A fizzy sound followed by a rattle ensues.

'Simon?' I call over the interference. 'It's me…'

'Olivia,' he says, somewhat frazzled. 'Thank God.'

'What's wrong?' I gasp. 'Is it the kids?'

'Yeah,' he says, and my mind begins to race with images of hospitals and morgues. 'They want *spaghetti bolognese* but we can't remember which sauce brand you buy.'

Oh, FFS! 'I don't buy it, Simon. I *make* it.'

Silence.

'But I don't know how to do that,' he says accusingly as if I'd refused to teach him for years.

'Then buy any sodding brand you like,' I say, not quite as snappy as I'm actually feeling, what with the scare he's just given me, but still.

'Hey, what's the matter with you?' he snaps back.

'Nothing,' I say. *You only bring out the worst in me, is all.*

He huffs. 'How's your mum doing, then?'

'Splendidly,' I answer. I'm the one with all the issues, apparently. But I say nothing. The less Simon knows about me the less he'll have to nag me about. 'She's getting vitamins for her bones but she's actually quite tickety boo for her age.'

'Good, good.'

And because he's not talking or asking me anything else about how I'm doing, we go through the usual spiel, pretending it's a normal conversation.

'How are the kids?'

'Fine.'

'How's school?'

'You should ask them, they never tell me, Olivia.'

'I mean, are they doing their homework? Going to their afternoon activities?'

'Olivia, you know I don't know these things. I'm usually at work.'

'How's my dad?'

'You should know, you speak to him every day. Ask him.'

All this until I decide that, bar any emergencies, we really don't need to continue this agony of a conversation. Thank God I can call Markus for truthful updates. As a matter of fact, he's more reliable than my own husband and he doesn't rattle my cage. So all in all, there's really no reason to keep up the charade of calling Simon every few days, when all he does is give me a hard time.

'Right, then,' I say.

'Right, then,' he echoes. 'Talk if there's a problem?'

So he really doesn't want to talk, despite the fact that we have two kids in common. What does that tell us about our marriage? 'Yes,' I reply, trying to hide the relief in my voice as we ring off.

Goodness me, when had this happened to us? I mean, I knew it had been happening over the past five hundred years or so, but when had it started? And why didn't we do anything to correct the course of this off-kilter relationship? I mean, is it only me, or do other women experience this spouse-to-roommate syndrome too?

Because that's what Simon and I have become. And he's not the fun kind of roommate, either. You know, the one that makes you laugh? There is literally nothing left for us to talk about outside the kids and the bills (both of which I sort out myself).

And while I'm thinking about it, my phone rings again.

'Hey, you…' comes the deep voice I'd recognise even after a million years.

'Hey, Markus,' I chime, happy to hear his voice.

'Wait, what's wrong?' he asks. 'I can hear something in your voice.'

I sigh. Where do I start? 'Uh, the doctors here think I need to wear a CPAP mask. I've had anxiety attacks that leave me gasping for air at night.' There, I've told him and not my own husband. Nothing surprising there.

'Then wear it if it's going to help,' he says. 'Anything to get you back in shape.'

'But it's a noisy machine…'

'It does its job, though, Livvie.'

'But once I start wearing it, I'll be wearing it for the rest of my life,' I counter.

'Not necessarily. Just try it and see how it goes.'

Markus is always so practical. No beating around the bush, no insecurity of any kind. If there's a problem he solves it. End of.

'And that's it?' I squeak.

'That's it.'

'Hmmm…' I say.

He lowers his voice. 'Livvie?'

'Yeah?'

'Whatever happens in your life, I've got your back.'

I know he has. But just hearing him say it makes my throat tighten and I let out a high-pitched 'Thank you.'

'You're welcome. Okay, I was just checking up on you; now go and book that machine before they run out. They're all the rage nowadays.'

I laugh. 'Okay, Markus. I will. Good night…'

'Night, *skat*.'

The next morning, just before breakfast, I find a text from Cassie! I can't believe it! My fingers are actually shaking with excitement as I open it.

Jen is having a party for the class and then a sleepover. Dad says I have to ask you if I can go.

Nothing else. No *Hi, how are you*. No *Please*. Nothing.

'Is that a text from Loverboy?' my mother asks as she's towel-drying her hair, fresh out of the shower.

'Who?'

'Oh, just the gorgeous man you work with.'

'How do you know he's— Never mind.'

'Your father sends me pictures of you all.'

'Right.'

'So it wasn't him? Something's got you smiling.'

'No, it was Cassie.'

'Oh, well that's great, Olivia!'

I purse my lips. 'Not really. After weeks of radio silence, now she wants my permission to go to a party.'

'It's better than nothing. Maybe it'll be a good chance for her to blow off some steam?'

I snort. 'Hardly. She's not going.'

'Oh. May I ask why?'

'It's not to punish her. All things being equal, I would have normally said yes, but not this time.'

'Why?'

'Well, where do I start? I'm assuming the party is for the class and the sleepover is strictly for the girls, but I know her friend's family. Jen is the daughter of Gemma and *Brian*, a real prize of a man whom no one likes – and for good reason. Apparently he lets his daughter smoke and drink, although only at home and strictly under his supervision, but even so… and he's way too friendly with Jen's friends.'

'Ouch.'

'Exactly. Plus, Gemma works night shifts as a doctor at the A&E, meaning that she is hardly ever home in the evening, leaving Brian in charge. *And* Jen has two older brothers, both of whom have turned out to be real creeps.'

'Oh, my!'

'Exactly.'

'Jesus…'

I put my head in my hands. 'I should not have left her in such a delicate moment of her life.'

There is an awkward silence between us, but then she says, 'So what are you going to do?'

'There is no way that she can go to that party and I'm going to have to be the one to tell her because Simon is completely useless at parenting. And—' I bite my lip. 'Then she'll hate me even more.'

Mother thinks about it for a moment. 'Have you ever considered that maybe she doesn't hate you? And that maybe she just doesn't appreciate your mothering her?'

'But I *am* her mother…'

'Of course, but she's used to you being the boss and setting all the rules.'

'But that's what mothers are for.' I realise the irony of our conversations and that she is giving me pointers once again, but it's slowly becoming less awkward with every heart-to-heart chat we have.

'Yes,' she concedes. 'But perhaps you might want to make yourself a little more vulnerable to her.'

'What do you mean? She needs me to be the strong one.'

'Absolutely, but if you explained to her why you're uncomfortable with her going, she might see things from your point of view. Show her your own fears, that you're afraid of what might happen, beyond her control. Tell her that she's too precious for you to risk anything, and compare your fear with one of her own worst fears.'

'Huh. I'd never thought of that before. I'm usually so stressed about her safety and everything that I never really stopped to think about it from her point of view.'

And this coming from someone who has only ever considered things as a daughter desperate to avoid her mother's mistakes. Maybe I am too strict because my mother never was.

'I guess I'll give it a try. Thank you, Mother.'

'You're welcome, Daughter,' she says with a smile. 'See you on the terrace for breakfast?'

I am actually starting to not hate her. She is wise, so much wiser than she used to be when I was young. And she's happy, now. Maybe one day I'll understand and forgive her completely. It feels like we are on the right path.

'I'll be there,' I promise as she goes back to her own room to change.

I figure there's no time like the present to get the bad news out of the way as it is a Saturday morning and Cassie's probably lounging around in her room.

'Yeah…?' she says when she picks up.

Oh, Jesus. I can see that this is not going to end well.

'Cassie, sweetheart, can you put the video on?'

'Why?'

'Because I want to see you when I talk to you.'

'I haven't showered yet,' she says.

'That's okay.'

She groans, there's a blur and suddenly her face fills my screen. She's still sleepy and her hair is in its usual bedtime ponytail atop her head. Her pjs are on inside out. She's the most beautiful thing I've ever seen.

'Hello, sweetheart,' I say. 'I miss you.'

She suppresses a snort. I suddenly realise how difficult things must have been for my own mother, dealing with a stroppy teenager who refused to speak to her. At least Cassie has answered the phone and switched the video on. I never wanted to speak to my own mother for twenty-two years. Perhaps I had indeed been a bit too hard on her. After all, I'd never asked for her side of the story. But now I know that there's always a second side.

'So can I go?' she says. 'To Jen's party?'

'About that,' I say, 'I've been thinking. I'm not comfortable with the situation.'

'What situation?'

'Well, for instance, is her mum going to be there?'

'You know she works nights…'

'And what time are the boys in your class going home before the sleepover?'

'I don't know…'

'Well, that's it, you see, Cassie. I'm… not comfortable with any of this.'

'What exactly do you think I'm going to do, Mum? Spoke marijuana? Have a drink?'

Among other unmentionable things, yes. 'It's not you that I don't trust,' I reply, following my mother's advice. *Be honest, be vulnerable.* 'I don't trust Jen's father to look out for you. I don't like the atmosphere in that house and frankly, Cassie… I'm terrified.'

Silence. 'Of what?'

'That someone is going to say or do something to you that they never would do under normal circumstances in a civilised environment. You're too precious to me, and I would never forgive myself if something happened to you.'

'But nothing's going to happen…'

'How can you know for sure, Cassie? I was your age once, and I remember all too well being in a hurry to grow up and surrounding myself with people who I thought were my friends, people I loved but who instead,' I swipe at a tear, 'took advantage of my innocence and trust in them. I don't want the same to happen to you, Cassie. I don't want you to make the same wrong choices I did.'

For a moment, she is silent and I can hear the cogs turning in her mind. I'm surprised we've been on the phone this long at all.

'So basically, you're saying no, and giving me a whole bunch of reasons why you're saying no. You don't trust me to tell off anyone annoying me.'

My heart sinks to my feet. 'Sweetheart, please try to understand…'

'What if Uncle Markus takes me?' she suggests.

'Uncle Markus? He can't sit in on a party all night…'

'There's no need to, all night. He can make sure all the blokes have gone.'

Yeah, only to come back when they see he's gone. I don't think so.

I take a deep breath. 'Not this time, sweetheart. Next time, I'll be there to chaperone you myself. But this time, I'm going to have to say no, for all the above-mentioned reasons. I'm sorry, but I'll make it up to— Cassie?' But the screen has turned black. She's hung up on me. Fantastic. So much for being vulnerable.

15

'That's round one,' my mother says when I relate the conversation to her at breakfast.

I lift my head over my cup. 'You mean there's more?

'Oh, most definitely,' she assures me. 'Now that she knows you're human, too, you can pull back a little.'

'What?'

'Don't be desperate to connect. It translates as your wanting to have control over her.'

'But I *do* want control over her,' I argue. 'Not like she thinks, obviously, but she's my *child* and I need her to know that I care.'

My mother raises her hand. 'She knows that now. So let her come and find you. You've set out the bait. Now she needs to bite. If she comes willingly, then you've got her.'

'A bit like you inviting me here, I guess...?'

'Touché,' she says, smiling. 'Did it work?'

Does she mean, can I actually forgive her, rather than just shut her out of my heart and get on with it?

I put down my cup and look up at her. Actually, not only do I not hate her so much anymore, I'm starting to enjoy her company. Yes, she's choc-full of flaws, but who isn't?

I nod. 'I think it did,' I whisper, and she takes my hands in hers, her own eyes moist, and she laughs. 'We're being silly, aren't we?' she says and I realise that she's not very good at taking her own advice. She lost me for over twenty years. And now she has been able to try and make amends. Something in me has shifted. I don't know what exactly, or why, but suddenly I see things in a different light.

'So how was the CPAP experience for you?' Dr Severini asks me as soon as I sit down opposite him. I swear, he seems entertained by my life. How professional is that?

'A walk in the park,' I lie.

'Compared to what, life at home?' he offers.

This guy has me down pat, so I roll my eyes. 'Really? Is that going to be your angle? That things are that bad at home?'

'Aren't they?' he insists. Between him and Markus, I'm running out of places to hide from the truth.

I shrug. 'Not really. I have my kids, my father and my business partner.'

'Aha, we have a new entry, then. Tell me about your business partner.'

Aha, indeed. If I start talking about Markus, this shrink will suss me out immediately. As if I needed telling that lusting after your best friend is a no-no when you're married (to someone else) and have kids.

'He's all right,' I concede.

'So it's a man. Are you attracted to him?' he persists.

Who on earth wouldn't be? 'How is that in any shape or form relevant?' I counter.

'You know it is. It's what's missing at home.'

I open my mouth. How does he *know* these things? Are all his female patients the same woman over and over again, with different names and different faces, but basically loaded with the same problems?

'So, are you attracted to him?' he wants to know.

I shrug again, not liking where this is going. If I say yes, I'm officially a Mary Magdalene. If I say no, I'm a liar.

'*Everyone's* attracted to him.'

'But you especially. Are you in love with him?'

Aaaarrrggghhh. When is this torture going to *stop*?

'Of course not.'

'Okay, change of subject,' he says. 'I can see you're not ready to talk about him yet. How are things going with your mother?'

'My mother? Actually, much better. She's giving me some advice on how to deal with Cassie.'

He nods. 'That's good.'

'Basically I'm getting a crash course into my future with Cassie if I don't give myself a good sorting out. If I don't make an effort with my mother, I could meet the same fate when I'm older. Hell, Cassie's already more ruthless with me than I was with my mother. If I don't sort her out now, when we're older she'll cart me off to some old folks' home where I'll be painting watercolours and still trying to finish *Ulysses*.'

He looked up, impressed. 'You're reading *Ulysses*?'

'I read some of it at university. I never got past the 'Sirens' chapter. It must have been the flirty barmaids pissing me off.'

'Olivia, to know you is to be entertained.'

'So I've been told.' I shrug. 'It must be my suitcase full of happy memories, Doctor.'

When I get back to my room, I can hear my mother laughing through the wall. I never ever remembered her laughing that loudly when I was growing up.

'Oh, you monster, you!' she cackles. 'And what did he say? Really? I told you how to handle him. Try it my way next time! You will? Good girl!'

Ah, Mother and her relationship advice. She's always got a full-proof solution for some desperate friend. I wonder how she got to be such an expert?

'And remember, Cassie, girls never chase boys!'

Cassie? Did she say *Cassie*? As in *my* Cassie?

'Sweetheart, if you want Liam to find you interesting, you just need to be mysterious. *Indifferent*. It gets them every time! Now you be a good girl and call me back tomorrow, okay? I want to know how it goes. Nonna loves you! Talk tomorrow!'

What the hell is going on here? I can't even get my daughter to answer a call from me, and here she is having conversations with my mother? About boys? I didn't know there was a boy on the scene!

So I knock on my mother's door.

'Come in!'

If I go in there, I know I'll lose my rag. I just know it. So I merely poke my head round the door.

'Mother, was that Cassie on the phone?'

She pushes her hair away from her face, eyes on the Berber rug. 'Cassie…? Uhm, yes…'

Well, at least she's not trying to lie her way out of it, I'll give her that.

'You know, Mother, you've got more front than Brighton. You knew that I was trying to speak to her. Why didn't you tell me you two were talking?'

'But love, I thought you knew. We always talk,' she says. 'At least three times a week.'

'What? Since when?'

'Since always. Oh, don't make that face, Olivia. You should be happy that she talks to *someone* about these things.'

'Yes, Mother, but that someone should be *me*.'

'What can I say? We have a lot in common. We get along.' She bows her head. 'Which is more than I can say for the two of us, unfortunately.'

Oh, I can feel it. A biblical migraine forming right behind my eyes. *Breathe. In. Out. In. Out.* I have to get out of here before I get into an argument with her. So I take another deep breath. 'I'm going to have a shower now, Mother. I'll see you downstairs.'

'Okay,' she says meekly. She has chosen not to argue either. Good. We're making progress.

Or, I thought we were. How could she keep this from me? She knows I've been struggling in my relationship with Cassie. Not because I've told her, but because Cassie has. I wonder what not-so-charming things she's told her about me?

As it is, I need to know more. I'm certainly not giving my mother the satisfaction of asking her about my own daughter's life, and I can't trust Simon's discretion as he is like the proverbial bull in a china shop. Nor do I want to worry Dad, so there is only one solution. I call Markus.

'Did you know that there's a Liam?' I ask as soon as he picks up.

'What?' he says.

'Liam. Does it ring a bell?'

'You mean the bloke Cassie likes?'

'Does everyone but me know about this?' I whine, raking my hand through my hair.

'Who's everyone?'

'My mother.'

'Oh. Well, they talk often, don't they?'

'Okay, now I'm officially the worst mother on the planet. How did I not know about this? How do *you* even know about this?'

'Easy, Liv, don't get angry. She probably didn't want to upset you.'

'So she goes behind my back instead?'

'She's not, really. I mean, they see each other every summer. It's only normal for them to develop a relationship.'

'How often do you talk to your grandmother then?' I ask.

'Every Sunday, actually. When she gets back from the market we have a chat.'

'Oh.' Christ, am I that self-centred that I don't know these things about the people I care about? 'Right. Sorry. Where is Cassie now?'

'She's out with her friends. George has gone to pick her up.'

'Out where?' This is getting out of hand. I should know where my daughter is at exactly every moment of the day, even if I'm an hour ahead.

'At a cricket game…'

'Since when does she…? Oh, I get it. Liam's playing, is he?'

'Yes. Listen, Liv. I understand where you're coming from. But you can't force her to talk to you if she doesn't want to.'

You know when your child is being fractious and you tell them that you would *never* have answered back to your mother the way she is doing? Well, that's a line I have never been able to use while raising my children, for obvious reasons.

So all I can come up with now is: 'Wow. Whatever happened to old-fashioned discipline?'

Markus is silent for a moment. 'Tell you what. I'll have a chat with her. See what I can do, okay?'

To have someone else, albeit your best friend, intervene on your behalf is humiliating. But all I can do is accept. And make mental notes so that next time it will be different.

'Thank you, Markus. I owe you one. Or a hundred...'

He chuckles. 'No worries. It'll all be okay. She'll grow out of this phase and you'll be back to being besties before you know it.'

'Yeah, maybe,' I say. 'Thanks again.'

'Talk tomorrow?'

'Of course,' I assure him. Who understands me better than Markus?

Simon hasn't called since the spaghetti sauce debacle. Now, I'm used to him doing this occasionally when I'm at home because God knows how unreliable he is at the best of times, but this? I'm out of the country and he totally ignores me? I know he's alive because Joe has answered my texts, bless him. Cassie has elected to continue to ignore me as she does when I *am* at home.

So I bite the bullet and call his mobile again, and I swear the ring has a new-found, ominous tone. Good!

'Hi, Simon. How are things?'

'Fine,' he says. 'The kids have finished their homework.'

'And you?' I ask.

'I don't have any homework.'

'Seriously, Simon.'

'Seriously, Olivia.'

'Can I talk to them?'

'They're out.'

'Where?'

'At the movies. With your dad and your buddy.'

'Markus?'

'*Him.*'

The implications of that 'him' were endless. Simon doesn't like Markus because:

He is jealous of his looks, success and general attitude towards life;

He is jealous of the fact that the kids always talked about him and wanted to include him in all their activities. In the evening we would all (minus Simon) have dinner together. And on weekends we would invite him to come round to hang because we loved him and not because, as Simon puts it, 'That poor sod doesn't have a life of his own.'

He is jealous of the fact that Markus and I sometimes spend a good eighteen hours together at a time, albeit for work.

He is jealous of the way Markus and I have bonded over the years and is afraid that our friendship might turn into something that would endanger his position as my lawful partner and head of the family.

Scratch that. I was just having a laugh. Back to reality and this dreary telephone conversation we're having. I want to say something meaningful, something that might remind him that we were a team, once. 'So a movie, that's nice,' I soldier on. 'Which one?'

A sigh. 'I don't know, Olivia. Why do you even care?'

'I beg your pardon?'

'I mean, you left, so...'

'Simon, the fact that I left doesn't mean that I don't care about my kids.'

'Ha. That's rich from you.'

Of all the things to say. Trust him to use my issues as ammunition against me. 'What's that supposed to mean?'

'It means whatever you want it to mean, Olivia. I'm done arguing with you.'

'Actually, Simon, we don't argue. You and I never talk. Or rather, I talk and you don't even listen.'

'Here we go...'

I take a deep breath, ready to launch into yet another tirade of accusations as to why he's so distant and uncaring, but then I stop, suddenly completely, absolutely *saturated*. I've had enough of all this fruitless bickering that always leaves me looking like I'm the witch. What's the point in sparring with someone who isn't even listening to you, but whose instinct is to oppose you as a matter of principle, no matter what you do or say? Simon and I are past being at loggerheads. I'm so over all of this.

'You know what, Simon? I'm hanging up, now. Goodbye.'

'Yep,' he says. And that's about it from him for now, apparently.

Tonight is *1970s Nostalgia Night.* Everyone is wearing clothes I wouldn't be caught dead in but that, apparently, bring back happy memories for the guests, particularly the Villa dei Respiri Ladies, as I've dubbed them, my mother included.

There are crazy outfits and wigs and I'm assuming they are impersonating some Italian singer at karaoke. I catch a few titles and look them up on the internet.

There is one singer from the sixties, a certain Mina, who is amazing. Taller than most women, lithe and extremely classy and sexy at the same time, she has a voice that tells a million stories. I look up the lyrics in English and read of difficult relationships and heartbreak and loving an immature man who is never available; it reminds me somewhat of Adele's songs today. Even the blonde hair and long lashes and gold lamé dresses add to the similarity but the voice is different. Mina's is velvety, more delicate but just as powerful.

Rather than just singing the words, she seems to be telling stories from her own life, shaking her head at her own mistakes and laughing at her own naivety, but vowing to recover. I can relate to that, as could so many women in the sixties, as divorce, I read, was not legal in Italy until 1970.

I learn that Mina was and still is an active icon. Back then she challenged society by having an affair with a married man and was subsequently kicked off the major television networks for 'moral reasons'. But she didn't care, and soon, as Italy was finally breaking its own taboos, the public clamoured to have her back. And come back she did, with a vengeance.

Now over eighty, she lives somewhere in Switzerland and can be seen wearing her iconic look: a pair of huge shades and her hair pulled back tight in a sleek ponytail.

There have been singing rivals over the years in the names of Iva Zanicchi, Ornella Vanoni, but no one has ever come close to being the icon that Mina was and still is today.

I make a secret playlist on my phone because I want to discover all the work of this remarkable woman who seems to have life figured out. I might even learn something about love and life from her.

From the corner of the room I watch my mother as she plays her favourite Mina song, 'Se telefonando', on the piano. It's about a woman who wishes she could end her relationship over the phone to make it easier, but realises that, in fact, it is already over. Remind you of anyone?

My mother is so into the song and so intense, almost as if making love to the piano, her voice mellifluous. Almost too much so. She truly is talented, though. There is nothing she can't play or sing, and I would know with the number of times she's performed in public while I watched from the shadows, wishing I had half of her talent.

16

June 1st

June 1st is my thirty-fifth birthday. (Which had been one of Simon's arguments to try to make me stay home. Luckily, I won.)

The first thing I see when I open my eyes is a huge pink bow. Tied to a humongous photo album.

'Happy birthday to you!' Mother sings, thrusting the thing in my face. 'Happy birthday to you! Happy birthday, dear chickie! Happy birthday to… you!'

I sit up, groaning inwardly. It's a miracle in itself that I've made it to this age with my sanity intact, but this would throw anyone over the edge.

'Open it!' she chimes, clapping her hands. 'It's a photo album'—no kidding?—'full of all the years together that we've missed out on! This way there will be no gaps in the years!'

I stare at her. She's all happy and chirpy as if she had just said something tremendously clever and thoughtful. I'm supposed to be okay for all the years spent without a mother because now I have past pictures of her? What could I possibly say to someone who is so self-centred she doesn't understand what an utter insult this gift is?

'Err, thank you, Mother. I'll have a look at it after I've got some caffeine in me.'

I hadn't known, in fairness, when I accepted the invite to the wellness clinic that I would, in fact, be spending my thirty-fifth birthday with my mother, only to be reminded of the other twenty-one birthdays that she hadn't been there. And now, despite many years having gone by, I don't want to think about it because it hurts too much, on this day in particular.

A re-run of all this festiveness is performed by her friends in the dining hall over breakfast, followed by a huge applause as if I'd done something really, really special, like discover the cure for cancer. Everyone is crowding me so I can't even have my breakfast in peace without having to stand up to return the hugs or handshakes and slobbery kisses from the elderly men. Not to mention the offers of lunch down in town, or a ride on the Ferris wheel or an ice cream or dinner with these over-zealous people who are all my mother's friends and not actually mine. It's not even ten o'clock and I'm already wondering how I am going to get through this day.

An hour later, I'm summoned to retrieve a huge bouquet from Interflora that has arrived at the main desk and I'm all smiles on the way there. The card is signed by the kids, Simon and my father.

I'm somewhat disappointed that I haven't received even a measly card from Markus, seeing that we *design* the bloody things.

Did I offend him in any way when we last spoke? I know I can be a real pain sometimes. Why am I like this? Why can't I forgive and forget? Why can't I let things go? In any case, I can't recall pissing him off.

No. Today's my birthday and I am going to enjoy it. No regrets or remorse or grudges. I'm going to hike back upstairs, have a shower and put on my prettiest dress, be extremely polite to my mother and enjoy my time here with all the other guests who, actually, are quite friendly and certainly mean no harm.

Luckily my mother is busy all morning with her physiotherapy, her shrink, etc., and has had to delay all the celebratory stuff to the evening, which gives me ample time to come up with an escape route. Perhaps I could hitch a ride into town with one of the waitresses?

With the day completely open to me now, I could go for a walk but I've already changed, even put on make-up and a nice pair of heels I never thought I'd wear. Even my hair is making an effort today. Tonight, when the kids are back from school, I'll call home and thank everyone for the beautiful flowers. Even Simon and Cassie will have to be nice to me on my birthday, right? All in all, I can earnestly say that today, the Gods are smiling down on me...

And speaking of... my Scandinavian God is finally calling me.

'Hello?'

'Happy birthday, *skat*,' comes his deep, warm voice over the phone.

'Thank you. Did you know I almost ended up in tomorrow's papers?' I say to Markus.

'Really? What did you do?'

'I was doing this obstacle course thing in the gym with the doors wide open onto a natural terraced cliff. I was running so fast that inertia kicked in and I couldn't stop. The panic doors leading outside were open because it was hot and I ran through them and almost off the cliff. I swear I thought I was going to die. Imagine the titles in the papers: Crazy Brit throws herself off the cliff to get back at her suddenly needy mother.'

'Jesus, Liv. You want to be careful.'

'Gotcha!'

'What?'

'I'm just kidding!'

'Jesus, Liv, you scared the crap out of me. What the hell would we do without you?'

Quite the opposite stance to the one Simon would take. I swallow a whole world of words back and instead recite a Danish proverb Markus once taught me:

'*Ingen ko p å isen!*' Meaning, literally, 'no cow on the ice' as in, everything's okay, don't worry.

'You have a very good memory for languages,' he says, pleased with me.

'*Tak*,' I thank him in Danish, just as he taught the kids and me. Even if Simon thinks it's a ridiculous waste of time and effort because we're not actually going to Denmark, are we?

'So what are you doing today?' he asks.

'Oh, not much. No plans whatsoever. My mother, for some crazy reason, has all morning booked, so she says we can't celebrate until the evening.'

'Good. So maybe you can spend some time with me, then.'

'Have you got all this time to chat?' I ask.

'I've got all the time in the world,' he says, and the line goes dead.

Great, just great. 'Markus? Markus, are you there?'

'I'm here,' he says, but his voice sounds less tinny. Almost as if—

'Hello, you,' he says. But the line is still dead. I turn around and there he is, his jacket over his shoulder.

'Markus?! What… what are you *doing* here?'

'You didn't think I was going to let you spend your birthday without me, did you?' he says, giving me a great big bear hug. I hug him back, inhaling his familiar scent. It's his real smell because he doesn't wear cologne. I can't describe it, but it's delicious. Something between soap and freshly cut grass and loads of testosterone. My oestrogen recognises it instantly.

'How long can you stay?' I ask, breathless with surprise and elation.

'Just the twenty-four hours, unfortunately. I need to be back.'

'Is my dad okay?' I ask. 'The kids?'

He looks down at me. Finally he says, 'Your family is fine. Relax, Livvie.'

'Of course, sorry. You'd tell me. How silly of me. You wouldn't be here, right?'

'I can only stay a short while because I've got a huge shipment to get out next week. So what do you want to do?'

Stresa is an almost three-hour journey by car, but totally worth it. Resting on the Western bank of Lake Maggiore, it is one of the most beautiful and elegant places I've ever seen, with stunning views of the lake and the Alps, while elegant period and historical villas dot the lake promenade from where you can almost touch the Borromean Islands.

It's famous for, among other reasons, the Stresa music festival, for Villa Pallavicino which is a beautiful historic mansion with a zoo and luscious gardens.

In Stresa, there's also a cable car running up to Monte Mottarone with gorgeous views of the Alps and the old town with charming narrow streets, hotels, sidewalk cafés and restaurants, not to mention sophisticated and elegant palazzi ranging in colours from cream to mustard to ochre all the way to pink, topped by the typical Italian terracotta pantiles. Throw in the balmy breeze and you have everything you could ever want on a day out.

I'd heard all of my mother's friends boasting about having spent some torrid nights in the most exclusive hotels there. I might not be getting a hotel room but I sure as hell can get lunch with Markus, who's come all the way just to see me.

We spend the morning hiking up and down all the cobbled lanes, stopping for a meal in a narrow side-street café that only has three tables. We both order fried polenta topped with a ragout sauce made with minced meat, mushrooms and onion, a true luxury. All this washed down with a bottle of Nebbiolo wine.

'I miss everyone,' I confess.

'They miss you, too.'

I snort. 'Even Cassie?'

'Especially Cassie. She hasn't been the same since you left.'

'You mean she's kinder?'

He thinks about it. 'She's more… fragile.'

I sit up. 'Should I come home?'

'No, no,' Markus assures me quickly. 'I think the distance is doing you both some good. You get a respite from her attitude and she understands what it's like without a mother.'

But I hardly think that Cassie's suffering without me.

'It's not the same, Liv,' he whispers.

'What's not the same?'

'As you and your mother.'

The man knows what I'm thinking at every turn. 'This is different,' he says. 'Cassie doesn't know it yet but she respects you.'

'I respected my mother. Until she showed me her true colours.'

'You haven't forgiven her yet?'

'For ambushing me on this trip?'

'For everything. Just open up your heart to her, Liv,' he urges.

'Oh, Markus. I wish I could. I mean, I can be civil and all, but truly, honestly forgive her? I just… can't.'

'For your family's sake? For George's sake?'

I narrow my eyes. 'Why, what has Dad said to you?'

'Only that he wishes you could forgive her.'

'I don't know how *he* even managed to do that. She literally walked out on him with no warning, whereas with Simon, *I* should win a medal for my staying power and—'

There. I've said it. Loud and clear so I can never go back on it. I am *struggling* to stay with Simon. Big time. Of course, I could have told someone else instead of Markus. Even if he knows me inside out, now that I've said it, I can't pretend that I haven't.

Silence.

'I know you're unhappy, Livvie.'

'It's fine,' I insist, trying to claw back some shreds of my composure. 'I love my life. I love my children. I love my home.' But we both know that's not enough.

I am a grown woman. If my mother wants to stay in Italy

where her life is perfect, let her. She'd given up the marriage to my father and the family battle years ago, whereas I still have plenty of fight left in me.

And it makes me laugh (no, it actually infuriates me) how Aldo's grandchildren call *her* Nonna, Grandma, when she hadn't even earnt the title of 'mother'. There is nothing grand about her and her mothering in the least. What had I been snorting when I'd agreed to spend the best part of two months here as a gift from her?

'Come here, *skat*,' he whispers, pulling me up against his side. It's nice there. My own private nook. I can leave all my problems there and it's okay with him...

For dessert, we order the Margheritine di Stresa, biscuits topped with icing sugar that don't sound like much, but those with a fine palate will appreciate. Me, I'll eat anything, so I trust the waiter's advice and am I glad we did!

After lunch we go up in the cable car to Monte Mottarone for the famous view. The breeze is much cooler up here, and Markus gives me his jacket in a chivalric gesture that destabilises me. I was having fun, but to feel his arms around me while he settles his jacket about me is... new.

On our way back to the car we pass many more shops. We are in an expensive area with designer labels.

'Come with me,' he says, taking my hand and pulling me into a shop.

'What...?'

'For a little souvenir,' he says, his eyes all mischievous.

'Oh, you'd better watch it,' I say. 'I have a feeling that you're not going to find a five-euro keychain in here.'

'Good, because that's not what I'm looking for,' he replies.

I am standing at the men's end where all the hats are. He'd look good in any of them, of course. 'How about this one?' I suggest, but he's off talking to the shopkeeper, so I continue my perusal of accessories such as gloves, wallets, scarves, all with prohibitive prices. Best to get out of here asap.

'Did you find anything?' I ask.

'Let's go,' he says quickly.

'You haven't stolen anything, have you?'

He bursts out laughing. 'Why would you think that?'

'I dunno, I just…'

He stops and we are at a railing over Lake Maggiore. It is just gorgeous and I want it to last forever. 'Here,' he says, pulling out a small packet from underneath his jacket. 'This is for you. Happy birthday, *skat*…'

I must look shocked because he laughs again. 'Go on, open it.'

'I… thank you, Markus, but I hope you didn't buy it in that store where everything costs an arm and a leg…'

'Just open it already.'

'Okay,' I say obediently. It is a Ferragamo silk shawl. It is absolutely gorgeous, with blues and greens that seem drawn from the lake, and gold and silver flecks that look like the sun glistening off it. 'Oh my God…'

'You like?'

I look at him, then at the scarf, then at him again.

'I love it, Markus! Thank you!' I say, willing back the tears because I'm not going to bloody cry on my birthday.

He peers down into my face. 'I didn't mean to make you cry,' he says.

'Oh, no, it's not you, Markus. I guess I'm just tired.'

'Then let me drive you back,' he whispers. 'You can take a nap before the festivities continue. I've got to go and find my hotel anyway.'

'Okay,' I agree, the idea of him leaving killing me.

It's sunset by the time we get there. Everyone is milling about, waiting for drinks. 'Do you want to come in and have a drink?' I offer.

He shakes his head. 'I have some more driving to do, better not.'

'Okay…' I hate goodbyes, but this is it.

He seems to hesitate. 'Liv, is there anywhere we can talk in private?' he asks.

'Oh?' We've been talking non-stop all day. I take his hand, leading him to the chapel. The last mass of the day is finished but the church is never locked overnight. Something to do with Italian trust and faith. Bless them.

We sit on a pew at the very back, like two kids in a cinema theatre wanting to snog. I mean, *I* want to snog him big-time.

'So what's up?' I finally ask.

He studies his shoes. 'You remember Lilja, right?'

Aarrrghhhh, my one fly in the champagne! She's gorgeous and almost as madly in love with Markus as I am, and they've been on and off more times than I care to count. She's determined to get him and there's nothing I can do to stop her.

'Y-yes…?'

'Well, she came to my house the other day…'

'From Denmark?' I say, secretly admiring her. The girl has spunk.

'No. She is moving to England. Precisely, Canterbury.'

Oh no, no, no! That's the end of us, or at least my version of it. He'll never have time for… whatever it is we are doing here – friendship? Family? Ah, yes, business. Because he is first and foremost my business partner.

'That's nice,' I say as someone places an Oscar into my hands and the audience applauds. Meryl Streep is happy to have lost to me because I've done a brilliant job. 'What about her work?'

'That's the thing. She wants to work for us.'

What!? A thousand alarm bells go off in my mind as my heart shoots up my throat and out of my ears.

'But I said no,' he informs me, still looking at his shoes.

My head snaps around so hard I can hear it click. 'And why is that?'

Markus shrugs. 'Because what we have now is good. Right?'

'Right,' I'm quick to assure him. 'It's perfect.'

'I mean, we wouldn't want that to change, would we? Unless…'

'Unless what?' I prompt.

'I mean, Simon has no say in the company, right?'

'Of course not. You know that, Markus.'

He shakes his head as if to toss an invisible weight off his shoulders. 'Right. So I don't want her to be a part of this, either. A part of… *us*.'

I swear his eyes have changed. They've got darker as he stares into mine. Is he…? Does he…? This can't be! He's never looked at me like this before!

'She wants to move in with me,' he whispers.

I can hear the loud thump as my heart hits the bottom of my stomach. I move away from him as if he's caught fire. 'Oh! And… you? What do you want?'

He half-groans. 'I want a simple life. Lilja is anything but simple. She's impossible to please, unreliable, everything that drives me nuts.'

I nod, trying hard not to let any of my own emotion seep into my voice. 'So, uhm, what does that mean?'

He sighs. 'That she is not staying in my house. I can't stop her from moving to Canterbury, of course, but please don't believe anything she says about us being a couple right now.'

'Why would she tell me?'

'Because she may feel entitled to stick her nose in our business.'

'Why?' I ask.

'She just thinks that sooner or later something permanent will happen between us.'

Well, at least she has that illusion. Me, I've got nothing.

'But it's going to happen, with someone or other, sooner or later,' I say. Markus has loads of women, but he keeps it casual. Could *you* walk away the morning after begrudging him anything? He and his casual partners always agree that that's what it is. A casual fling. All the times he's been 'on' with Lilja, he's never talked about it as if it's anything serious. But what he doesn't understand is that one day someone's going to get him. He can't continue dodging bullets all his life, can he?

'Yeah, well, maybe,' he says, draping an arm around my shoulder and bringing me closer to him. 'It's cold in this chapel, isn't it?'

'Spoken by a wannabe Viking,' I titter, caught between wanting to die and never wanting to leave this spot. How long can I keep this act up?

'It's late. I should go back to my hotel now,' he says, yawning.

'Yes, you should,' I agree, but neither of us makes a move. Something between us has shifted. I can't quite say what, or how, but something is different. The way he's looking at me. The tone of his voice. We have been close friends for years, but now, hanging in the space between us is something new, undefinable. Something I wish I could name, but haven't got the heart to.

I rest my head on his shoulder and it feels like the most natural thing in the world. If only it wasn't so late, he could stay longer. And if only we weren't both absolutely knackered, we could talk for ever and ever…

17

I must have closed my eyes for a few minutes because when I open them, an entire congregation, including the priest, is staring down at us, whispering.

'Did they have sex, do you think?' someone hisses.

'Hardly. These pews are too narrow. And hard.'

'How would you know? Have you tried it yourself?'

Holy shit. 'Markus!' I hiss, shaking him. 'Wake up! Markus!'

'Wha…?'

He opens his eyes and stares up at the old biddies now grinning down at us.

'Am I dreaming or are there people hovering over us, Livvie?' he whispers conspiratorially.

'No dreaming,' I assure him. 'We fell asleep!'

'Erm, *Signora* Dawson,' the priest says. 'A word, if you don't mind…'

Trust me to attract unwanted attention wherever I go. I have been here but a few weeks and already I've got a reputation. Catholicism has well and truly judged and condemned us to burn in the eternal fires of hell. But that's nothing – just wait until Dr Severini hears about this. He'll have a field day.

Markus is waiting by his car, his hands stuffed into the pockets of his jeans. He looks like he's waiting for a bollocking, poor sod. When he sees me, his hands come out of his pockets and he splays them before me apologetically.

'I'm so sorry about that. I guess I'm a bad influence.'

I shrug. 'It's fine. He believes me, and we haven't broken any rules, really.'

'I'm glad. I wasn't planning on getting you into any trouble, but there it is. Sorry. At least we slept soundly.'

And then it hits me. 'Hey, you know what?'

'What?'

'This is the first time I have slept soundly since I've been here!'

'What?'

'I slept the whole night without waking up with anxiety attacks! Thank you, Markus!'

And then he finally grins that sexy grin of his. 'Anytime.'

We hug and I don't want to let go. To be honest, I could quite frankly hang onto him for ever. 'Thanks for coming all the way here, I really appreciate it.'

'It's nothing. We'll call you tonight when I get in,' he promises.

'Does my family know you came?'

He smiles sheepishly. 'Uhm, just your dad. I don't think Simon approves of our friendship as it is.'

I snort. 'That's putting it mildly. But he's not jealous.'

'No, of course not.'

'He's just jealous of you, as a person. Not of us. Because there is no us. In that sense, I mean.'

'Of course,' he agrees. We stand in awkward silence for a moment. 'Maybe I shouldn't have come.'

'No, I'm glad you did. It's not every day that a girl has a best friend like you.'

'BFF,' he says.

'BFF,' I agree as a thousand knives slice up my heart from the inside. He bends down to give me the lightest kiss on the cheek and it's all I can do not to shiver in sheer pleasure.

'You're going to miss your flight, go,' I say, wrenching myself away from him like some medieval damsel who has forsaken her lover to save his life or some other heartbreaking situation. I completely get it.

With one last, painful (for me) hug, Markus gets into his rental and drives down the slope, disappearing round the first bend.

With Markus gone, the emptiness is so heavy I know I can't go on living this way. I need to sort myself out. I can't be feeling like this, so bereft and impaired, when at home I have a husband. The mere thought of him should cheer me up. But it doesn't and I need to be honest with myself. I don't have a husband in Simon. I haven't for a long time.

I need to speak with him. Make it clear to him that we can't stay married. I owe it to myself to be free. And Mina's song, 'Se telefonando', the one about the telephone break-up, pops into my mind again.

'So the word is out!' My mother beams as I inch my way to my bed, my back absolutely shot by the night spent on the pew. '*Tell!*'

'There's nothing to tell, Mother,' I say as I ease myself down on the bed. I never thought that if we ever slept together (genuinely *just* slept) it would be *this* devastating to my body.

'Nothing to tell? Oh, come on, Livvie. It's me you're talking to. I can see it from miles away. You are in *love* with him.'

'Mother, I hardly think that's appropriate.'

'Why not? We both know that Simon isn't the one for you. God knows I've told you so many times…'

'You mean you've told *Dad* so many times.'

'I had to,' she says simply. 'But you went and married him anyway.'

'I was pregnant, Mother…'

'So what? Lots of women have babies on their own. In fact, being with Simon is practically like being on your own, isn't it? It's a good thing that Markus is in your life.'

It figures that my mother would encourage me to leave my husband. If I still had any doubts about it, now I know I can't. I can't do to my kids what my mother did to me. I'll have to try to be happy some other way.

'Okay, Mother, first of all, Markus is just a friend.'

'Rubbish. Your father told me the way he looks at you.'

'What?'

'Everybody can see it. This man is in love with you, too.'

'How can any of you say that? The truth is, Mother, if you really, really want to know, Markus feels sorry for me.'

She stares at me.

'That's right. He feels sorry for me because my life is a mess.' The fact that it was partly her fault is by the by.

'Livvie, that's life. It is a mess. But you know, it can also be a beautiful mess if you let it.'

A beautiful mess? Only she could come up with something like that.

'Live every day, Livvie. Be happy. Fight for what you want. No one has the right to take anything away from you.'

You did, I want to say. *You took from me the joy of living. You took away my trust in you, and my self-confidence. You took my entire childhood away from me, leaving me scared, embittered and enraged…*

And then I get it. 'You knew he was coming, didn't you?' I ask.

'Of course! Your father told me. That's why I made myself unavailable all day.'

Well. I guess she did get me what I wanted for my birthday after all: time alone with Markus.

'Aren't you coming down to breakfast?' she asks as I pull the sheet over my head.

'No,' I whisper. 'I need to sleep now.'

'And dream of Markus?' she sing-songs. 'You do that. And think about what I said. Only you can make yourself happy.'

The news is all over the place. My mother's friends are ecstatic that I've dared to break the no-sex-on-the-premises rule. They think I've been swinging from the chapel chandeliers with Markus, only to land, exhausted, onto a back pew to sleep it off. I'm literally a legend among the cleaning staff and the waiters, and even the managerial staff, who normally just say *Buongiorno* in the corridors, are now saying *Buongiorrrrnoooo!*

'Tell us, tell us, tell us,' Carla begs, taking me by the wrists to sit me down at the breakfast table. 'Elsa saw him. She says he's *bellissimooo*!'

'He is!' my mother agrees. I turn to glare at her. 'What?' she says, the picture of innocence. 'I've seen the pictures your father's sent me.'

I roll my eyes.

'So has he committed or was it just sex?' Lucia wants to know, clutching at her very expensive pearls.

'Neither,' I answer, yawning.

'Mamma mia, he's really done a number on you, *sì*?' Maria exclaims.

If only. I wish he'd come to tell me something crazy like he loves me, but no.

And my mother's friends, they're dying to hear it, too, literally elbowing the others out of the way so they can be the first to hear stories of my love and passion for Markus. But there's only one tiny detail.

'Ladies, I'm *married*!' I remind them.

'Pffawww…' Carla says. 'Marriage! Do you know what that is? A rescindable agreement once he's taken the best years of your life!'

'Act now, or you'll be sorry when your breasts are dangling on the dinner table, you don't recognise your face in the mirror and you haven't got the energy to do what you could be doing *now*!' Maria says, patting my hand. 'To hell with morality. Enjoy your life while you still can!'

'And this is your religious group?' I quip, and they all roar with laughter.

'We all got married for love when we were in our twenties, *bella*,' Elsa says. 'We helped our husbands in their careers, raised the family, organised their social lives, made them look like the greatest men on earth while behind the scenes, we were the ones doing all the work!'

Lucia leans in. 'We chose the wrong man for love and had to stick with him for fear of losing our reputations. But now I say to hell with reputation, where is my life? My happiness? Your mother was the first one to rebel against society. She is a trail-blazer!'

Now *that* was a word I wouldn't have used to describe my mother.

The next day my mother and I are scheduled to have a joint session with Dr Severini. I know it's her doing but I've decided to go with it.

'So...!' he says as I sheepishly walk in and take my seat. He is smiling gleefully this morning. He's over the moon, as you can imagine. A crack in my armour, now that's something to talk about! Which confirms my opinion of him. But I want to see how far he can go. Plus, talking to him is better than not talking at all, right?

Of course I feel like an impostor, but it's also fun to see how the world would react to a woman who's betrayed her shitty husband (info courtesy of my mother, no doubt) for a man the likes of Markus (info courtesy of the congregants who caught us in sleeping).

'There have been new developments, I hear,' he debuts.

I lean forward. 'Did my mother tell you that? Is that what this joint session is all about? And are you even allowed to acknowledge that crappy gossip?'

'Ah, but *is* it?' he counters with a twinkle in his eye.

'What is wrong with you?' I ask. 'You're supposed to be an objective shrink.'

'I am. I was given objective information by a proper source and I have drawn my conclusions.'

'Again, I did not have sex with Markus.'

'I never said you did. But there is no way you would fall asleep with a man you're not in love with.'

Busted.

'So now the question is, Olivia, what are you going to do about it?'

Terrific question. What am I going to do about it? Absolutely nothing.

That's when the door opens and my mother saunters in. I can't remember her ever being on time. Not once, and today is no exception.

'Did you tell everyone that Markus and I are a thing?' I ask her before she even gets a chance to sit down.

She looks up from her bangles, smiling. 'What's that, love?'

'I said, did you tell everyone that Markus and I— Oh, never mind. It's not like anyone will believe me after *your* masterpiece of a story.'

'I haven't said a thing to anyone. They came to me, and I simply said that Markus is a lovely man and a good friend to you.'

'Yeah, right…'

'But if you want my opinion I think he's the right bloke for you.'

'Mother, please listen to me carefully. I am a married woman. No, it's not perfect, but no marriage is. Will you please tell her, Doctor?'

But he only beams at her. What is wrong with everybody here? Why is everyone under her bloody spell?

'Mine is,' she interjects. 'Because I chose well. I followed my heart, and you should, too.'

'Well, not all of us have that blessing,' I snap. 'We don't always have a choice.'

She looks up at me with those enormous eyes. 'Everyone has a choice, especially when they believe they don't. It's never too late, Olivia. Leave him. The kids will understand. We will all support you.'

I get to my feet, unable to believe what she's just said. How dare she judge my life? How dare she tell me what to do? *She* will support me? This is so rich!

'My marriage may not be perfect. But it's my decision whether to stay or go because it affects the people I love. But you wouldn't understand that, Mother, because that's exactly what you did to us all those years ago.' I am so angry I want to spit. 'And here we are, *Mother*. Just... Full circle. Right back where we started. You throwing me under the bus once again. I wish you weren't my mother, because being your daughter has caused us all nothing but pain!'

And with that, I march out of the session. Dr Severini and my mother are just perfect for each other. And how professionally is my shrink behaving? I really should report him.

I'm still shaking and my blood pressure must be through the roof. So much for a *wellness* clinic. This place is a bloody death trap!

I go for a walk in the park to blow off some steam. Luckily, the few people that I come across know better than to stop me for a chat. Not today. Perhaps not even tomorrow.

I've had enough of all this. It's bad enough that my mother thought it was okay to book me in here, adding herself as one of the features. And in adjoining rooms, to boot.

But she also thinks she can tell me what to do, after all these years. When I was little she didn't care, and now? It's like she's come down on me in one fell swoop to try and correct all the things she doesn't like about me. And everyone here pretty much thinks that I'm an immature, ungrateful daughter who can't keep her own husband, when in reality she's the one who gave up her husband and children to be with someone else. Who's the selfish person now, eh?

I've had enough. I need to get out of here pronto.

18

After that joyous conversation, I spend my time sitting by the brook at the end of the clinic's property, in the shade of a copse of trees. I'm going to book myself a flight right out of this bedlam and go home, where I'm needed, if not actually appreciated, by my kids. Because I certainly don't need my mother.

I spend hours there, and it's past dinner time by the time I decide enough is enough. I wish Markus was here to fall asleep next to me on this bloody hard bench. Markus makes everything so much more bearable.

Sighing, I get to my feet to face the music. I'm going to go into the dining hall, head held high, and I'm going to enjoy my meal and then frogmarch myself back upstairs early while my mother holds court to all her friends. She'll retire very late, as always, and I'll pretend to be sleeping, as always.

On the way, I decide to have my dinner brought up to my room to avoid the gaggle of women entirely, but the joke is on me because my mother is already there waiting for me.

'Come on, Livvie. Let's discuss this like two proper adults.'

'Two proper adults?' I gape. 'You want to teach *me* how to be a proper adult?'

'Livvie, you are my daughter and I think we should be able to have a civilised conversation.'

'Oh, come on, Mother! Do you really expect me to believe your new-found motherly love, that you want to be my mother again? That you actually *care*?'

She blinks at me. 'Of course I care. I always have. Olivia, I never stopped being your mother. I know you feel like I abandoned you, but I always kept in touch, sent letters, postcards, gifts, invited you to come visit. When Joe and Cassie were old enough I invited them over for the holidays. I did everything I could to not lose you...'

'You did? That's funny, because all I remember is crying myself to sleep wondering why my mother left. You didn't care enough to stay with your family, where you belonged! I had to go through puberty without you! Do you know who bought me my first bra? That's right, Dad! And do you know that when I got my period I didn't leave my room for five days? No, you don't, because Dad would've spared you that sense of guilt. Why, I just don't know!'

Now that I've started I can't seem to stop, every feeling I've been pushing down over the past few weeks – or decades – spilling out of me. 'I'll never be able to understand why you get the accolades as if you'd been there the whole time, every single day, through good and bad, like a real mother. But you weren't! It was Dad! Always Dad, every single day of his life! And where were you if not with your Italian boyfriend, eating granita and sipping limoncello!'

And then, it happens. My flighty, heartless mother's eyes fill with tears. Real, big, plopping tears. And then she begins to shake, letting out a loud, feral cry that seems to come from her gut.

'Look, Mother, I'm sorry. I didn't mean to yell at you. I'm just upset. I take it all back, okay?' I sigh.

I'm more than aware that this was always our dynamic while she was living with us. She did something to upset me, but when I gave her grief for it, then she got upset and it frightened me so much to see her come undone that I would always be the one to apologise in the end. But the only way to break that cycle was to stay away from her.

'Do you really think that I left you so light-heartedly?' she whispers. 'That I didn't cry *myself* to sleep for the choice I'd made? That my heart didn't ache for you, every time your father told me something had happened to you? Do you think I didn't suffer when Mitchell died? Or when you were bullied? Or that I didn't want to fly back and shake Simon senseless until he saw what an amazing girl you really are behind your snarky, I-don't-give-a-shit exterior? Do you think I didn't blame myself for how you'd changed? Of course I did, Olivia! I felt exactly the same way you are feeling now with Cassie.'

'That's not the same, Mother.'

'Probably not. But it feels the same,' she informs me.

Well, she's got me there.

'I know I've been a terrible mother, and that you still hate me despite our best efforts.'

'I don't hate you, Mother.' Also because, I've learnt these past few weeks, that hatred takes up a great deal of energy and I am exhausted by it.

'Are you sorry you came?' she asks timidly.

'No, of course not…'

'It was cowardly of me, not coming back to England and instead insisting you came to us. But you never wanted to. You never even wanted to speak to me, and it made me suffer. It wasn't your fault, of course. I was the adult, and I just dumped all that on you. I'm so sorry, sweetheart. Can you ever forgive me...?'

Her huge eyes have become two alpine lakes of tears. I want to reach out and comfort her, but I haven't got it in me just yet. She needs to understand that we'll get there, I'm sure, but I need time.

'I forgive you, Mum...'

'Thank you, sweetheart. I truly appreciate it. I know I was selfish. What a thing to ask of a young girl! And what you must have thought of me.'

Oh, I have many thoughts.

'Even Aldo said that if I was so miserable I could go back to England for months at a time if it made me feel better... or even for a year or two.'

He loved her that much? Simon had a hissy fit when I told him I was going away for two *months*. Of course, there are husbands and there are *husbands*. It figures she got two good ones and I'd got the crap one.

'So why didn't you come back, then?' I ask, trying to keep it civil.

She sniffs and laughs at herself while dabbing at the corner of her eyes, but all her make-up is gone. She looks better without it, anyway.

'Because I knew that if I did, and then left again, I'd destabilise you even more, and George was adamant that you didn't suffer anymore. And I guess also because I was absolutely terrified of coming back to face you.'

'But you always sent me invitations,' I say.

'And you finally answered!' she says with a nervous laugh. 'And I'm glad you did!'

'Yeah,' I mutter. 'I am happy to be here, even if it doesn't always seem that way.'

'It is beautiful here, isn't it?' she says.

I look around us, from the mountains to the pine trees to the lake below and the little boats bobbing from shore to shore.

'It feeds the soul. I've never been to such a beautiful place before. And this place… it takes my breath away. Thank you for inviting me here to stay with you.'

'It's my pleasure, Livvie.' And then silence, followed by: 'Oh, to hell with it. I told myself I was going to be honest with you, so I'm going to.'

'What?' I ask. 'What is it?'

She sighs. 'I was looking for the right moment to tell you, chickie. I… have breast cancer.'

My breath catches in my throat. 'M-mum…'

Her eyes moisten as she squeezes my fingers delicately.

'Oh my God, *Mum*…'

'It's okay, chickie,' she soothes.

At that, I splutter. When was the last time she'd called me that without my baulking?

'Oh, Mum, I'm so sorry!'

'Livvie,' she says, clearing her throat, but her voice is still feeble, so different from her singsong voice only a few hours ago. 'It's just one of those things, honey.'

'But why?' I blurt out. 'You don't smoke, you exercise…'

She shrugs and smiles. 'Oh, well, who knows? You just have to take it on the chin, whatever life gives you.'

'H-how far…?'

'I've already done a few rounds of chemo. Lost my hair and grew it back… Now we wait and see what's what until my next check-up. But I want to go back home to Sicily now. Will you come with me? For a while?'

I can't believe it. My mother has… cancer? We were only just getting to know each other again! It can't be over just like that, after all these years of not talking to her!

'Yes,' I whisper, my voice cracking. 'Of course I'll come with you, Mum.'

'Thank you. If I'm not asking too much… I know school is not out yet, but… the kids don't have any exams. Maybe your father could come with them—?'

'Absolutely, Mum. We'll all come.'

'Thank you,' she repeats. 'I'm so happy, all of us under one roof again, after all these years…'

Happy? She's… happy?

'Oh, chickie, wipe your tears. This is the way it's meant to be. I'm sorry I've been such a disappointment.'

I shake my head. 'That's in the past, Mum.'

She smiles and reaches out to caress my face. She hasn't done that in over twenty years. Because I had never let her. I had never answered her letters, never accepted her invitations to Sicily. I had simply erased her from my life. And now she is battling to save hers.

'You know, love,' she says. 'I don't want you to make a big mistake.'

'W-what do you mean?'

'Please forgive me if I insist, but it's obvious that Simon is not the man for you anymore. Maybe you loved him in the past, but now it's over, and that's okay. You can always start again, find a new love. And based on what your father tells me about this Markus, it looks like you already have, am I right?'

'You've just told me you have cancer and you want to talk about my love life?'

'Of course, why not? Your love life is important. It's part of your happiness. And it's so much more interesting than my boring diagnosis. You're not only a mother. You're also a woman. Don't ever forget that, chickie.'

Up until now my father and I had only texted, except for my birthday. And now I understand why. You can hide behind a text, but not so much when talking on the phone. Even today his voice is sad, despite his efforts to sound chipper.

'Hi, Dad, how are you guys?'

'We're all tickety boo here, love. How's your mum?'

'She… told me about her cancer.'

'Oh, *sweetheart*.'

'Yuh…' I manage, not knowing what else to do. But it's important that all cards are on the table now. I sniff, unable to speak around the lump in my throat.

'Will you finally forgive her, pet?'

'Yes, of course…' I whisper, reaching for the tissues.

'Good girl.' I can practically hear him smiling over the line. He must have been waiting for this moment just as long as my mother has.

'She's asked that we all spend the summer with her in Sicily.'

'Of course. We'll make arrangements to come out as soon as school is out.'

'Thank you, Dad.'

'Now. Are you okay to talk to Joe? He's about to come in.'

'Ooh, yes please,' I croak.

'Hi, Mum!' comes his sweet little voice.

'Darling! How are you?'

'We're great, Mum. We miss you but we're in good hands. Grandpa and Markus are hilarious.'

'I'm so glad. How is football?'

'We played our last game this season. And we won!'

'I'm so proud of you!' I chime. 'Not because you won, but because you gave it your all!'

'Thanks, Mum! Do you want to talk to Cassie?'

'Of course!' (I hadn't dared ask.)

'Okay, then. Bye, Mum!'

'Bye, love, I'll see you soon!'

And I wait for him to put Cassie on.

And wait.

'Er, hello? Cassie? Cassie, are you there?'

'I'm *here*,' she says as if I'd been hollering into her ear for hours and she can't stand the sound of my voice anymore.

'Oh, hello, love. How are you?' I ask tentatively.

'Fine.'

'How was the movie?'

'All right.'

'How's school?'

'Fine.'

'And the girls, are they doing well?'

'All right.'

'Miss me at all?' I venture.

I can *hear* her rolling her eyes. Okay, not true. She groans.

'I miss *you*,' I confess.

'Right,' she says.

'Cassie?'

'*What?*'

'I know you're angry at me for something. But remember that I love you. Very much.'

Again the groan. 'Right. I have to go now.'

And that's the end of that. No *How are you doing? Are you feeling better? We miss you.* Nothing. What does she care? Because I had decided to come out here in the end. What's it to her how I am doing?

I am afraid that she will resent me for leaving for a long time to come, just like I still resent my mother, albeit the circumstances were different. I'm also afraid that, being my daughter, she may have inherited my anger issues. I'm almost always angry and I certainly don't want my only daughter to be the same. I don't want her to be this sad, bitter person who will eventually sabotage her own life and happiness, not to mention that of those around her. I want her to be the opposite of me.

To get my mind off that call, I ring Markus's phone.

'Hey, you,' comes his beloved voice over the Alps to caress my heart. 'How's it going?'

'Meh,' I confess. 'Not too good.'

'Talk to me.'

'My mother's just told me that she has cancer.'

He releases a long breath. 'Jesus, Liv, I'm so sorry.'

I dash the tissue over my eyes and reach for a new one. Lucky I have a jumbo box with me. 'She wants me, Dad and the kids to be in Sicily with her for the summer.'

'I'll sort out the flights for you,' he offers.

'Thank you. Do you… think you might be able to make it too? Even for a brief spell?'

'I'll be there, sweetheart. You can count on me.'

'Thank you, Markus.'

'I'll see you soon, *skat*.'

'So what's on your mind today?' Dr Severini asks me as I sink into his chair. 'You seem different. Was it your mother's presence last time that annoyed you?'

'My mother has cancer,' I blurt out.

'Yes, I know. I'm so sorry.'

'You knew?'

'Well, Susan and I have been having our own sessions recently. We've spoken about her diagnosis several times.'

'Right. So everybody here knew before me and—' I rake a hand through my hair. I realise that I had no right to know anything about her as I haven't spoken to her in twenty-two years. And now I'm paying the price. But I don't intend to pay for my childhood for ever.

'Perhaps this is a good time to start repairing your relationship,' he suggests. 'It's not healthy to hold on to all this anger. If not for her, let go for yourself.'

If anything, I am all the more angry towards her, and myself, for all that has happened between us. I am angry that it had to go this way. I am angry that she waited all this time to force me to speak to her by inviting me here. She could have found a better place. And a better time. I am angry all over again, period. But I can't take it out on her anymore, of course. It's time to fight my demons head-on, by myself. So I get to my feet.

'Dr Severini, I'm very sorry, but I won't be coming back.'

'Oh?'

'I've finally realised that I can do this by myself. I know what to do now. Goodbye and thanks for the laughs.'

The look on his face? Priceless.

When I get back to my room, I flop onto my bed. So much for therapy being cathartic. In my case, it's exhausting. All those feelings roiling around, threatening to come to the surface.

That's when my mother knocks on the adjoining door.

'Livvie, can I come in?' she calls.

'Yes,' I answer, trying to stifle my tears.

She opens the door and pads over to my bed, sitting on the edge.

'I am glad that I've told you the truth about my health. I want to always be honest with you from now on. I have so much apologising and explaining to do,' she says. 'And so much to make up for. I know that. I've known it for all these years, but I hoped that eventually time would relieve me of my sense of guilt.' She turns to face me more fully, her expression fearful but vulnerable. 'But is there any way that you think that, as two grown women, we may reconnect once again? Can you really find it in your heart to forgive me, Olivia? Only now, seeing you as a grown woman, do I realise how much I've missed out on. I have been so selfish. But I want to make amends for all the hurt I've caused you…'

My eyes are suddenly flooded with tears and my throat is tight. Can I truly forgive the person who's done me the most damage in my life? Can I forgive my mother? I wipe my eyes and nod.

Without a word, she spreads her arms and I fall into them, and we both sob inconsolably.

Over the next few weeks Mum and I spend some quality time together. We go for short walks and long sits. We get massages and pedicures and manicures and anything that we can do together, side by side, that is not too strenuous for her. Now that I know, I see I should have figured out the tell-tale signs, like her cough, her moments of frailty, her hunger for life and laughter. And Dad's insistence on my coming out here.

I take her out to Stresa where Markus took me, and we have a leisurely meal on the lake in the shade of a huge tree that seems to be growing in the water.

We chat and laugh. We joke about Dad's idiosyncrasies, like all the puzzles he's started but never finished, and his obsession with trying new recipes when he never used to lift a finger in the kitchen when she was around. There might be, here and there, a moment of awkwardness about her absence as it is a big part of our past, but we push on past it, because none of that matters in the face of her disease.

And I find that, although we can't cram twenty years into two months in Villa dei Respira, my stay here has explored almost every avenue of this unusual mother–daughter relationship. And through its peaks and troughs, I am finding it easier to navigate the difficulties, but I also understand a little bit more about my relationship with Cassie. Granted, my relationship with my daughter is founded on a different basis, but many dynamics, many twists and turns, are very similar to my relationship with my mother.

As I am both a mother and a daughter, I am beginning to understand how to be better at each role, something I'd never questioned before. I thought it was supposed to be something that just came naturally, but I have learnt that there are unspoken rules of interaction when dealing with both my daughter and my mother.

'I can understand why people would want to move to Italy,' I sigh as we are finishing up our lunch in the restaurant overlooking the lake. Our vegetarian lasagnas are simply mouth-watering, and today we have decided to live a little and share a bottle of Barolo. Why the hell not?

Mum puts her hand on mine. 'Is that something that you might ever consider?' she asks softly. 'Or are you happy in England?'

I wonder what it would have been like if my father had moved us to Italy to be closer to my mother. Not that that would have made any sense, chasing the woman who left you halfway around the world, but maybe he had at least considered it for my sake.

Could I live in Italy? Absolutely. But my father? Would he want to at this point in his life, even if he and Mum have managed to remain good friends? And Cassie? She would absolutely hate me for even suggesting moving out of her beloved Canterbury. Joe would follow me anywhere, my baby. I know that. But would it give him what he wants and needs from life? He is passionate about his football. Maybe I could get him into a good school with a good team?

And my business? Okay, let's cut to the chase. I could run the business from anywhere, but would I want to run it without Markus? Would I want to live in a different country than him? Even if he has his own life and future plans? I have to accept that even if we always live in the same place, there will come a time when I won't be able to see him every day, and that I have to get on with my own life. Because, in any case, my priorities are Cassie and Joe. Anything else is just a bonus, really.

And then I realise that I haven't even given Simon a thought. Which really says it all. I can't see myself living with him for the rest of my life. Maybe I am more like my mother than I thought.

I look up at her. She's waiting for an answer. 'Could I live in Italy? Personally, yes. But I have to put Cassie and Joe first.'

And I bite my lip. I didn't mean that to sound accusatory in any way. It's just what mothers say and do. Put their kids first. But the past is in the past.

Mum is still holding my hand. She gently squeezes it. 'All these years, Livvie, I've been thinking about what I did to you. I was a horrible mother...'

I shrug. 'It's okay, Mum.'

'No, it's not. Yes, you had your father, but a girl needs her mother. I understand that now. I didn't before, because I never had my mother around. But you needed me, and I left.'

I can feel the pain rising in her voice and I squeeze her hand back. 'Mum, I think I need you now more than I did back then.' And that is the truth.

'I've learnt so much about you. I needed this, Mum, even if I didn't want it. I needed to know that you love me.'

Her huge eyes are glistening. 'Oh, my darling,' she whispers. 'I never stopped loving you. Never...'

My breath catches as I push a sob down.

She laughs. ‘Okay, let’s not embarrass ourselves here, yes?’

I nod as I look around at the other diners. ‘Let’s not, indeed! Fancy some dessert?’ I suggest.

‘Abso-bloody-lutely! Tiramisù for me,’ she says.

‘Sounds like a plan!’ I agree as I catch the waiter’s attention.

19

The next day we are in the entertainment hall waiting for the dinner announcement.

Mum sits at the grand piano, listlessly caressing the keys. And I just *know* what's on her mind. I may not have spoken to her all these years but it's perfectly clear to me.

'That day… when I left… I want to make it up to you, chickie,' she says. 'I'd like you to sing that song, if you would like?'

I can tell that her shame is still burning, especially now that things are slowly mending between us. It's something that she hasn't been able to deal with, a nagging sense of guilt that has been plaguing her all these years.

I watch her, panic rising inside me as she tentatively plays the opening chords of 'our' song. Before I realise what's happening, she begins to sing the song ever so softly, under her breath, like she used to while teaching me.

I listen as she finishes the first verse and looks to me for the second. I open my mouth, for her, but nothing comes out. She smiles her *you can do it* smile at me. I did sing it before, when I was on my own that day. But can I do it again, with her playing the piano like she was supposed to have done? Is this what it takes from both of us, to come full circle and erase the past?

So I begin to sing, under my breath, softly, uncertainly. Mum is still smiling, encouraging me, and before I know it, I'm a teenager on that stage again, still full of trepidation. Only this time Mum is there to back me up. We haven't done this in twenty-two years and I don't know how many more times we'll get a chance to do this together, if at all, but I'll be damned if I don't do it now.

Because this is our official atonement. The moment where everything changes for real, in every way. If I can do this with her, *for* her, it will mean that I have well and truly, finally forgiven her. And I also know that somewhere along the line I've grown out of my pain. And perhaps even my anger. Because there are more important things in life. There is life itself. And the memories we make with our loved ones, those who touch us the deepest and are always the ones who hurt us the most, without ever wanting to.

Before I know it, I am singing along, singing every word with feeling as her own voice drops in order to let me take the lead. I remember all her silent gestures. I know exactly from the look on her face that I'm doing well, that I've sung that particular section exactly the way it should be sung. I can see from her face that she is proud of my voice, but also that she is proud of me, and of us. We have come a long way since the night of the school talent show.

It's time for the climax of the song and, perhaps because I'd sung it recently, I really manage to knock it out of the park once again. Only this time I'm not alone.

As I bring the song down to its conclusion, there is a loud crash.

I open my eyes and whirl around. Behind us an entire crowd has filled the hall, with the Respiri Ladies in the front line, clapping and cheering like there's no tomorrow.

'That was absolutely amazing, Olivia! And you didn't even warm up first!' Mum says, getting to her feet to wrap her arms around me, and we hold each other as the crowd continues to go absolutely bonkers. 'Thank you, chickie! I've had the time of my life!'

'Me too, Mum!' is all I can say as I'm still winded. 'I never thought we would ever sing together again.'

'Never say never, you see, love?'

I nod as tears stream down my cheeks. Happy tears, for once.

The next day, another crazy thing happens. I get another message from Cassie:

Hi Mum, how are you? Everything is fine here. School is boring as usual. Talk tonight?

Now, I know that my mother is behind this and that this is certainly not a spontaneous gesture from Cassie. She probably rolled her eyes and finally, after much insistence from my mother's part, capitulated. But I still can't help being absolutely beside myself with joy! Though I rein myself in a tad. I don't want to look too desperate and therefore, in her eyes, pathetic. So I type back:

Lovely to hear that all is well. Yes, happy to talk tonight. Seven p.m. your time?

To which she immediately answers:

Ok.

Better than nothing, I guess. I'm grateful. I'm also grateful to my mother. So I tell her.

'Aw, chickie, I have no idea what you're talking about!' she says with a smile and a wink.

That's her way of doing things. But if it means that Cassie is willing to talk to me again, I'll take it, thank you very much.

I don't need to tell anyone how happy I am all day, bouncing around like a duck on springs. I can't help smiling to myself. This time I'm going to be cool. Not be needy or too smother-y. I'll listen to what Cassie has to say and I'll support her.

Unless, oh crap, is there a particular reason she wants to talk to me? She knows how I feel about sleepovers and wild parties. Has she… done something? Nonsense. Cassie is a clever girl. She would never get into any trouble. Unless Liam has anything to do with it? Okay, now I'm officially worried. But then again, if something were wrong, Markus or at least my mother would have given me a heads up, right?

Seven o'clock is never going to come soon enough. I'm tempted to call her now, but I stop myself. It would only annoy her anyway.

So I book myself a massage. God knows I'm tense enough.

The massage room is a different one this time. It's done up in shades of burnt orange and rust and deep yellows. On one end of the massage bed there are low, thick, scented candles burning. The masseuse is a small woman, but I soon find out, much to my joy, that she has the most powerful hands I've ever known.

'Tense, *sì*?' she prompts.

'Yes,' I murmur back, already plunging myself into relaxation mode. Out with all the bad thoughts. I mean, there's really no need to worry. I would know if something was wrong, right? A mother knows these things. I would feel it in my bones. Which, come to think of it, I do.

'Untense your shoulders, please,' the masseuse whispers.

'Sorry,' I mumble back.

Of course I could always nip back there for the weekend. It's only a three-hour flight, at the end of the day. I could be there in time for Saturday brunch and stay with my family all weekend and fly back Sunday afternoon. Just to make sure everything's okay. And that Cassie isn't in distress. This Liam bloke... are they together? My mother had said, *Let him chase you*. Is she stalking him? Of course not. Well, at least I know they are not an item. Because once that happens and he's bad news, there's no getting rid of the scum. But he hasn't dealt with me yet. I'll sort him out. I'll show him he can't just crook his finger and boss my baby girl around. I'll teach him what respect looks like—'

'Mrs Dawson, your shoulders. Please.'

'Sorry,' I whisper, trying to breathe calmly and willing myself to focus on this lovely massage. The oil smells nice. Rosemary? Rosemary reminds me of Christmas. Funny, because cinnamon should remind me of Christmas, but last year Markus baked something with cinnamon around Easter and it sort of stayed with me. Next Christmas, I would like to… next Christmas. What is going to happen next Christmas? Will my mother be around?

I can't even think of her not being around, even if we have many, many issues still to resolve between us. It would be nice to have them – her and… Aldo – over at the house. We could decorate the oast house and throw a lovely Christmas party with friends and family. Or we could spend it in Sicily with Aldo's family. I have no idea what the future will bring and it's driving me crazy.

This is ridiculous. I'm here having a massage in one of the most exclusive resorts in the world, and I am worrying about things that are totally beyond my control. I can do nothing about my mother's health right now, save keep her company and attempt to fix the twenty-two-year rift between us. Nor can I solve any of Cassie's problems, whatever they may be, until I speak to her later. But I can't help but wonder—

'Mrs Dawson, please try to relax…'

'Yes, sorry, sorry.'

'Turn over, please.'

I do as I'm told and let her work on the rest of me.

Seven o'clock finally rolls around and I am practically jumping out of my skin. My daughter has never phoned me unless she needed something: a lift, money, school supplies, clothes, etc. But then again I have never been this far from her. I know exactly how she feels. Even if I'm not the first mother to take a much-needed break for my mental health, I still feel guilty.

But I am literally doing it for them. So I can be a better, calmer mother. A little pain for a big gain and all that. I only hope that this will be the first of many spontaneous connections between us. I don't expect a call every week, but once or twice before I leave this paradise on earth would be nice. Maybe I could come back here with her, one day?

My mobile rings and I pounce on it. 'Hello, Cassie...' *I sound pleased but not desperate.*

'Hi, Mum...'

'How are you?'

'I'm fine. How are you?'

'Just fine, thank you, darling.'

She sounds okay. Meaning, she doesn't sound like she's being pushed around. But she does sound listless. 'So how are things?'

'Oh, you know. The usual.'

'Yeah?'

'Yeah...'

'And school? How's school?'

'We had a few tests this week. I think I actually did well.'

'Good for you, I'm glad, Cassie. I never doubted it.' *Supportive but not smother-y.*

Silence. She's not revealing anything spontaneously any time soon.

'Any boys... on the horizon?' I ask and curse myself. Have I blown Markus's and Mum's covers?

'Actually...' she says, hesitating.

'Yes?' I say, holding my breath. *This is where she tells me that she's engaged to be married or something. Calm down, you idiot. Cassie's not engaged. She's a teenager, for Christ's sake.*

'There is one guy. His name's Liam.'

'That's a nice name.' God, could I sound any more lame? 'Is he nice?'

'Yes, he is. I like him, Mum.'

'Good, good. And does he like you?'

'I'm not sure. Sometimes it seems like he does. Other times, he seems… distant.' I don't respond, not wanting to push her, so she continues. 'He's coming over to study for our French test next week.'

'Did you ask him or did he ask you?' Important to understand the dynamics, right?

'He asked me. But I'm not so sure if he wants to study with me because he thinks I'm smart, or because he likes me as a girl.'

Ah. 'Well, Cassie, you have the brains and the looks. There's nothing wrong if he likes you for both of these qualities.'

'Yes, but… what if I help him with his schoolwork and then he doesn't ask me out?'

'Then you will be friends.'

'But I want to be more than friends…'

Oh, my goodness, my little girl has grown so fast! When did this happen? I clear my throat.

'Well, honey, your nana says that good things are really worth waiting for, you know? And she's right.'

'So you don't think I should give him a little push?'

'Oh, absolutely not. Boys don't like being pushed. They get frightened if someone tells them what they want. Just be friendly as usual and if he really, really likes you, he'll make the first move.'

'But what if he's too shy?' she insists.

I don't even need to think about it. Simon was shy and look what I ended up with, someone without an ounce of initiative. 'If he's too shy he'll never get what he wants. Remember when you wanted to join dance classes but you thought you weren't good enough, but in the end you asked anyway?'

'Yeah?'

'Well, they wanted you to join too but they weren't sure you were interested. Remember that?'

'Yes.'

'So, then. If Liam really likes you enough to be a very good boyfriend, then he'll find a way to tell you. If he doesn't make the effort to overcome his shyness then it will always be you making all the effort.'

'Oh. Yeah, I guess you're right. I'll just have to wait and see, then.'

'Yes, but not for ever. Someone else might come along. Someone who is really crazy about you and who goes out of their way to tell you.'

'That would be nice.'

Yes, it would, indeed.

'Mum?'

'Yes, darling?'

'I *miss* you...'

It's all I can do to stop from bawling. 'I miss you too, sweetheart.' *Shall I jump on the next plane? Ask me and I'm there, sweetheart...* 'But we'll see each other soon. Nana would like us all to go to Sicily for the summer. Would you like that?'

'You mean... you'd come too? To Sicily? To stay in Nana's house?'

Hot tears form behind my eyes while my throat swells with unexpressed emotions. I should have done this years ago, but instead I let life pass me by, when I could have forgiven. I would have so many memories now, with my mother and father together and the kids. But I was stuck in my ways and there is nothing I can do to get any of that time back. All I can do is move forward.

'Yes, Cassie. I'm coming, too.'

'Mum, are you okay? Your voice is weird.'

'Uh, yes. I think I'm just having allergies.'

Silence. She is sounding me out, the clever girl.

'So you and Nana are really getting along, then?'

'Oh, absolutely, darling.'

'I'm so happy, Mum! This summer we can all swim in the sea together! They have a gorgeous mansion above the beach and there are these tiny stone steps carved into the cliff and you go down, down, down and the sunsets are amazing and so is the ice cream and—' She stops, and the silence is filled with something unspoken.

'What is it, sweetheart?'

'What made you change your mind about Nana?' she wants to know. Nothing gets past this one.

I take a deep breath. 'If you love someone, deep down in your heart, you have to forgive them. Family and friends and love are what life is all about. Not just school or work or success.'

'I know,' she whispers. 'Will Dad be coming too?'

'Uhm… I don't think so, honey. Your father is very busy and summer is a very busy time for him.' Busy. He's always busy. That's his middle name, Busy.

'Right,' she says. She doesn't sound too distraught. 'Can we bring Markus? He's never been to Sicily before.'

'Of course. Nana won't mind.'

'This is so cool, I can't wait!'

'Neither can I! Give your brother and Grandad a hug for me, will you?'

'I will,' she promises.

'And call me whenever you need, even if you think it's not important. I'm here for you always, Cassie.'

'Thanks, Mum. I love you.'

I almost stroke out on her last sentence. It's a good thing she can't see my face because I'm sure it's purple. I'm about to be overwhelmed. 'I love you too, darling,' I say and hang up as a sob escapes me. My little girl! She's back! I haven't been this happy since Joe was born. Now all I have to do is solidify our relationship.

And the one with my mother. Family above all else.

The next day I expect Mum to want to stay at the villa to relax, but she is determined we go out shopping. The first place we end up is a music stand by the lake that sells instruments and old vinyl records. There is just about everything there, from Italian folk music to her favourite albums by Mina. She picks them up, one by one, placing them in chronological order and singing me bits of each.

'We'll take them all,' she tells the stall owner, who wraps them up and puts them in a paper bag.

'Is that every single one of Mina's albums, then?' I ask.

'Yes. For you.'

'For... me?'

'Yes. I already own her collection. But I noticed you were enthralled the first time you heard her songs, so...'

'Mum… thank you so much. I'll learn every single one,' I promise. I already know more than a handful thanks to Spotify, anyway.

She winks at me. 'And now, my dear, lunch is on me. I wonder if we can find somewhere that makes fried polenta? I'm starving!'

And she links her arm through mine as we wind our way through the little *osterie* on offer.

That night we are both tired, so opt to have dinner in my room while lounging in our pyjamas and sifting through some photo albums she's brought along from Sicily. I prepare myself for another jump into her unknown past, but the photos are all of Joe and Cassie holidaying in Sicily through the years. I shouldn't be surprised to see all those pictures, but seeing entire photo albums full of moments of my children's lives – moments I wasn't around for, where they look so happy and carefree to boot – certainly does have an effect on me.

And to think that they have all these memories with my mother and Aldo, an entire life I don't know about, makes me question my past choices. I could have found a way to forgive her sooner, to enjoy these precious moments with my children. But no. I had to play the hurt diva and divide my family in two, even spending two entire weeks of the summer away from my children because I refused to give my mother any sort of satisfaction.

I could have travelled with them, seen their faces light up as they saw the island for the very first time, or heard their squeals of delight as they splashed into the sea for their first swim of the season every year. But no. I had to be me. Well, I've certainly learnt my lesson now.

The next morning I wake up late. If I don't hurry I'll miss breakfast. So I have the quickest of showers and rush down the stairs to the east terrace where we usually eat.

'Olivia!' someone calls from behind me. I turn to see Elsa, followed by the rest of the Respiri Ladies tripping over themselves.

'Susan's had a fall!'

And then I see a small crowd of people surrounding my mother.

'Mum! Mum!' I call, rushing to her side. She has already been hauled onto a gurney and into an ambulance. She looks awful, like all the blood has been drained from her face. Lying there, she looks half her size, and so defenceless! A wave of gut-wrenching pity and fear washes through me. I was angry at her for half my life, but I never wanted anything to happen to her. I have never, ever, not even in my darkest, angriest moments, wished her any harm.

'Come,' Carla says. 'My car is out front, we'll follow the ambulance...'

20

The Respiri Ladies sit with me in an uncharacteristic silence the entire time the medical staff are tending to her, bringing me coffee, water, a shawl, but I refuse everything. They send each other worried glances but remain quiet.

About an hour later a Dr Angeli finally comes out to talk to me. 'We've notified her husband.'

'Thank you.'

She's seen it a million times before, I'm sure.

'We'll let her sleep. I'll have someone call you when she wakes up.'

'I'm not going anywhere,' I say, my face scrunching into a knot so I won't cry.

The doctor nods, briefly touching my arm. 'If you need anything at all…'

'Thank you.'

'Come back to Respiri and get some rest,' Maria coaxes softly. 'One of us will keep guard and come and get you the minute we have any news.'

'It's okay, thank you,' I assure her. 'You go and get some rest. I want to be here when she wakes up.'

They nod, but Lucia and Carla remain, agreeing on shifts so that I'm never alone.

I should call Aldo to follow up on the call from the hospital. But I don't have his number, because I've never cared to speak to him. I should have had it, in case something ever happened, shouldn't I? Well, today it happened.

I call my dad.

'Sweetheart,' he says. 'Don't worry about a thing, I'll ask Markus if he can bring the flights forward.'

I'm grateful for that, of course.

'See you as soon as possible, okay? Hang in there, my darling.'

I can do nothing but accept it. And wait for her to wake up.

I am sitting outside her room with Elsa and Carla now, who have brought fresh coffee and a jacket for me.

And still there is no one there to ask about my mother, as the occasional nurses scurrying to and fro don't stop, doors clicking open and shut behind them. I don't dare disturb them. Every time a door opens I jump, tunnel-visioning on their face to try to glean any info at all.

I have been told to relax, and that I will be informed. But I can't relax, of course. I need to stay with my mum. She should be up and about, annoying the crap out of me with her endearments and encouragement and not in a hospital bed. So I'll stay right here until someone can tell me how she is doing.

I've tried to distract myself by studying the pictures of the Alps on the walls over and over again. By now I know each and every ravine of these mountains. Then, about three hours later, Lucia nudges me, and in the corner of my eye I see a man running down the corridor. He is in his late sixties, looking very trim and elegant in a pair of sand-coloured trousers and a white shirt with long sleeves folded, and not rolled, up to just under the elbow. He has salt and pepper hair, bright blue eyes and a square jaw. It's not until he's reached me that I recognise him from the kids' pictures.

It's Aldo Amore, my mother's husband. Behind the elegant stance and well-tailored clothes, there is pure terror on his drawn face. But he recognises me and hurries towards me. I jump to my feet, instinctively grabbing his outstretched hands. They are warm and solid.

'Aldo...'

'Olivia! How is she?'

'I don't know, they won't tell me anything!'

'Come with me,' he says to me and Elsa, taking my arm, and we follow him down the corridor to a small lounge with sofas scattered around a coffee table with some carafes and porcelain cups.

He knocks on a door, speaks briefly with a nurse who pokes her head out and nods. Then he comes back and pours us some steaming coffee. I wrap my fingers around the hot cup, gathering what comfort I can. Because inside I am frozen to the core with fear.

'They will give us some information as soon as they have it,' he says softly. He speaks English fluently, his accent not as marked as I'd always imagined it. He is obviously a well-educated man, with poise and innate elegance; the negative picture of him I'd formed in my head had clearly come from a place of anger, and I'd pegged him completely wrong.

There is no cloud of pungent aftershave surrounding him, no ostentatiously expensive suits and shirts and colourful ties that I imagined every Italian wore. Obviously the stereotypes living in my head have misled me to conjure up an image of someone who couldn't be further away from reality.

And I never imagined that someone so put together could ever fall in love with a mess like my mother. And yet, here he is. There is truly someone for everyone.

'Th-thank you,' I whisper.

'Drink,' he says as he pours himself a glass of water. 'There is so much to say, but you need to take care of yourself, too. We won't be of much use to her if we're both in a state.'

I nod, too frazzled and exhausted to utter another word.

This is insane. Two months ago if you'd told me I'd be sitting across from Aldo The Homewrecker, drinking coffee and taking his advice while agonising over my mother's well-being, I wouldn't have believed you.

Another hour later, a doctor finally approaches us and we all jump to our feet in unison. '*Adesso è sveglia. Potete vederla, due per volta.*' She's awake now. You can see her, two at a time.

'*Grazie, Dottore.* Come, Olivia,' Aldo says, and I have to ramp up my energy to keep up with him shooting down the corridor with the vigour of a twenty-year-old, scurrying after him until he stops at a room on the right. The door is open and immediately his face changes.

'*Amore mio*,' he breathes, smiling at her from the door.

'*Amore mio*,' my mother whispers back.

He moves aside for me to go in first despite the fact that he's just flown in to see her. It's such a kind gesture towards me, especially when I know how badly he wants to be with her. So I nod him onwards, staying on the threshold. He looks down at me, reaches out to squeeze my hand and rushes to her side.

They are speaking in whispers, but you don't need to hear what they are saying to feel the love between them. It is so tangible that it comes off in waves, reaching me and wrapping me up in their warmth, so intense and intimate that I have to look away.

It's not right. Life should be lived to the full. Sixty-five years old is not old, especially in her case, as vibrant and cheerful as she is. And yet, here she is, with this disease. *Cancer.*

I drop my head in my hands, cursing myself over and over for not knowing, for not understanding, for not even thinking that one day she was going to die.

I don't know how long Aldo is in there for but when he comes out, I can see that he is barely kept together by what can only be love. My heart goes out to him.

I get to my feet. 'Aldo...'

He guides me to the door. 'It's all right. She's got a broken leg and a slight concussion from the fall. She wants to see you, Olivia. Go...'

I swallow the huge boulder in my throat and nod, not wanting to let his arm go, not wanting to go in there but at the same time desperate to see my mother.

My lips are shaking but I force myself to stay calm. Like Aldo had maintained his calm in there, I can't let her see how upset I am, either. It could have been worse. Much worse. I know it might get worse later.

She is attached to a monitor and a drip. The sheets are up to her chest and her arms are on top of the blanket.

'Hey…' she whispers, her eyes the only bright part of her face.

I rush to her bedside. 'M-Mum… how are you…?'

She rolls her eyes. 'I'm fine, chickie. I just tripped over my own feet, silly me. I'm so sorry I scared you. But the good news is that I can go home forty-eight hours after they put a cast on my leg. And I can't *wait* to hug the kids. They love Sicily in the summer. They like to play and picnic on the beach. They love to eat tons of watermelon and throw themselves in and out of the sea all day…'

She knows them well, after holidaying with them since they were little. Holidays that I missed out on because of my stupid, ridiculously staunch anti-mother campaign. I could just kick myself now.

'And promise me you'll never give up on Cassie. She's a real gem, you know? She's just like you, chickie…'

I cover my mouth with my hand and nod again, tears streaming down my cheeks.

'Oh, darling, don't cry. All will be well. But I do need you to do one last thing for me. I need you to throw away any bad thoughts in your life and make a break for happiness. Life is so, so short, Livvie. Live it to the full! Tell Markus how you feel about him.'

'*Mum—*'

'Let me finish, Livvie. Your father tells me that man loves you.'

'He doesn't. But I don't want to talk about that right

now…'

'Then we'll talk more, later,' she whispers. 'Go back to the clinic and pack. I'm feeling better already, and in forty-eight hours we'll fly south.'

I nod and delicately kiss her brow, wishing I had done it a million times before, day in, day out, before her skin lost its youthful glow. Twenty-two years. I threw away twenty-two years of having her in my life. I know I had my reasons, and I truly had conviction in my behaviour, but now, faced with the possibility of losing my mother, it all seems so silly. It was my choice, and mine only, not to let her make up for leaving. I could have had a life with her. A life of phone calls, visits, holidays, jokes, fights, fits of silly laughter, shopping, lazy days on the beach and all those little things that mothers and daughters do.

Aldo shoots to his feet as I step out into the waiting room.

'She wants to go home. And she wants my family to come…' I tell him. 'We'll be there.'

He nods. 'Yes, yes, perfect. Thank you, Olivia. It'll be good to have her back. I've missed her so much…'

'You gave her up for two months, knowing she wasn't well… so she could spend time with me?'

'Oh, Olivia. We owe you so much. We owe you a lifetime of happiness that we've managed to pack into twenty-two years so far. If we are meant to be happy for a little while longer, I'll take every single day with gratitude.'

I look at the man who, despite everything, cares about how I am. Because my mother cares. She does. With all that's been going on in her life, she is worried about me. Me, the daughter who never forgave her.

'She came up with the idea of inviting you to Respiri

to spend some quality time with you before she broke the news to you.'

'I feel so guilty…'

'Nonsense. Come,' he says. 'Let's get you back to Respiri. I'll make arrangements for you to come home with us.'

Come home with us. It sounded so foreign to my ears. And yet, I knew that I couldn't possibly pass up on spending some more time with my mother and this lovely, kind man.

There is so much I want to say, so many questions I need to ask. But the most important thing now is to get my family here to spend as much time as possible with Mum. And Aldo. Unable to speak, I merely nod.

From what I can see, Aldo is, as my dad has always said, an absolute gentleman. He is soft-spoken, kind, generous, so very similar in fact to him that I wonder what he has that my father doesn't, apart from the money.

Because now, thinking about it, I can't see my mother as a gold-digger. It is so blazingly obvious to me now that she loves this man as much as he loves her, and an indescribable emotion pervades me. I don't know what it is, but I am moved to see that someone else has loved my mother the way my father did. I'm also feeling sorry for my father, who's lost the love of his life to another man, a man whom he has nothing but respect for, as if nothing had ever happened to break his heart.

'I'm going to call my dad,' I sniff. 'Do you want to speak to him?'

Aldo nods. 'Yes, please, Olivia.'

I dial his number and he answers on the first ring. 'Livvie? How is she?'

'She's okay for now, Dad…'

'Ohthankgod. We'll come out on the next flight.'

'Okay. But... can you please not tell the kids? I want to tell them myself, but not until I see them.'

'Will do, love. Is Aldo there?' he asks.

'Yes, of course. Here, I'll pass you over to him.'

Aldo takes my phone and listens, nodding. 'Operation Limoncello underway, George... Okay, then. Call me when you've landed.'

'What's that?' I ask when he rings off.

Aldo sighs. 'It's the plan to bring all of you back under one roof with your mother. Your parents and I have been friends for ever, since long before you were born. And we all decided that if and when one of us was ill, the other two would be there to support them. So now, as soon as your mother is ready, we'll all go home to Sicily and spend some quality time together. And have some good family talks.'

'Okay,' I say obediently. Aldo inspires true confidence. And he commands respect. With a quick hug and a promise he will be back to pick me up tomorrow for another visit before we all leave together for Sicily in two days, I go to my mother's hotel room and sob until there's nothing left inside me.

There is a knock on the door. It's the Respiri Ladies, who file in one at a time. Upon seeing what I'm doing, they begin to retrieve stuff from the drawers and help me pack. They are like family, doing everything that family would. I know the secrets that would destroy their marriages, and yet they have put their trust in me, simply because I am Susan's daughter. In the space of only a few weeks, they have all taught me about freedom and life, silliness and happiness. I am indebted to them all for this.

'I want to thank you all,' I whisper. 'For being my mother's friends. You have kept up the laughter and she is truly blessed to have you.'

They shush me and hold me, rocking me back and forth as a new batch of sobs comes to the surface.

After the Respiri Ladies have retreated back to their own rooms, and the packing is finished, I lie on the bed, exhausted. All I want to do is fall asleep, give in to the exhaustion, but then I hear my phone ringing.

'Olivia? Finally, I've been calling for hours...'

'Markus,' I gasp. Just the sound of his voice makes me feel stronger. 'I'm sorry...'

'How's your mum?'

'Hanging in there,' I answer, my voice catching in my throat.

'We're already at Gatwick, but there's a problem with the flight.'

That's all we need. 'Why, what problem?'

'Apparently Mount Etna in Sicily is spewing ash. If it gets any worse we'll have to fly to Palermo instead of Catania, which will add hours to our journey.'

'Oh my God...'

'I'll let you know how soon we can take off. But I'll find a way. Just hang in there, okay?'

As if he could see me, I nod, unable to speak. 'Yes,' I finally manage to say.

'Okay, honey. See you soon. Stay strong.'

'I will,' I promise. I blow my nose and catch a few breaths before I call Simon.

'Hey,' he answers immediately. 'How are you doing? How is she?'

I'm surprised he even cares enough to ask. 'She's okay for now. Thanks for letting the kids go,' I reply.

'No worries. If you need anything…'

'We're okay, thanks, Simon.'

'Well, I guess I'll stay here and hold the fort, then…' he says. It's the most sensible thing he can master, at this or any other time.

'Yes, thank you, Simon. I'll let you know what's what.'

'Okay, Olivia. Give your mother my best.'

As if he even knew her. But that's all on me, I suppose. 'I will. Thank you, Simon.'

We ring off, and the call has left me sadder than before. Again.

Mount Etna has, of course, delayed us a few hours as well. We encounter the dark smoke that has been spewed into the air, but the pilot assures us that the winds have changed and we'll be okay.

Mum is at the back of the small medic helicopter that Aldo has chartered. There is a doctor and a paramedic on board. We are allowed to sit with her provided we don't press her to speak or to stay awake as she has been sedated for the duration of the trip so as to avoid any further stress on her system.

This is absurd. Two days ago we were all having drinks on the terrace as usual, and now it's a nightmare.

Up ahead the sky has become black and for a moment I baulk. I had no idea this could happen, but Mount Etna is immense, taking up the entire view. As I watch in a daze, the winds blow away the smoke in some places, granting fleeting views of the volcano. We are far enough to be safe, but close enough to see the plume of smoke that has created a large, dark cloud, almost like a chef's toque.

At the centre I can barely make out a horrific-looking, huge, gaping crater, ready to swallow you up if you dare to get too close. And then I see nothing more until we touch down on solid ground.

This is my first time in Sicily. I should have come before, when I'd been invited, for all those summers. I should have come and made light of the situation, while we were all much younger and less vulnerable. I should never have allowed my family to divide in the summer. I should have done so many things that I didn't do. I only hope it's not too late.

21

Sicily is nothing like you'd expect. It is the exact opposite of Northern Italy, where everything is regulated and scheduled and seamless.

As soon as the doors of the helicopter ambulance open, the first thing that hits me is the heat. And the fragrance in the air. Lemon, orange and tangerine blossoms, to be exact. Where Villa dei Respiri sat above a calm lake among secular pine trees and an organised botanical garden, Sicily is a glorified chaos of the senses.

It's crazy that you can actually smell flowers instead of the fumes so typical of airports. Then, on a second breath, you can smell the grass and the trees in the copse that you have to walk through to get to the car park. And if you look up, you will see Etna towering over you and the city.

An ambulance is there to meet us. Aldo has certainly planned this Operation Limoncello well. I'm glad he and Dad have had the foresight to be so organised. They must have been planning this since the moment Mum got her diagnosis.

Aldo takes my hand as the ambulance doors open and the staff transfer my mother inside. Aldo and I sit next to each other as the medic team go over their procedures and Mum is finally strapped in,

I watch Aldo as he takes in the scene with pained eyes and I squeeze his hand. He truly loves her, and I'd be completely lost without him right now.

'She'll be okay,' he says to me, squeezing my hand back. 'She saved my life, you know? She tried to stay away, but then she came back as a match as my kidney donor, and she couldn't stay away, knowing that I would die if she didn't fly over that very night. She gave up your happiness for my life, and I am so ashamed of it.

'She could have returned home after she donated her kidney to me. But instead, she stayed. And I didn't ask her to go. You must know that she loved your father very much, and she still does – just not in that way. But he is a good man, and he understood. I think he always knew. I'm so sorry, Olivia. But you know, she really wants to try and atone with you…' his voice catches in his throat, '…before it's too late.'

'Oh, Aldo! What can I do to make up for all of this? For how horribly I've behaved for all these years! I didn't know…'

'There will be a lot to do at home. We have a lot to face. We must be strong, and we will be.'

I nod, swallowing back my tears. 'Thank you, Aldo, for loving her so much.'

'You can relax now, Olivia. We're finally home.'

My mother and Aldo's home, Villa Gelsomino, is an antique villa on the southern coast of Sicily. The northern side faces a vast countryside of green wheat swaying in the warm breeze, and endless orchards yielding summer fruits, while the south side teeters over a cliff facing the Mediterranean Sea. There is a staircase leading to the beach carved into the rock, the one Cassie told me about, and a handrail to hang onto.

The stone walls of the façade are carved into ornate Baroque columns, while many sculpted faces and animals festoon the balconies. It is a noble's family home, a thing of dreams. The house staff pauses in the entrance hall, hushed in respectful concern as they take our bags while Aldo quietly debriefs them. I look around, taking in the cool interiors, the marble floors and the relaxed elegance surrounding me. My mother has been living a life of luxury, here, adored by a man I didn't know. She has an entire life that I knew nothing of.

The staff immediately splinter off to their duties. It is obvious they, too, are a part of Operation Limoncello. Some of the medical-support staff are to stay in the house until she is better. A maid, Filomena, has been assigned to me, she explains as she ushers me up the stairs.

'*Signor* Amore wants your room to be close to your mother's so you can visit her any time you want,' she tells me.

'Thank you.'

'There is a button by the bed in your room. Anything you need, you call me, please.'

'Will you be taking care of my mother as well?' I ask.

'No, that is the honour of Concetta, the chief of staff,' Filomena explains. She sounds like she's ready for anything. They all are, and I am so grateful to them. And to Aldo.

A few hours later, after I've showered and sat in silence with Mum, who is still sleeping, my family arrives.

I know that my father has kept the secret, but my children are no fools. They have sensed that something isn't quite right and Joe is puffing his chest out, trying to be brave, while his lower lip is trembling with the anticipation of bad news.

On seeing me, both Joe and Cassie throw themselves into my arms.

'They guessed something was up,' my father says apologetically. 'They were terrified that something had happened to you, so I told them about Susan's leg. That's all they know.'

'Mum,' Joe says. 'Are you okay?'

Cassie says nothing. She's buried her face into my shoulder and she's not letting go.

'It'll be all right, sweethearts,' I whisper to them both. Joe nods, believing me, while Cassie is shaking like she's about to come apart; my father looks as if he's aged ten years since I last saw him.

'George!' Aldo whispers, taking a long step forward and pulling him into his embrace.

They seem as if they had been friends their entire life and I am humbled by the respect and affection these two men have for each other. They share a love for my mother, of course, but I am not prepared for the intensity of their relationship. As far as I know, they've enjoyed a degree of civility fuelled by my father's yearly visits to accompany my children. I had no idea that a true friendship had developed all these years while I stewed in my bitterness.

These two men, through kindness and civility, have managed to navigate through many very difficult years thanks to each other's help. *Despite* having been rivals. They simply put it all behind them and got on with it. Now Dad's kind words and his friendship with Mum and Aldo despite everything are beginning to seem feasible, if not yet quite making sense to me. I still need to understand how, and why, it all happened.

'Are you good, my friend?' Aldo asks my dad, who wipes his eyes and nods.

'Yes, I am. Look who I've brought you,' he says with a smile and Aldo opens his arms to my children who practically fly into his arms, kissing his cheeks and calling him 'Nonno'.

'Welcome back, little ones,' he says, his voice tender but his face drawn by too much worrying.

And then, with an audible hitch in my breath, I turn and see Markus in the doorway. He's hanging back, not sure of how much time to give us.

'Markus,' Aldo says, holding out a hand. 'So glad you are here with us. This is a time for family and you are family.'

Markus slides me a look and it's all I can do to keep myself from throwing myself at him like that damsel in distress.

'I wish it were a happier time… I've heard a lot about you,' Markus says.

At that, Aldo chuckles and points at Dad. 'From this one, yes? Don't believe a single word. Now, let's get you all fed, you must be starving and exhausted. Come, come into the living room.'

Living room is an understatement. It has an enormous, white, circular sofa with a huge coffee table in the centre absolutely covered with local Sicilian food. I am grateful that we don't have to all sit at a table because we are all too exhausted and I have no appetite whatsoever, but I must admit that Aldo and Mum's cook has done them proud.

There are antipasti of every sort, from aubergine and Parma ham tidbits, to ham- and pesto-filled puff pastry. There are mini sandwiches and salads and risotto and caponata and arancini, the rice balls Mum loves so much.

'Children, it's important that you eat so you are nice and strong for your nonna, *sì*?' Aldo instructs Joe and Cassie, who reluctantly sit down and pick at the food. 'Everyone, please, Susan will have my head otherwise.'

I sit next to Markus, who passes me a plate on which he's put a few canapés and savoury muffins.

Aldo pours George a shot of limoncello and they both drink simultaneously, as if they've rehearsed this for years. Perhaps they have.

'So what happens now?' I ask Aldo.

'I've hired the best nurse in the province to tend to your mother,' he answers, drained. 'Don't show her you're worried. She wouldn't want you to be. Just be jovial when she wakes.'

My father nods. 'Thank you, Aldo, for loving her so much.'

Aldo exhales. 'Thank you, George, for your support and friendship all these years. It means so much to us.'

This exchange has moved something inside me even if I can't explain it. Unconditional love. Consideration. Forgiveness. I could take a page out of their book.

That night when I tuck Joe into his bed, I hold him closer, tighter and longer than I usually do, which everyone at home jokes is long enough as it is. But tonight, and for always, I will hug him so he will never ever doubt what he means to me. And I know he doesn't, because he basks in the warmth of my love.

When I get to Cassie's door, I hesitate. Too much, too soon? Is she too upset? But then I tell myself this: no one knows how long we have, and which hug may be our last. Bad things happen all the time and I want to give as much love as I can. So I knock on her door, half-expecting her not to hear due to her ever-present ear buds.

'Come in,' she calls.

I open the door to see her just as she's tossing some tissues into the wastepaper basket. Her eyes are red from crying and when she sees it's me she springs towards me.

'Mum,' she says. 'I was going to come and find you.'

Now that alone is a huge improvement. I am only sorry about the circumstances that have brought us to this.

'How are you feeling?' she asks softly.

I shrug, debating whether to continue the *I'm invincible* charade or simply be honest. And then my mother's words come back to me: *Let yourself be vulnerable around her.*

I sigh. 'I'm frightened, Cassie. I don't want to lose my mother now that I've only just found her again. And I feel guilty for not forgiving her.'

And then she wraps her arms around my middle. 'I feel the same way with you, Mum. If you died…' I can hear the words catch in her throat.

'I'm not going anywhere, sweetheart. You're going to have to put up with me for a very long time.'

'You promise?'

'Absolutely, darling.'

And we stay there like that for a long time. In her embrace I can feel the love that she has for me and that I have not felt for years now. And it's like a broken dam, with all our emotions coming out in a torrent of tears and fierce hugs.

Once both children are asleep, I see Markus on the west terrace, admiring the sunset. He is standing away from me, his back straight with tension. I know it's been tough on him, too. He is, alongside George, the backbone of this family.

He turns and sees me. 'Hey, you,' he says, opening his arms for me, and I'm in them like I was always meant to be there. It has been a day full of emotions, and now these open arms completely undo me and I am sobbing again.

'She is ill and there's nothing I can do. I can't believe I've wasted so much time. I've been a real child. Everyone told me so. You told me, Dad told me, but I wouldn't listen and now it's too late!'

'Hey…' he whispers, taking my face in his hands. 'It's never too late. Your mum knows how much you love her. Mums have that sixth sense, you know?'

'But I've been absolutely horrible to her!' I cry inconsolably. 'How could she possibly believe that I actually *do* love her?'

'She just *knows*. Just like you know that Cassie loves you, despite her past behaviour.'

'Okay,' I whisper into his chest.

'She's missed you terribly, you know?' he says.

'Really?'

'Oh yes. She became very needy, asking us for help with things that she normally does on her own, you know? It was due to your absence; it was so obvious. She realised she'd been taking you for granted.'

The next day, I spend all my time at my mother's side while Markus is playing with Dad and the kids down on the beach. From up here they look so tiny. Mum is sitting up in a wheelchair, a light sheet over her cast, and insists on being wheeled out onto the covered veranda facing the sea. There is a round marble table out there and elegant wrought-iron chairs topped with thick white linen cushions that pale in comparison to the ones at Villa dei Respiri.

'Would you like a glass of water, Mum?' I ask as I reach for the carafe. There is also iced tea with real lemons and mint, but I can't bring myself to touch anything. The night has not brought me peace and wisdom. If anything, I am even more afraid for her now.

She shades her eyes to look down at the kids on the beach who are now building sandcastles. She smiles. 'Don't mind if I do, chickie.'

I nod, determined to keep my eyes dry, and pour her a glass, holding it up to her.

'I'm all right, I can drink on my own,' she whispers.

'I know,' I lie, and let her take a few tentative sips.

'Hmm, cucumber, my favourite,' she says and we laugh.

I sit down next to her, my eyes scanning the glistening Mediterranean before us. I've never seen anything so beautiful in my life, and in that moment I wonder what her life here is usually like. Her days must be so serene, passed contemplating the beauty of the world from up here.

With a man that adores her, many friends, a beautiful villa in paradise, it's easy to think that everything is always tickety boo. But now I realise that she was very troubled by leaving us the way she did, and by our subsequent lack of a relationship.

'So… *Markus*,' she says, nodding to him as he races the kids to the water's edge to get some more water for their castles. We can hear their laughter all the way up here, so soothing at such a difficult time. Children do that. They soothe you when you need them the most.

'Markus, yes.' I'm not quite sure how to justify his presence, but I know that the kids will have banged on and on about him every time they came to visit.

'I'll be very happy to finally have a chat with this gem of a man,' she whispers, winking at me.

I feel a surge of love and gratitude for Markus, for being my rock. Wild horses wouldn't have kept him from accompanying the kids and Dad. I truly don't know what I'd have done without him. He's like… the air I breathe. My family. And I know I'm going to have to learn to lean on him less, and not be hurt as he leaves to live his own life.

One day he might get married, or move on and form his own company. And then I'll probably never see him again. The thought terrifies me.

'You know, Livvie, sometimes life throws us some bad stuff. But then, in a sort of fateful, chaotic way, it suddenly rewards us for putting up with it in the first place.'

'Mmph…' I say, eyeing her surreptitiously.

'In the past few weeks, I've got to know you, the real you, Livvie. After I left you, you were so…'

'Angry?' I offer.

'Yes. Of course I don't blame you. I was the only one to blame. You were just a young girl and I renounced watching you grow. It's criminal, and so many times I've told myself that the cancer was what I deserved for being such a shit mother.'

She looks at me, then looks away as her eyes fill up with tears.

'I was a mess, mentally. Now I'm okay upstairs, but it's my body that's giving up on me.' She snort-laughs. 'You just can't have it all, can you? Well, at least you are here. You all are. For the time being. It's going to have to be enough.'

One thing is certain. I'm not going to leave her, not as long as she wants me here. We have spent too much time – *years* – apart, and all the while I fed myself a version of my mother that was incomplete. I want to get to know Susan Amore, the optimistic, beloved-by-all woman that she is today.

22

Over the weeks, Cassie starts spending less time with Joe and the men outdoors and more with Mum as she undergoes another round of chemo. She seems to be doing much better already. They talk in her private parlour room for hours on end, and often there's laughter. Sometimes I'm called upon to have a chat, so as not to leave me out, I suspect, because those two have a bond that I can only dream of.

In my heart, there is a pang of hope that Cassie isn't indifferent to the world after all; that she is touched by things both good and bad. Because no strength lies in not allowing yourself to be touched by emotions and events in life. It is the good times, but also the harder ones that tell us that we are truly living by knowing the differences between joy and tragedy.

Cassie seems to understand my mother's illness, and is eager to get as much quality time with her as possible, which to me indicates that she is maturing and appreciating people and things much more. I am happy that they are getting the best out of each other.

Wandering around the villa after one of these chats, I end up on one of the terraces facing the Mediterranean Sea. My father is sitting there, alone, overwhelmed and depleted of all his energy. I wrap my arms around him just as his shoulders begin to shake and he finally lets himself go into a long-pent-up sob.

'Oh, Dad!' I whisper, holding him and suddenly it's like I'm comforting Joe.

For years my father has been my rock, my true north when I needed him most. And for years he has ignored his own pain and simply got on with life without his own love. A bit like I am doing.

'Don't cry, Dad,' I whisper. 'It'll be okay, I promise you. We're all here together now.'

'I'm not crying just for your mother, pet,' he sucks in his breath. 'I'm crying for you, too.'

'*Me?*'

'I'm crying for the life that you'll miss out on if you don't act now.'

He means my marriage. Which is far from being my priority right now. It's really all that obvious to everyone, I know. And yet, I have to try and make light of it for as long as I can, or at least for now, for the kids' sake.

'Dad, it's okay…'

'But it's not, sweetheart. Haven't you learnt anything from our mistakes? Do you think you're going to live forever? It goes quickly, you know, love, so pick up the phone. Tell Simon you don't love him anymore. He'll accept it. He already has an inkling, hasn't he?'

I shrug and swipe at a tear. I'm not crying for Simon, of course. I'm crying for all the time we waste in our lives trying to do the right thing. I'm crying for all the years that I could have been, if not happy, at least independent and free to love whomever I chose. Not that there could ever be anyone besides, well, you know who. And I'm crying for my parents' sacrifices.

'Will you think about your old dad's words?' he asks and I kiss his cheek.

'I will. Thank you, Dad.'

'Do it tonight. Tomorrow is another day. It could be a brand-new day for you. The first day of the rest of your life without Simon.'

'I will,' I promise. And I find that I mean it.

I retire briefly to my room for a heart to heart with Simon. I know I shouldn't be doing it over the phone, but honestly, we're just slowly pulling out each other's teeth. Why not curtail the agony? So I dial his number.

He answers on the fourth ring. 'Hello, Olivia.'

'Hi…' I breathe, my heart pounding. How do I do this? Can I actually do this over the phone? Doesn't he deserve a better approach? He still is, after all, the father of my children.

'How's your mum doing?' he asks, interrupting my internal debate.

'She's okay for now,' I say. It's nice of him to ask, even if he's never met her.

'Right,' he says. 'So, when will you and the kids be coming home?'

'I don't know, Simon. We'll probably be out here a little longer.'

'Right. Well, in that case, I'll say yes to a conference in Florida.'

'Florida?'

'Yes, at Disneyworld. The firm's booked a block of rooms for a week.'

'Oh. Right.'

'You don't mind, Olivia?'

'Not at all. Actually, Simon—'

'It's okay, Olivia.'

'What?'

He sighs. 'You want out. And frankly, so do I. When you get back, we'll figure out something fair for the kids. I don't want them, or you, to suffer. Okay?'

I can't believe I'm hearing this. I'm stunned into silence.

'Let me ask you something,' he continues. 'Is Markus there with you?'

I roll my eyes. How many times have we had this conversation? 'Not with me per se, Simon. He's with the family. He practically is family.'

'Did you ask yourself even for a moment why I wasn't invited?'

'Because you never… cared,' I defend. 'Anything that has ever had anything to do with my family, you weren't there for me, Simon.'

At the other end, I hear a sigh. 'Would it have made a difference? Would you have loved me more?'

'Would *you*?' I ask. 'I did everything I could so that you would love me, Simon. I gave you two kids, a home, the best years of my— Never mind. We'll talk when I get back. I'm glad that you want to do this properly, with no animosity.'

'I haven't been the best husband, I know. I guess I owe you that much. Give your family my best, Olivia. I hope your mother goes into remission. I truly do.'

'Thank you, Simon. Take care.'

I hang up and dash my knuckles over my cheeks.

It's past midnight now and the house is quiet. As I pass Markus's door, I hear him speaking in urgent tones and can't help but stop to listen.

'No, Lilja, I haven't told her yet. It's not the right time; her mother is very ill. Yes, I know there's no time like the present, but stop rushing me. I'll lay it down easy but right now she's not ready, okay?'

I freeze in my tracks. *Her.* And she's obviously impatient about something. Oh my God, it can only be one thing. She has finally made inroads into his heart. Convinced him that if she can't join our company, they should start their own, and start their own life together, and he hasn't got the heart to tell me.

This is it, the moment I've been dreading for ten years.

I can't even think of how we're going to manage without Markus. He is my wingman, my partner in crime. I could have done none of this without him. And now he's leaving, taking my heart with him, and there's nothing I can do. He must do what's best for him, even if I know that she will never love him like I do.

Because I love him for the person that he is, not just his looks or his talent. I love him for his laughter, the twinkle in his eye, the way he breathes deeply instead of getting angry at a problem or an annoying person. I love him for the way he sees the world: a good place where he needs to do his best. I love him for how he embraces my dad at the end of a long day to thank him for his help, how he cheers up my children when they are down and how he takes the drama out of my daily life whenever I get too upset.

But I can't love him only because he makes our lives better. I have to love him also because he should make his own life better.

This is how life works. You find people, you lose people. It feels like a crazy merry-go-round that never stops, but we must learn to find peace in all the confusion.

I can't tell Markus about my feelings because that would only be a spanner in the works of his own life. Besides, there's someone else I need to concentrate on now more than anyone else. She needs to hear my feelings more than Markus right now.

The rest of the house is dark but for the light in the corridor opposite Mum's room. The nurse sitting in an armchair in the corridor assures me that she is sleeping peacefully. I poke my head in, observing her from the door lest I wake her up.

Aldo is there, asleep, his head on her bed and holding her hand. He hasn't left her side except to give us some alone time. He's so in love with her it makes my heart ache. Theirs is a love that I'd failed to understand. She'd given him a kidney, part of herself, for him. I would do the same for Markus, only he'll never know. Markus and Aldo have a lot in common. A quiet assurance that everything will be all right, even if it might not be.

And my mother… she looks so small, almost like a young girl, with her long blonde hair pillowing her head. She has always been so beautiful, with high cheekbones and well-defined features. She's breathing evenly. Tomorrow we'll talk some more. I'll tell her about my call with Simon. She'll be proud of me.

Aldo stirs softly, then lifts his head to check on her. He feels her forehead, then gently kisses it, smoothing back her hair and caressing her jaw as a tiny sob escapes him. We both know he's not worried about her broken leg, but about what might happen down the line. It's too much to watch and my breath catches in my throat. He turns around and sees me. He makes to get up, but I rush forward and place my hands on his shoulders to make sure he stays where he is. Where he belongs.

And then, before I know it, my arms encircle his shoulders and I plant a soft kiss on his cheek. It is sandpaper-y, as he hasn't had time to shave or groom himself as he usually does. Usually he is impeccable, judging from the photos and everything Mum's told me about him. But now he's a wreck.

Surprised at my gesture of affection, he covers my hand with his and squeezes it gently.

'Thank you for loving my mother so much,' I whisper and he bites his lip and nods.

'She loves you so much, too, you know,' he whispers back.

A big boulder has lodged itself in my throat, so I only nod.

There is so much more to say. I have so much to apologise for. My selfishness. My stubbornness. My lack of empathy. I could have got over it as an adult. But I'd preferred to play the victim. And now I might even lose my mother when I've barely started to know her. I thought I knew her, but it turns out that so many sides of her were completely unknown to me. I could have relented and forgiven her all these years. I could have accepted her invitation to Sicily to get to know

Aldo and his lovely family. I could have had a second, Sicilian family. But I refused it.

'Tomorrow,' he says. 'We will all talk. There is a trust in your name that you—'

'Please,' I say, stopping him. 'You're right. There is so much to say in the next few days. Let it not be about money.'

'I understand, Olivia. But your mother and I want you to have it. For your and your children's sake. You are going to need it if you decide to really follow your heart. Don't make our same mistake. Don't wait too long.'

I sit in silence. I don't know what to say. All I know is that things will never be the same again.

23

I am twisting and turning in my bed, my head full of the notion of freedom on a double level. Freedom from my loveless marriage, and freedom from my anger towards my mother.

After all these years, I don't have to pretend for the kids' benefit that everything is okay with Simon. I'm finally, finally free. So then why do I feel like sobbing my eyes out? I should be relieved, not… derelict. But once again, I have failed.

Because I have tried and tried, all these years, to fix things. To make it all work despite everything. But his negative attitude today after a long day made it difficult for me to feel close to him. To feel that *oneness* that I have always craved since I was a child and my mother left.

I had always told myself that I would be different, that I would be a better wife and dedicate myself heart and soul to my husband and cater to his needs, and all those unrealistic goals we set ourselves at the beginning of a relationship.

If you have children, or financial problems, or meddling

in-laws or anything at all that could possibly disturb your relationship, it will happen.

Love isn't, nor should it be, a vacuum where you and your partner live an all-exclusive, all-consuming, symbiotic existence where you annihilate yourself just to see them smile. It doesn't work that way, and women are becoming more and more conscious (thank God) of this since their grandmothers stopped pretending they liked to bake in full skirts and high heels.

Life is not a TV commercial where everything is perfect and where the soufflé always rises to perfection. Most soufflés sink, while others stay downright flat from the beginning, no matter what you do. We have no control, and the sooner we realise that not everything is our fault, the better.

So what if we can't be there every night to greet him at the door with his favourite slippers and the paper? We're not his pet dog, trained to focus solely on him and his needs. We have a right to live our lives as well, despite our behaviour being disturbing or annoying to him. So what if I wear my eyeliner a little thicker than usual, or not at all. So bloody what! We are going to continue being who we are, and the sooner that they (and our judgemental children) realise it, the better.

I am angry. I am angry with Simon, but more so with myself for letting him peg me into that hole that I don't fit in and never will! And I'm angry with Cassie for not trusting me enough all these years to be her mother the way I could be.

And no, the irony of the fact that my daughter and I are a repeat of my mother and myself is not lost on me. I can see the similarities there, of course. And all the time I have been telling myself that it was just a coincidence, that we were different because I really loved my daughter and that it wasn't going to happen to us, like a drunk person driving against motorway traffic and reassuring his passengers that he is fine and that everything is okay. How wrong I've been!

How many sleepless nights I had, battling with myself, wishing I had the courage to do what my mother did and get out of this nightmare of a marriage, while on the other hand knowing that if I did, it would have an effect on my kids.

I'd told myself I would wait until they were older, but every year that went by and his attitude worsened, I knew I was just faking it. Until just now, when faking it was no longer an option. For whose benefit anyway? The kids have seen our interactions, or rather, lack thereof. So what am I going to tell them? How is Joe going to react with his father leaving?

And Cassie! I've barely just got back into her good books. She is not going to be happy to learn that her parents are divorcing.

So it's pointless to try and hide it, or worse, pretend everything is okay. That would be the worst betrayal. Like my parents. Up until my mother had left, I had no idea that things were really bad. None at all. It had happened out of the blue, like lightning on a clear day.

Unable to sleep, I grab the silk shawl Markus bought me in Stresa, wrap it around my shoulders and tiptoe down the marble staircase to the kitchen where I grab a bottle of white wine from the wine cooler. Aldo won't mind. I push the French doors open and climb into one of the plush outdoor armchairs, drinking directly from the bottle.

'Couldn't sleep either, huh?' comes Markus's voice from the dark corner opposite me.

'Jesus, I didn't see you,' I hiss. 'What are you doing up?'

'Same as you,' he whispers, clinking my bottle with his bottle of beer. 'Hot night, isn't it?'

'Stifling,' I answer, breathing in the heat coming off the still sea. Not even a wave to send a flitter of air our way.

'The garden smells nice, though,' he says. 'I love the jasmine. It's so pungent at night. You hardly notice it during the day.'

Like my inner voice. During the day, I suffocate it. But at night, all the truths come out. 'I just got off the phone with Simon,' I say as I take another swig of wine.

I can hear him turn towards me in his chair. 'And?'

'It's over. When we get back we'll discuss the T&Cs. But he said he's not going to fight me. I think he's going to Florida with someone else.'

'So soon?' Markus asks nonchalantly.

I put my bottle down on the table and shrug. 'Who knows? It may have been going on for ever. It would certainly explain a lot of things.'

'You mean between you and Simon?'

'What else? Even this patio table knows that we were never a good fit, and that we are doing the right thing by separating.'

'Are you convinced of that?' he wants to know.

'That I've done the right thing? Absolutely. I was unhappy, Markus. You know it.'

'Good for you, Livvie,' he says, getting to his feet. 'Well, I'm going to hit the sack now. I've been out here for a while already. Good night.'

'Oh? Okay. I thought you might want to hang.'

His hand comes down on my shoulder. 'You need to do some hard thinking now. Ask yourself what you really want to do with the rest of your life.'

I want to spend it with you, Markus. If I could only say it. But I can't. I can't lose him just because I have a big mouth. If I still want him in my life, even in the form of texts from Denmark, I have to stay quiet about my feelings for him. Because it would be awkward. Even if he hasn't got the heart to tell me because of Mum's condition.

But he can't stay here for ever, can he? He has a life to live, a new relationship and a new business to start, so—Wait a minute. Has he got a new business to start? Or is he going to want to keep this one and buy me out? Because our business is flourishing. It would be stupid to leave this partnership just now that things are going fantastically well. So that's it. He wants me to leave. But he hasn't got the heart to ask me right now.

Well, maybe I should make it easy for him, like he has done for me, all these years. Because his half of the business has done wonders for mine. And it's only right for me to acknowledge that much and let him have it back. Tomorrow. I'll tell him tomorrow.

'Uh, okay. Good night.'

'Night, Livvie.'

And that's the end of that. No talk-athon through the night like in the chapel, or endless shooting the breeze with him. None of that. I have to say I'm pretty miffed about it, but what right do I have over his time? He's changed and it's probably because of Whatshername, who's threatening to move to Canterbury, if she hasn't already.

Of course, it would have been a great story if I'd come right out and told him that I've left my husband for *him*. That would've been a real corker. But life doesn't always go the way we want it to. Markus isn't there to solve my problems or to make my life better, no matter how much I actually may think that he does.

Markus is my wingman, no doubt. My rock. But there is a huge difference between being buddies, amazing buddies, and... *soulmates*. I mean, *he* is *my* soulmate. Always has been. But I'm not his. And when he does marry Lilja, I will positively die of heartbreak.

The next morning, Dad and Aldo walk down to the village café and return with granita e brioche, a breakfast whim for Sicilians. It is basically an antique custom, to dip your brioche into a freezing glass of granita, which is basically like a lemon slush. Lemon is the original flavour, but there are also others, such as coffee, chocolate, almond, any kind of fruit, pistachio, etc.

'Everyone, gather round before it melts!' Aldo calls from the dining patio overlooking the sea as a maid is busy setting the table for all of us.

'Ooh, looks yummyyyy!' Markus says while fake-wrestling Joe for the best seat.

'Here you go, *cara*,' Aldo says, handing Cassie a glass heaped with lemon granita which she takes with a huge smile.

'Thank you, *Nonno*!'

Nonno. Grandpa. It feels so strange to hear her call him that. All these years my children have been coming here, they have built a rapport. They are, in effect, family, Aldo and the kids. Even the staff have been doting on them for years, with laughter and memories of every single visit. There are pictures all over the house to testify to the happy times: Mum in a swimsuit on the beach, her hair drenched and happy while she holds each of my children under an arm in a warrior pose. They look so young and carefree.

Or the photo from Aldo's nephew's wedding, my kids dressed in the most adorable clothes, Cassie with pink little roses in her hair. Things I hadn't bought. I'm sure Dad would have told me they would have been going to a wedding in Sicily. But in those days all I could concentrate on was how much I missed them while they were abroad with their grandmother.

I had had all sorts of nightmares and it had been Markus who'd convinced me that letting them go away for a couple of weeks in the summer was good for them. But not so much for me, because, apart from missing them, when they returned they were always so full of stories about where they'd been, what they'd seen, and all the people they'd met. Not to mention how much fun they'd had with Nonna and Nonno, and how much they loved them and were looking forward to going back, year after year.

And I suddenly realise that perhaps one day their grandmother might no longer be around to play with them. Sooner or later, her body might let her down, and it could eventually be the beginning of the end.

This morning the kids, tanned and relaxed from playing on the beach the day before, have reverted to a more solemn version of themselves. They understand that things aren't going too well with their grandmother.

'Can we see Nonna?' Cassie says, eyeing me.

'Of course you can, darling,' I answer. 'Just as soon as you finish your breakfast.'

'Is she going to die?' Joe blurts out and all eyes swing to his face.

'We all die eventually, Joe,' Aldo says slowly, putting down his spoon while trying to hide his hurt. 'It's part of life. But if your life has been good, you leave a good memory and people think about you long after you are gone. That's why it's so important to be happy as much as you can.'

'Absolutely,' Dad agrees. 'So let's remember to love our friends and family even when they hurt us without meaning to. In the end, love is the most important thing in the world. Right, Markus?'

Markus, who has been watching me the entire time, puts his spoon down and wipes his mouth. 'Absolutely, George. You are both right. Love is the most important thing.'

And that's when I just know it. He's going to tell me about Whatsherface later. I can see it in his eyes. But I'll be cool. I knew this moment was coming. He couldn't be an un-catchable bachelor for ever, could he? Even George Clooney eventually married. And look how happy he is.

Silliness aside, I am trying to prepare myself for it. We'll have to dissolve the company, of course. Because there's no way I'm letting *her* dictate what I'm doing, despite Markus and I's promise to each other about excluding partners from our business decisions.

In the afternoon Mum wants to sit on the terrace facing the sea again. She is also expecting Aldo's side of the family to visit.

They come in dribs and drabs so as not to tire her out. They don't stay too long, and although I can't understand what they're saying in Italian, they are all laughing, Mum the hardest of them all.

'You take care of yourself and we'll see you next week, Susan,' Aldo's cousin, or at least I think that's what she is, says (in English, presumably for my benefit) as she delicately kisses Mum on both cheeks. 'If you're lucky, I'll have some more gossip for you!'

Mum chuckles and pretend-shoos them all away.

It is so evident that she is well-loved by his family. Throughout the years she has forged friendships and bonds with his people who consider her to be one of them.

Now I finally see my Mum for what she is: a loveable, sociable person whom, once you get to know, you can't help but love. Every laugh or look or hug that's she's received this afternoon is filled with love and I can't help but chastise myself for how I've treated her. As bad as she'd been, she was still my mother.

24

Oh, if we only knew what's going on behind people's smiles: at work, in the street, at a random café. We are all, to one extent or another, suffering from something. Bereavement, mental illness, the breakdown of a marriage, the illness of a child. There is so much in this world that makes us vulnerable.

But if we are kind and understanding of other people's weaknesses and problems, we can face things. I think of the woman at McDonald's the afternoon I lost it. Her kindness opened a portal to emotions I didn't even know I'd had, where fragility and a lack of self-confidence blocked everything else to keep me unhappy. It is a constant battle we are all fighting, sooner or later, in our lives. A battle against disease or despair. There's so much to cause us all grief.

And yet, there is also so much to bring us joy: watching my children rolling around in wet sand, shrieking with laughter. Finally sitting and chatting with my mum without any sense of oppression in my chest.

Despite my mother's illness, I can't help but feel that the other shoe has dropped, but for the better. It has brought us all together under the same roof, something that I would have never thought possible. Most of all, it has brought us closer. It has made me realise that we are all family, no matter how many years or miles separate us.

Aldo and my mother will always be a part of me, and this beautiful home, filled with love, is already giving me some of the best memories I'll ever have of my family. It's not the beauty of the home, though, or the brilliance of the sea, or the fragrance of the salty waves mixed with jasmine and juniper at night. It's the sense of calm and togetherness, as if nothing, not even grief, could break us.

For the first time in my life, despite the horrible news of my mother's illness, I feel so close to her. Gone is the anger and the bitterness that I harboured in my heart, replaced by an immense feeling of love, and belonging – something I haven't felt for many, many years.

And Cassie: ever since my family arrived she has been surprisingly loving and respectful, linking her arm through mine and asking me how I am when I least expect her to. Her grandmother's illness has touched her much more than either of us had expected. She has grown up, almost overnight, like the maturing fruits hanging on the branches in the orchard outside.

In the afternoon, while everyone is napping to avoid the intense heat, I debate whether to go for a swim. Instead I decide to go for a stroll through the villa's orchard. Under the vast trees I walk in the shade as a gentle breeze caresses my face and dress.

There are more trees than I can count, of all kinds. I wouldn't be able to tell what they are if not for them bearing their ripe, fragrant fruit. There are cherry trees, pear trees, peach, apricot, figs, persimmons, grape vines with big, fleshy, purple grapes and big, bright green grapes. I pick one off the vine and pop it into my mouth and, oh, my goodness! I never knew that fruit could be so tasty! I can almost taste the sun and the sea in them.

Further ahead is the vegetable patch with tomatoes, courgette, lettuce, onions, potatoes, carrots, leeks, spring onions... and some plants I'd never seen before in my life. At the end of the tomato patch is a long trestle table covered in what looks like sun-dried tomatoes. They are covered in a transparent mesh to keep off the dust and birds, I assume. I taste this, too, closing my eyes to concentrate. I actually *can* taste the sea in them, with their salty, tangy flavour!

Nearby is a row of figs drying out, all strung together, almost ready to be put in mason jars, but I prefer to pluck one, a black one, off the tree. I peel it and dig my teeth into the soft purple flesh and almost swoon.

Up above the magpies are circling, impatient for their turn at the luscious bounty, soon followed by the swifts, which have arrived, hurtling through the air, drunk on the thermals. I look to the south, on the other side of Villa Gelsomino, where the seagulls are crying. I never noticed any of this beauty back home, trapped as I was in the daily routine of our life.

Here, in Sicily, you can almost forget yourself as you enjoy the beauty of your surroundings and the very air you breathe as everything around you whispers of the past. And the reason why you had to leave home.

How interesting it must have been for Mum when she came to live here for the first time. How odd everything must have seemed to her, so different from Old Blighty. For one thing, she left on a rainy day. I can imagine her touching down in Catania and having Aldo take her to this beautiful home, to the first day of her brand-new life. I forgive her for abandoning us. I can appreciate now why she felt she had no other choice. She had to look after herself and Aldo. Sicily must be a cure for all that ails us: its natural beauty, slow pace, never-ending summer lunches under a carob or mulberry tree that lead to naps on a hammock.

I can't keep this going anymore. I have to let Markus go. It's not right. I have to tell him. I find him on the side terrace, his favourite place. There is a small lava rock tabletop painted by Caltagirone artists in brilliant Sicilian colours. He is sitting in one of the two black wrought-iron chairs facing the sea, his head to one side in thought. It looks like he's sinking into the chair.

He looks absolutely forlorn, and despite the fact that I could be mad or hurt, I feel for him. I just want to give him what he needs and deserves. He has a right to live his own life with his new girlfriend rather than be tethered to me and all my personal baggage. He's done enough for me and my family all these years. As much as it kills me, I have to let my wonderful, loving, caring Markus, my partner in crime, my wingman, go. Time to let him take his freedom back…

'I know what's going on, Markus,' I declare as I sink into the chair opposite him, my back to the sea.

His eyes dart to mine. 'And what's that?'

'I overheard you talking to Whatsher— Lilja.'

'Oh. And...?'

'Well, I think she's right. It's time.'

He sits up. 'What do you mean?'

I shrug. 'We've been friends and business partners for over ten years now, Markus. Let's be honest with each other. It's time to move on to the next phase of our lives.'

'And... you're ready for that? I mean, you and Simon have just finished, and the kids will be going through a tough time, so...'

'No, of course I'm not ready. And neither are the kids. But it's only natural, now...'

'Are you sure, Livvie? I didn't want to say anything just now, with your mum like this. I didn't want to complicate your life.'

'Complicate? Oh, Markus, my life was all the better because you came into it. I really mean that. And I will always be grateful to you for it.'

And that's when he reaches over and pulls me to him, taking my mouth in an urgent kiss.

I am so shocked I actually jump in surprise. But I am also instantly brain-dead, except for the fireworks behind my eyelids. I have wanted this forever and ever. I have fantasised this moment in oh-so-many ways.

I have imagined us, lip to lip, body to body, *this*, happening outdoors, indoors, in the sea, high up on a mountain, at work, while I was looking my best and even my worst in my pyjamas while pigging out on ice cream on the sofa after everyone's gone to bed.

I did not expect him to kiss me on the mouth, just now, like this!

'Livvie...?' he whispers.

'Hmmm?'

'Say something. Please.'

I clear my throat. 'Well, uhm, that was one knee-melter of a kiss. Thank you.'

'And you kissed me back. Do you know what that means?'

'That you're okay with this?' Because I'm not. I love him and I don't want to let him go!

He laughs. 'Yes, because I am crazy about you, Olivia. I have been since I met you at that market ten years ago.'

'What?' I almost yelp. 'You have... those kinds of feelings for me?' I'm afraid I've misunderstood. Transplanted all the scenarios of what I've ever wanted to hear all these years right into this one, final conversation. But I haven't. I know I haven't.

'Uh-huh...' he assures me.

'Then why the hell do you want to go?'

His dark eyebrows knit. 'Go? Go where?'

'Back to Denmark, with Lilja.'

'I don't want to go back to Denmark, let alone with Lilja!' He laughs again, and I feel my confusion deepen.

'Then what is it that you told her you didn't have the courage to tell me?'

He throws his hands up in the air with a pained groan. 'She was urging me to make a stand and tell you about my feelings for you! I love you, you nuthouse!'

In response, I punch him lightly in the chest as if he'd just pulled my leg by telling me I'd won the lottery.

'I had absolutely no idea!' I cry out.

'Because I never told you! I couldn't, could I?

I consider it. 'I guess not.'

'And you?' he wants to know. 'Do you have any feelings for me?'

'Only since the bloomin' day we met!' I blurt out and his eyes widen.

'But I had no idea!'

'Because I never told *you*!' I echo him. 'I couldn't, could I?'

'Shut up...'

'Seriously! You didn't know?'

'How could I? You never gave anything away.'

'Only because I was – am – married! And I had no idea you were... are you sure you're in love with me? And not Anya, or Maya, or any of those gorgeous girls hounding you twenty-four-seven?'

He laughs, shaking his head. 'You never stop, do you? I have been hiding my feelings for so long now. I didn't think I'd be able to do it any longer. But I couldn't tell you. Not while you were with Simon. I didn't want to be your rebound.'

I stare at him. 'Rebound? Markus, I have been killing myself all these years, waiting for the kids to be a little older. I didn't want them to suffer. So I waited and waited, and in the meantime things with Simon went from indifference to *total* indifference.'

'And here we are now,' he says, ducking to kiss me again, his face flushed with excitement. 'I'm so happy I could sing! Is that too twee?'

'Definitely! But I love that you are twee.'

He checks my face. 'You don't seem too fussed, though, about this jaw-dropping revelation?'

'I'm still in shock!' I laugh.

'Think nothing more of it,' he says, wrapping his arm around me and coming in for another one of those knicker-melting kisses. Oh, go on, then!

It feels so strange and new, to be in his arms the way I never had been before, in such an intimate embrace, chest glued to rock-solid chest. And yet, I know it's right. It's a bloody miracle, and apart from my kids, it's the best thing that's ever happened to me. And speaking of—

'I know what you're thinking,' he says.

'What's that?'

'You're worried about telling the kids.'

Busted. 'And my dad…'

'Please. Your dad would be over the moon.'

'You're right. He's been badgering me for years to get a move on and take my life back.'

But of all people, it surprised me that he would be the one to give me such advice. When my mum had suggested it, I'd baulked at the idea, of course. But when he ever mentioned it, it sort of made sense, if it hadn't been for the simple fact that Markus was (and still is, in my opinion) completely out of my league.

'But right now, with your mum like this, it's probably best not to take centre stage…?'

'You must be joking,' I say. 'If I told her that it would boost her energy levels. She's been badgering me about you for quite some time now.'

'Has she?'

'Oh, yes. She'll be thrilled.'

'So we tell her then?'

'And my dad and Aldo, of course. But not the kids. Not yet.'

'Yes. In time, after your divorce, we'll break it to them gently,' he suggests.

I snort. 'Good luck with Cassie.'

'You don't think she'll accept me into the fold?' he asks, his brow furrowing.

'Oh, you're already in the fold,' I assure him. 'Though I think it'll take her some time to accept her mother sleeping with someone who isn't her father.'

'Ah, *sleeping*… niiiice…' Markus drawls, pulling me closer to him and nuzzling my neck. And that's it. I've completely lost my train of thought. 'Come, let's go. We need to talk. I found a secluded beach, further down. Away from indiscreet ears and eyes…' He winks, and I practically swoon.

I pause, processing his words. Am I ready for this? Am I ready to actually, emotionally and physically, let go and have sex with Markus, with everything that's going on? Technically, Simon and I have broken up. I am a free woman. So it's not a betrayal. Later, we'll tell my parents. But for now, all I want to do is walk on the beach with Markus, hand in hand, talk and laugh and be free to be happy and finally, *finally* love him.

Which I do. And I am mind-blown. Markus is so tender yet urgent. And oh my God, *passionate*! I've day-dreamed of this moment since I first laid eyes on him, letting myself go to naughty thoughts during our first business dinner that very evening in Copenhagen. While he talked about merging our businesses, like a love-starved, love-struck schoolgirl, all I could think of was merging our bodies. And our lives. I never thought that this day would ever come, and now that we're here, I am going to make the absolute best of this.

Even if I am worried sick about Cassie's reaction. I mean, let's be honest. She sees him as part of the family, like my brother or something. She would be utterly appalled by any notions of an attraction between her uncle Markus and her own mother.

'She'll be fine,' Markus says when I confess my worries to him. 'Eventually, at least.'

Much – and I mean *very much* – later that day, while the kids are on the beach with two of the staff, Markus and I return unseen to the house via another path to break it to the adults. Mum is the first to react, and she does so with such grace and happiness.

'Come here, you two,' she whispers and holds us to her. 'I could not be happier, knowing that my only daughter is with a man who has proven himself a true gentleman and truly in love. Markus, welcome to our weird but loving family!'

'Thank you, Susan,' he whispers back, patting her shoulder. 'All I want is the chance to prove to her how much I love her and the kids.'

'You finally did it, you old stick!' Dad chimes, clapping him on the back. My mother is beside herself with joy as she clings on to me.

'You will be very happy together, sweetheart. I know it,' she whispers to me. Her embrace feels good, and I want to stay there a little while longer. As long as I can. Perhaps to recuperate all the lost years, or perhaps it simply feels right. This is where I should be now that I'm ready.

'*Mum!*' comes a shrill cry from the living room door. There, standing in the hall, her face tear-stained and fists clenched, is Cassie. 'You and… Uncle Markus?!'

25

Oh God. Oh, crap, crap, *crap*. She's always been Daddy's girl and will always take his side first before she takes mine. Not that she ever has taken mine, but still. She will never be able to understand.

Markus is rubbing the back of his neck in embarrassment. I know he wants everyone to know, but this is not how I'd envisaged my kids finding out.

'Well, darling,' I start. 'Uncle Markus and I—'

'I saw you kissing! Are you a couple?!'

'Er—' I falter. How can I deny that one?

'Oh my God, I can't believe it!'

'Cassie—' I stop short as she launches herself at me, and I brace myself. But then she throws her arms around my middle.

'Finally!' she shrieks. 'I've been waiting for this for *ever*!'

'You have?' I ask, my eyes swinging to Markus as Cassie gives him a squeeze of his own.

'Mum, come on! Even a total stranger could see you two have been in love for a very *loooong* time! I'm just so glad it's finally happened!'

'Me, too, Cassie,' Markus says, his eyes gleaming.

I stare at her in awe. 'I can't believe you're okay with this.'

'Mum, in case you hadn't noticed, I'm a woman too, you know?'

'Oh, I know, I know,' I assure her, and I can't help the small chuckle that escapes me.

'I think that's our cue to leave you two to talk, then,' Markus says. 'We'll all be on the terrace if you need us.'

Cassie and I smile at each other. I sit on the settee and pat the seat next to me. She comes willingly and rests her head on my shoulder, and it's different and awkward and completely wonderful. It's almost too much, and I have to swallow a sob as I put my arm around her. 'Thank you for understanding, sweetheart,' is all I can muster.

'Well, to be honest, Nana and I have been talking.'

'Oh?'

Cassie shrugs as she begins to play with her bracelet. 'I guess I never realised how much Dad was making you suffer. I never thought about you as, well, having your own feelings and struggles. I only think of you as my mum.'

I put both arms around her now, my throat like sandpaper. 'That's just fine with me, darling.'

'No, it's not, Mum. You're a person. A woman with her own thoughts and fears and desires. Not just a meal dispenser and a maid.'

She is really starting to sound like my mother now. I am proud. Touched.

And then, she has a thought. 'Does Dad know about you and Markus, then?'

'Not quite. But just to be clear, sweetheart, your father

and I were already over. I think we have been for a long time.'

'Well, if you want my advice, tell him so you can get it all over with.'

I look at my daughter. 'When did you suddenly grow up?' I ask her, squeezing her even tighter.

I have the feeling Joe will be okay with this when we tell him. Whereas Cassie has always been Daddy's girl (as much as she could be to an almost absent father), Joe is *my* boy. He and Simon have never talked about their feelings, whereas we are both well-tuned into each other's thoughts. I'm sure Joe already knows how special Markus is to me, and I think he'll be happy to have Markus around even more than usual.

Of course, he might be too young to know all the ins and outs of my deepest desires, which is a good thing, but I think that he's pretty much au fait with the people I love. And, even if I couldn't see it, everyone around me has told me that the feelings between Markus and me are more than obvious.

'Nana told me about your boyfriend, Mitchell.'

My mouth drops open a little, but I recover quickly. 'Did she now? What else did she tell you?'

'Lots of things about when you were my age. The dropping out of school and, the smoking…'

'Cassie,' I whisper. 'I was going to tell you myself, when you were old enough to understand…'

'It's okay. I've been a right pain in the arse, I know that, and I'm sorry. But now I understand that you had it bad when you were a kid, and you deserve to be happy. So I'm happy for you. We love Uncle Markus.'

I can feel the tears threatening to spill over. Who knew Cassie was so wise beyond her years? 'When did she tell you about my rebel years, then?' I ask meekly.

'A couple of weeks ago.'

There's no point in denying anything now. 'I remember what it feels like to be a teenager with no one to talk to. I was lost. I was lonely. And I was hurt. I'm sure you can relate to that, even if you have a much more ordinary family. You say that teens are never heard or seen. Well, I was one of those unseen girls.'

Cassie is still watching me closely. 'Is that why you did all that stuff? Why you went crazy? Because nobody would listen to you?'

'Because I didn't have a mother to guide me, darling. Of course, I had Granddad who was amazing. But I needed a woman's guidance. Someone who would get me from the inside, you know?'

'So you turned to Mitchell,' she says. 'Who loved you but apparently ruined your whole life.'

I smile. 'No, sweetheart. Mitchell didn't ruin my whole life. I made the wrong choices because I thought I had to be an adult. But I was still so, so young.'

'My age?' she asks.

'Yes. But it's different for you, Cassie. You have me. I had no one.'

'So you made mistakes because you didn't have your mum around to help you?'

'That's pretty much the gist of it. But let's not dwell on that. I'm starting a new chapter now. We all are.'

She sits up a little straighter, and I can see the cogs turning behind her eyes. 'Is that why you had those anger issues before you left for the spa? The dizziness? Everything?'

Again, I nod. 'And that's why I never want you to be angry with anyone without good reason. It can kill you on the inside, Cassie. It can take away your joy, your entire will to live...'

She sits in silence, thinking about it. Then she looks up. 'I don't want to be angry either, Mum. I never want to have to live another day in anger...'

'Oh, sweetheart,' I say, embracing her as she leans against me. She sobs and I quietly cradle her, rocking her like when she was a baby. This is good. I can feel all her tension unwinding. The pent-up anger and the false ideas are slowly dissolving with every catch of her breath.

'C-can we talk... some more...? Even in the future? Even about you and Dad splitting up? And Uncle Markus?' she squeaks against my chest.

I kiss the top of her head. 'Of course, love. Always. Whenever you want, I'm here for you. Whatever you need.'

She hugs me tighter, and it feels so good. There will have to be a lot of soul-searching and mea culpas on my behalf, but I know I am on the way to getting my baby girl back.

'How is Cassie?' my mother asks me from her daybed. She has insisted on waiting for us under the canopy on the terrace, with a view of the sunset. She is paler than yesterday. The doctor says it's due to the new round of chemo she's just started.

'She's all right now. We talked. It'll all be okay now...'

'I wish I had been there for you too, Livvie,' she whispers, a tear rolling down her cheek. 'I wish I'd told you the truth about Aldo when you were a child...'

I take her hand. 'Hush, Mum. It's all in the past. I have a lot to make up for in my daughter's eyes too, but it'll all be okay. We'll be a proper family now. You have nothing to worry about anymore.'

'And Simon?'

I shrug. 'Simon and I will be okay. Our goal is to do whatever's best for the kids, but they understand that we can no longer stay married.'

'And Markus?'

'He loves me. And the kids already adore him.'

As if on cue, the family joins us under the canopy, one by one. Aldo puts his loving arms around my mother and kisses her cheek, winking at me. My father sits on a chair opposite us and Joe climbs into his lap. Markus comes to stand behind me and kisses the crown of my head.

'Where's Cassie?' I ask softly.

'I'm here, Mum,' she whispers, coming to stand behind Markus and me, embracing us both.

'Hey. Let's take a selfie!' Joe suggests, jumping to his feet to set Cassie's mobile on the table facing us and rushing back to his seat. Once done, he starts taking more pictures of us, this weird, motley bunch that we are.

I smile and look around my new-found family as the sun begins its slow descent over the horizon. 'You did it, Dad. We are finally all under one roof,' I say.

Dad clears his throat and says, 'I did, didn't I?' with pride all over his face. 'It only took us twenty-two years, but here we are.'

'Thank you, George,' Mum says, smiling at him. 'You're my hero.'

For now, it's only the middle of the summer. We must live these precious, fleeting moments for as long as we have them. Because life can be a pain, but it can also be so, so beautiful. Life can be anything it wants. Life is precious. Life is strong. I believe it now. Every day, whether bad or good, is still worth living. As hopefully and as happily as we can. Together.

Acknowledgements

They say that you will never finish writing your book unless you plant yourself in that chair and pour your soul out. True. So I did, until the last drop of everything inside me went into it: hard work, love, patience, optimism and everything I could throw at it after a few very difficult years had left me as empty as a leaky hot water bottle.

I would have never written this book without the support of so many people.

First of all, my beloved DH Nick who picked me up, told me it was okay not to be okay and who encourages me on a daily basis and fuels me with endless cups of coffee and cake, year after year, book after book, while being my Alpha-Everything. I love you.

Also, my family and friends who believe in me unconditionally, and are quite brave in doing so!

Many thanks to my friends Francesca and Marisa who have been with me through the most difficult times of my life and who have made it all the more bearable. Life would be so much emptier without your deep and constant friendship. And boring without our midnight swims and endless antics! Love you, crazy ladies!

And let's not forget my work bestie Tiziana for cheering me on through the tough days at work and reminding me of what really matters: integrity, hard work, respect… and outrageously silly memes. Thanks for the laughs.

I would have never had the courage to continue writing had it not been for my amazing agent Lorella Belli of the Lorella Belli Literary Agency. Lorella, you really get me, and I'm so honoured to have a powerhouse like you in my corner. You have always been THE agent I wanted to work with. Thank you from the bottom of my heart to you and your amazing team for everything you do on a daily basis!

Many thanks also go to everyone at Head of Zeus, particularly my editors Holly Humphreys and Aubrie Artiano for picking up the slack, i.e., inconsistencies, spelling changes, eye colour changes and even name changes! And of course, for so much more.

Also thank you to everyone else at HoZ who makes everything work, including the cover artists (I always love my covers and this one is particularly gorgeous, isn't it?).

And speaking of beauty: Sicily has been and always will be a major inspiration for my writing. I have lived here longer than anywhere else now, and I feel so blessed to call this gorgeous island my home.

I would also like to thank my fellow authors, Holly Martin, Lisa Hobman and Caroline James, three brilliant authors of such heart-touching stories, for their support and words of encouragement. They've kept me company and allowed me to feel like a real writer even if I live far-removed from the writing world!

Also, many thanks to my very favourite bookseller, Liana, at the Agenda Bookshop in Valletta, Malta. She always makes sure the shop never runs out of my books!

And finally, to the dear memory of my baby sister Lidia who had a wicked sense of humour and sharp powers of observation without ever judging a soul. In one sentence she'd change my point of view to make me see the beauty and hilarity of life, in all its facets. Cancer took her away from us far too soon. She had an entire life to live, endless places to travel to and many more one-liner jokes to leave us in stitches. So I will try to live like she did, 'always looking at the bright side of life'.

And finally, I would like to thank you, my lovely, loyal readers, you supportive lot, you! If it weren't for all of you I wouldn't even be writing this. Or anything else, for that matter! Please keep believing in me, enjoying my stories and looking for my name on the shelves!

Gratefully yours,
Nancy Barone

About the Author

NANCY BARONE grew up in Canada, but at the age of 12 her family moved to Italy. Catapulted into a world where her only contact with the English language was her old Judy Blume books, Nancy became an avid reader and a die-hard romantic. Nancy stayed in Italy and, despite being surrounded by handsome Italian men, she married an even more handsome Brit. They now live in Sicily where she teaches English. Nancy is a member of the RWA and a keen supporter of the Women's Fiction Festival at Matera where she meets up once a year with writing friends from all over the globe.

Thanks for reading!

Want to receive exclusive author content, news on the latest Aria books and updates on offers and giveaways?

Follow us on X @AriaFiction and on Facebook and Instagram @HeadofZeus, and join our mailing list.